ARIEL'S ISLAND

SHARE YOUR THOUGHTS

Want to help make *Ariel's Island* a bestselling novel? Consider leaving an honest review of this book on Goodreads, on your personal author website or blog, and anywhere else readers go for recommendations. It's our priority at Hearthstone Press to publish books for readers to enjoy, and our authors appreciate and value your feedback.

OUR SOUTHERN FRIED GUARANTEE

If you wouldn't enthusiastically recommend one of our books with a 4- or 5-star rating to a friend, then the next story is on us. We believe that much in the stories we're telling. Simply email us at pr@sfkmultimedia.com.

ARIEL'S ISLAND

PAT MCKEE

To Donna,
who makes everything worthwhile.

"You taught me language, and my profit on't
Is I know how to curse."
—Caliban. (Shakespeare, William. *The Tempest*.
1.2.437–438).

ONE X

THERE WAS A BODY, DRESSED IN A SUIT AND TIE, impaled on the fountain in front of the law firm of Strange & Fowler. Pumps recycling water from the basin below were spraying geysers through the corpse twenty feet into the air, the water now red from the blood of the unfortunate and illuminated at the precise point of their apogee by perfectly timed spotlights. The sun was not yet high enough to glint off the upper stories of the building.

I was an associate at the firm, just trying to get a jump on the eighteen-hour Friday that lay ahead of me when chaos intervened in my otherwise orderly life. A riot of blue lights had hit me in the face as I turned the corner from my condo onto Peachtree Street. Dozens of pinging strobes and a mob of cops, EMT's, TV cameras, press, and on-lookers prevented me from seeing anything more until I got to the doors of the glass-and-steel tower that housed the firm. After a glance, I ducked inside, not succumbing to the curiosity of the crowd craning to see more. After all, dead bodies in Midtown Atlanta aren't that rare.

It didn't strike me until I walked into the building that he might be one of our own, when I heard indistinct whispers of a familiar name. My eyes darted from one end

I

of the slammed lobby to the other, trying to find someone who might know, and I saw one of the partners; the
blood seemed drained from his face as severely as from
the corpse in the fountain.

"Who?"

"I'm sorry, Paul, it's Billingsley."

"Good God. What—?"

"Suicide."

"No, it can't . . . he was just . . ."

"Must have jumped from the observation deck."

I turned to grab a passing security guard. I flashed
my ID.

"Yes, Mr. McDaniel."

"Can't you turn off—"

"We're trying. Everything's run by computers. No one
can figure out how to turn off the fountain, and the coroner
can't get the body out until we do—afraid he might get
electrocuted if anything is shorted out. The body's been
there over an hour."

"You can't let his wife see . . ."

"Too late. Cop saw his wallet in the water, fished it out,
and called her. Poor lady lost it. EMT's had to sedate her.
They just took her away in an ambulance."

"Can't we at least keep his kids from—"

He shook his head.

"Every TV camera in the city is out there. His kids are
likely watching it broadcast live on the hall monitors at
school."

"Damn. Damn!"

Billingsley.

I had worked with Frank Billingsley for the entire six
years I had been at the firm, most of that time on just

one case, *SyCorAx, Ltd., v. Milano Corporation.* SyCorAx came out of nowhere, claimed three key Milano patents, and hired Hector Cabrini—having recently won the largest judgment in state history against an airplane manufacturer—to recover lost profits in the millions and secure intellectual property worth billions. Milano tapped Strange & Fowler, Atlanta's most prestigious law firm, for its defense. I had started there as an associate, right out of Emory Law, just two weeks before the case was filed.

Suicide never makes sense to me, but this one made even less sense than others. Just this week Billingsley had given me first-chair responsibility for arguing a discovery motion filed by Cabrini, telling me he planned to leave the office early that day to watch his youngest son pitch his first high-school game. For the entire week before the game, Billingsley was pushing back appointments and client expectations to take the afternoon off—and was beaming the next morning with a count-by-count call of his boy's innings on his way to a win. This man was in full-throated enjoyment of his life, one of the last people I would expect to take his own.

The motion he gave me to argue was a low-risk skirmish. Not much more than a training exercise. Not evidence that he was clearing his calendar in anticipation of checking out on us. Billingsley expected we would have to turn over some of the contested business records that SyCorAx demanded, but the documents provided little additional information, so he was initially inclined to concede the motion. Rather than concede, I urged we should deliver the message to SyCorAx and its lawyers that they would get nothing more without a fight. To Billingsley's wary amusement, I jumped on the opportunity to argue

3

the motion as if it had been one being argued in front of the Supreme Court.

In my overly zealous preparation, I found the thing that so many litigators dream of uncovering: a previous statement in one of the hundreds of discovery letters from SyCorAx's lawyers that acknowledged the relative uselessness of the contested documents and conceded their retention in exchange for an extension of time to object to one of our requests. It was a gem buried under hundreds of thousands of pages of discovery—forgotten by both them and us as we moved on to other battles—until it popped up on my computer screen. When I told him, Billingsley was delighted, but he had an entirely different approach to how we should use it.

"All you need to do is call opposing counsel and tell them about this, I'm sure they'll withdraw the motion."

"I'm not so sure. Telling them about this letter will only give SyCorAx's lawyers an opportunity to prepare for it."

"So, your plan is to sandbag opposing counsel?"

"Sandbag! Hell, it's their letter. This motion is so frivolous I could make a good case for sanctions against them. Besides, I think it's more like an ambush. I want to discredit them in front of the judge, make them think twice before filing any more discovery motions—we've got to punch back at these guys."

"And how do you propose to do that?"

"Let them make their motion. Let them go on with the judge about how important these documents are to their case. I'm sure when they see me sent to argue instead of you they'll smell blood and lay it on for the judge. Once they've gotten as far out on the limb as they can get, I'll project their letter on the courtroom monitor with their concession highlighted. Judge Richards will slap them down hard."

"Risky. The judge could rule before you have a chance to respond. Judge Richards is notorious for that, particularly in discovery disputes. He hates them."

"But then, what have we lost? And we have a good chance to get some momentum moving into trial."

For a litigator, Billingsley was unusually risk averse. By the time I had any input in the Milano case, Billingsley had defaulted to a conservative litigation posture of damage control, all but conceding defeat while trying to minimize the monetary loss. It was a strategy that was anathema to the gunslinger courtroom style I had developed in the bit parts I had been given to perform so far, a style grown from a life lived with nothing to lose but everything to gain. As foreign as my approach was to Billingsley, he let me handle the hearing as I had planned.

My gambit worked so well that the judge not only denied SyCorAx's motion but excoriated its lawyers for bringing it. Message delivered. Momentum gained.

That was Wednesday. Thursday morning, after Billingsley finished telling me about his son's pitching debut, I gave him the results of the hearing. He was surprised but elated, so elated that he called Placido Milano to give him the good news. Placido had been the director of research and development at Milano Corporation and our prime contact with the company through years of litigation. We were fast heading to trial, and Placido needed to hear something positive. At $800 an hour and a thousand-lawyer law firm, he had a right to expect results.

Brothers Placido and Anthony Milano, who had inherited a controlling interest in the multi-billion-dollar conglomerate from their father, were absorbed in the business of the Milano Corporation, not in defending lawsuits. The Milano's work schedules and the time difference between Atlanta and the company's headquarters in Milan made it difficult for anyone in the firm to talk with them, much less meet. Placido and Anthony existed for me as disembodied voices on conference calls at strange hours, and even that was unusual. Both Billingsley and I were surprised when Placido answered the call.

"Fantastico! Splendido! Paul, I'm delighted your tactic worked. Frank, it's a great general who knows when to let his lieutenant lead the charge. I am hopeful this portends well for the trial."

That was yesterday, when it seemed Billingsley's life was everything anyone could want. This morning, he was suspended, transfixed, on a grand piece of artwork designed to project the prestige and power of Strange & Fowler. It was too much to comprehend.

I went to my office shaken and disoriented. The first thing that popped up in my inbox was an email from William Fowler, senior partner of the firm, requesting that I meet with him early Saturday morning. I suspected it was for him to introduce the new partner he had chosen to lead the Milano case. Billingsley's body hadn't even been removed before he was being replaced. But Fowler's reputation was all business; I was surprised he was waiting till Saturday.

At eight the next morning I was knocking on the door to Fowler's office. He invited me in. No one else was there.

Fowler's office was more a shrine than a workplace, the walls covered in plaques, recognitions, framed front-page newspaper articles, his desk and credenza strewn with mementos of past victories and recent honors. Fowler looked every bit the UVA linebacker he had been decades ago. He wore his full head of white hair longer than one would have expected, and at 72 his jackets fit more tightly than before, but he was still an imposing man. He remained seated when I walked in.

"Paul, you've done a fine job in the Milano case. I was particularly impressed with your aggressive strategy in the hearing this week. Frank told me about it before . . . well, before he passed. I've spoken with Placido and Anthony. We want you to take over the case as lead attorney."

Our eyes remained locked for a couple of seconds in silence—I was waiting for Fowler to say something else, like . . . "and Rem Smythe from corporate will be the partner in charge." Fowler was no doubt waiting for me to acknowledge his announcement. When it struck me that there wasn't going to be anything else, I could do little more than stammer.

"Sir, yes, Sir . . . of course . . . Mr. Fowler, thank you for the opportunity." Even though I had worked for years alongside him, I couldn't yet bring myself to address him by anything but "Sir" and refer to him in any way other than "Mr. Fowler."

There was more silence. I was thinking there had to be something else, but Fowler was ready to move on.

"Well, Paul, I think you have a lot to do. I don't want to take any more of your time."

That was it. In the next weeks I took the case in the opposite direction from where Billingsley was heading, convincing Placido and Anthony we could win the trial outright. By then many of my colleagues—and more than a few of the wags who wrote for the *Fulton County Legal*

Register, the daily gossip sheet that masqueraded as the official organ of the Atlanta legal community—had pegged my chances of winning the case at almost nil. "Paul McDaniel: Strange & Fowler's New Golden Boy, or Firm Fall Guy?" read Monday's headline after my promotion to lead counsel. The ensuing article opined that my lofty position with an elite law firm at the tender age of thirty had more to do with the firm's desire to have someone expendable to blame for what looked to be an unavoidable debacle rather than it had to do with any expression of confidence in my legal ability.

Some even suggested Billingsley's suicide was his final effort to avoid being tagged with a disastrous loss. "Billingsley knew the Milano case was such a dog," the gossip allowed, "that he killed himself before he lost the trial, rather than face Fowler after the verdict came in."

Worse, the stock market agreed. Shares of Milano Corporation that had traded at over one-hundred dollars prior to the litigation had plummeted by twenty-five percent after the suit had been filed. Now, with the trial looming and Billingsley dead, shares were selling for the equivalent of a sub-sandwich combo meal, and I was looking more and more like the story's fall guy. But by this point I was committed. Either the Milano case was going to be my career-making victory, or I was going down in defeat, having thrown every part of myself into the effort.

Maybe that was what Billingsley was thinking. Maybe that was how Billingsley felt in those last seconds, those seconds before he jumped: that he had given all he had to give.

TWO

"MR. McDANIEL, THE SUPREME COURT JUST gutted your defense. The decision in *Halo Electronics* came out this morning. Looks to me like there's nothing left of your case other than deciding how much money your client owes SyCorAx." The Honorable Judge Thomas Richards of the Northern District of Georgia glared over the rims of his glasses at me, only glancing at my opposing counsel. Moments before, Cabrini had entered the chambers glad-handing puzzled clerks and interns and hailing bemused assistants, already taking a victory lap while I sat grim, awaiting the judge. I had been lead defense counsel for Milano for less than a month, and it now looked as though the case was over before I had had a chance to file my first brief. What little momentum I had gained from the discovery skirmish had vanished.

Judge Richards had summoned us on two hours' notice to his magisterial chambers atop the Atlanta federal courthouse for an unusual Friday-afternoon meeting. Seldom did he allow business to interfere with his weekly outing to the Wolf Creek Trap and Skeet Club. But this afternoon he was seated at his desk. The desk looked like it had once belonged to a Renaissance Florentine Prince, and the regal impression Judge Richards cultivated was reinforced by

9

the city skyline displayed behind him—the gold dome of the Georgia capitol, the glass and steel towers of Midtown, the glitz of Buckhead in the distance. Judge Richards' glare intensified, his scowl deepened, his displeasure at the disruption to the order and pace of his calendar evident. He was only getting started on me.

"My usual practice would be to invite a Motion for Summary Judgment from the Plaintiff, but since trial is scheduled for two weeks from Monday, we don't have time for that. I believe it is best for all parties involved to allow you and Mr. Cabrini an opportunity to discuss settlement." Judge Richards motioned to his courtroom deputy who, like a half-dozen other minions, fluttered about the room awaiting the slightest opportunity to be of assistance to His Honor.

"Mrs. Ortiz, when is the next available trial date if we have to go forward with this case?" She displayed a hard copy calendar in front of the judge, pointing, commenting in tones meant only for him.

Cabrini used the opportunity to take a cheap shot. "Your Honor, I am happy for Mr. McDaniel to take all the time he needs to assimilate this ruinous precedent." But if there was anyone in the room who could be more condescending than Cabrini, it was the judge—who acted as though Cabrini had not even spoken.

"Gentlemen, our next available trial date is one month from Monday. I am continuing this case until then. I suggest you use this time to settle. If you don't, and we go to trial, I will be inclined to let the matter go to the jury on SyCorAx's claim for punitive damages." The judge's threat was the procedural equivalent of handcuffing me while Cabrini raided my client's treasury.

Most trial lawyers have had a ride on this train, railroaded by a judge, who had already made up his mind which side was going to win, and who wanted the case to go away without more work on his behalf. The only thing to do is to jump off before the engine leaves the station.

"Your Honor, Milano Corporation is not inclined to settle and does not wish to postpone the trial in this case." These were the first words I had spoken to the judge since we exchanged pleasantries upon meeting. Judge Richards yanked off his glasses, leaned across the desk, and shook his head with the same decisive exaggeration as if I had proposed an illicit liaison with his wife. Before he got another word out I pressed my point.

"All I ask is that you let me brief the issue before you decide. No one has had the opportunity to digest the ruling fully. I'll have a memorandum of law on your desk Monday morning."

"If you expect to try this case in two weeks, I'll need your Pretrial Briefs by next Friday." Judge Richards rose and tossed his glasses on his desk, signaling the meeting was over. He could still make it to Wolf Creek with plenty of daylight left. "And it's going to take a hell of a lot to change my mind." The judge disappeared into his private office.

Cabrini was out the door and heading to the elevators before I collected my briefcase, no doubt hurrying to tell his client of their extraordinary good fortune and my inexplicable stupidity. I was seen out by an intern, the lowest caste in the chamber's order.

I called Placido as soon as I got back to Strange & Fowler. From my glass-walled corner office the Federal Courthouse appeared short, squat, and insignificant in the distance forty-stories below.

When I told Placido what the judge said, he went off.

"Figlo di puttana! The only courts in the world worse than the Italians are the Americans. At least here you can buy a good result. I've been throwing money at this case for years! Why the hell am I still dealing with it?"

As soon as Fowler gave me a free hand, I developed my aggressive trial strategy based on the rock-solid precedent that the D.C. Circuit had relied on in *Halo* and sold Placido on it. But in an instant, the Supreme Court reversed the case, blew up my defense, and turned a winning strategy into an almost-sure loser. I had to explain to Placido how we got here—and more importantly, what I was going to do about it.

"Judge Richards called me and Cabrini to his chambers to discuss a Supreme Court decision that just came down this morning. It's not good. The judge is putting a lot of pressure on us to settle. I—"

"Settle! I'll never settle!"

"—I pushed back, and he is giving me this weekend to put together a brief to convince him that we still have a defense after the *Halo* decision."

"What's this *Halo* decision?"

"The Supreme Court made it far easier for a plaintiff in a patent case to get in front of a jury on punitive damages. They just need to convince the judge that we knew of the patents and intentionally used them. Cabrini has argued all along that Milano purposely pirated SyCorAx's patents, and we have been equally insistent that the patents are ours, and we can use them—"

"Of course we can, they're ours, we—"

"You need to understand, that position now plays right into their hands, or at least that's the way Judge Richards sees it. Now our exposure is through the roof—triple what it was before this decision came out. And the way Atlanta juries have been giving away other people's money, going forward with the trial is a billion-dollar roll of the dice."

"How can this be happening . . . don't they have to prove the patents belong to them?"

"Sure, but the judge is very close to ruling that the documents they've come up with are evidence of their ownership. I have no idea where they got them, but it's been enough to keep Judge Richards from throwing the case out. After *Halo* he's all but ready to rule for SyCorAx."

"Well, I'll discuss this with Anthony. And you . . ."

"I've got a brief to write, and I need to get ready for trial. And I don't have much time to do it."

"Ariel will give you all the help you need."

The principals' elusiveness would have made handling the litigation impossible were it not for Ariel, Placido's assistant, who had anticipated my needs for any arcane patent information supportive of the case and would provide it as soon as I requested it. I was convinced she could read my mind.

While I was concerned about the effect that a crushing loss in the Milano case would have on my client, my firm, and my career, it was my family—or what was left of it—that I was most worried about. My father was already gone, and the world had not been kind to my mother.

When I got out of law school, we both landed at the threshold of Strange & Fowler. I walked through the front door as one of its bright new stars, while building security found Mom half-conscious at the loading dock, clutching an empty bottle of Old Crow, demanding to see her rich son. As soon as I was drawing a paycheck, she began stays in a continuous stream of rehabilitation facilities—each of which she checked herself out of as soon as she sobered up, immediately to start drinking again. Without my support Mom had nowhere to go.

Now the aggressive trial strategy that I had urged Placido and Anthony to endorse appeared reckless in the extreme. It was my plan at trial to dare the SyCorAx lawyers to explain how the corporation came into possession of Milano's secrets. Without producing someone who had worked in SyCorAx's laboratory on the patents—I would argue—details about them must have been stolen from Milano.

The risk of this strategy was that all SyCorAx's lawyers had to do was to come up with a little old man from a dark lab who could claim with any credibility that he was the source, and the case would have been over. But I knew they couldn't produce that witness. At least they hadn't been able to do so throughout the years of discovery that I had used to turn over every corporate rock and shine a light under it. Until now the thing that kept me up at night was the fear that SyCorAx's lawyers had sandbagged me, knowing that my strategy was the only way for me to win and determining that at some critical point in the trial they would spirit a witness to the stand who would pull Milano's secrets right out of his hat.

That was a risk I was willing to take. What I had not anticipated was a Supreme Court decision that reversed years of established precedent, or a trial judge who felt my client's defense imposed too great a burden on his time at the skeet range. Now my strategy looked a lot like a direct track to the bankruptcy of Milano, an ignominious end to my short career, and my mother winding up on the streets again.

I contacted Ariel as soon as I finished with Placido. We never spoke on the phone and only communicated by email, but she was no more than moments away from a response to anything I needed. She assured me that she was available to edit the brief over the weekend.

After all night assimilating *Halo*, I had a first draft to her by noon on Saturday. I knew this was 8:00 in the evening Milan time and didn't expect a response for several hours, so I walked to my condo two blocks from the office to grab a snack and take a nap, planning to return in the late afternoon. That would give me enough time to get one more draft together and a chance for Ariel to look at it before emailing it to the judge Monday morning.

My phone pinged. I had just crashed on my sofa. It was 2:00 Saturday afternoon, and Ariel had revised the entire brief. I couldn't sleep now, turned on the coffee pot, and jumped on my laptop. Ariel and I went back and forth with drafts; she turned around her edits almost as soon as I could get out new drafts. At one point, when it was 3:00 in the morning in Milan and Ariel had just turned around another edit, I couldn't contain my curiosity. I was paid very well to do without sleep and turn in major briefs in a weekend, and I had no one at home to be responsible for other than myself. But this marathon writing session must have been a strain on Ariel.

"You don't have to do this all night. I'm sure you have family who're missing you."

"Paul, you are so kind to be concerned. But you don't need to be. I think you and I are a lot alike." It was a cryptic response, enough to pique my interest, but not enough to encourage further inquiry. I left it alone.

Ariel and I put in over 40 hours on the brief from Friday afternoon to early Monday morning, and I had a polished final version on the judge's desk before his coffee arrived. But even with our extraordinary efforts, I knew convincing the judge that Milano still had a defense was a longshot.

So I wasn't prepared for the call from the judge's chambers on Monday afternoon. It came from the same lowly intern who had led me out of the offices on Friday.

"The judge asked that I call you and Mr. Cabrini. He wants you to know that after reviewing *Halo Electronics* in the light of your brief he has decided to let the jury consider the issues raised by the defense. He also said we are going to honor the continuance of the trial for thirty days. Your amended proposed Pretrial Order is due in two weeks."

I wasn't going to question his radical change of heart. Somehow, I had persuaded the judge. Now all I had to do is persuade the jury, the lottery of human colloquia.

THREE

"OYEZ, OYEZ, OYEZ, THE UNITED STATES District Court for the Northern District of Georgia is now in session. The case of *SyCorAx, Ltd., v. Milano Corporation*, the Honorable Thomas Richards presiding. Be seated and come to order." The bailiff gaveled the proceedings open in Courtroom 9E in the Atlanta Federal Courthouse. Judge Richards' Courtroom was like all others in the building, designed for maximum discomfort—stark walls, no windows, wooden pews, searing artificial light, all arrayed before a judicial bench that towered over litigants like Oz over the Tin Man.

It was day twelve of a trial Judge Richards had scheduled for only one week. Anthony's son, Enzo Milano, grandson and namesake of the company's founder, groomed to take over the company, sat next to me at counsel table. Enzo was the face of the corporation, and this morning that face was ashen, lips dried and cracked, eyes shot, and hair disheveled. Depending on the outcome of today's deliberations, he either would be leading Milano Corporation into the next century or presiding over its dissolution. Judge Richards wasted no time and pressed hard toward the finish.

"Good morning, ladies and gentlemen of the jury. We concluded yesterday with the closing argument of Mr.

Cabrini on behalf of the Plaintiff, SyCorAx, Ltd. This morning you will hear from Mr. McDaniel on behalf of the Defendant, Milano Corporation. When Mr. McDaniel closes then Mr. Cabrini, representing the party with the burden of proof, will have one final opportunity to address you in rebuttal. After that I will give you the instructions on the law you shall apply in this case, and you will withdraw to begin your deliberations." Judge Richards peered down at me from the bench and announced my turn to address the jury.

"Mr. McDaniel, you may proceed."

Television and movies make it appear that lawyers' closing arguments are masterpieces of extemporaneous eloquence and logic, a combination of college debate and Shakespearean soliloquy. And some lawyers would like the world to think they are so brilliant that they can pull up all the facts of the case and arguments of the briefs off the tops of their heads. But the truth is, every word a lawyer says in front of a jury is considered, written, practiced, and mastered until a very-polished presentation sounds as though it just came to the lawyer's mind at breakfast. I was no different. I had practiced my closing for months. And I was sticking with my aggressive strategy. Either I was going to win it all, or I would soon be testing the job market. I stood and faced the jury without a note in my hands.

"Ladies and gentlemen of the jury, Mr. Cabrini's argument was about everything other than what is important in this case. SyCorAx's lawyer focused solely on his contention that Milano infringed SyCorAx patent rights. That's all he talked about. Why? That's all he has.

"SyCorAx's lawyer has missed the most critical step in his proof. His Honor will tell you at the conclusion of this case when he instructs you on the law that before SyCorAx can claim Milano infringed its patent rights, SyCorAx must establish it has the right to the patents in the first place. I contend that SyCorAx must show you how it developed these patents before it has any basis at all to claim Milano infringed its rights.

"So, let me bring you back to the heart of this case. You have heard days of testimony establishing that Placido Milano, the head of research for Milano Corporation, is directly responsible for developing three miraculous drugs that promise to end the scourge of HIV. These drugs are so innovative that the United States Patents and Trademark Office awarded Milano multiple patents. Though Milano invested tens of thousands of hours of its most-gifted scientists' time and millions of dollars in research funds, it is Placido's vision to make these drugs available free of charge to anyone who cannot afford them, much in the spirit of Jonas Salk who, generations before, made his vaccine available to all and saved millions from polio.

"Enter SyCorAx, more like the Martin Skink of this saga—the man whose company increased the cost of its life-giving drugs tenfold. It was only after Milano's groundbreaking work that SyCorAx came out of nowhere with its team of lawyers. They claim SyCorAx, not Milano, is entitled to the patents on those drugs. You haven't heard SyCorAx say they would provide these drugs free of charge to anyone. In fact, you have heard hours of testimony from SyCorAx's accountants telling you how much profit they expect to make from the sale of these drugs and demanding Milano reimburse it for its loss by paying millions in damages. You can be sure if SyCorAx is successful in this case, hundreds of thousands of people will be denied access to these life-giving drugs, just so SyCorAx can fill its corporate coffers."

It's usually right about here, when I have given the other side my opening punch, that I look around to see if it has landed. Until now I had been staring each one of the jury members in the eye, going from one to the other, hoping to catch a sympathetic look, and a poised, stylish, lady on the top corner of the box was nodding approvingly, ever so slightly. The rest were either fighting sleep or had their arms crossed, staring at the ceiling.

Through our jury research we knew just about everything there was to know about each one of the jurors. Juror number three, the stylish lady, was a retired English professor, divorced, with two grown children. Her former husband came to the marriage with a son with whom she grew very close and who was for a time her step-son—and who died of AIDS. When Cabrini asked if any jurors have family members with HIV or AIDS, she truthfully answered "No," otherwise he would never have left her on the jury. By reason of her education, interest, and personality, I was counting on juror number three to be a leader among the jurors—one who would lead them to a defense verdict. I was desperate for some positive energy from the jury, and I allowed myself to feel a spark of encouragement kindled by the attention juror number three was paying to my argument.

"But SyCorAx cannot prevail, not on the evidence before you. It has not brought forward any credible evidence that it developed these drugs. I challenge my opposing counsel, and I challenge you, ladies and gentlemen of the jury, where are the scientists and the lab technicians who supposedly did the research? Where are the accountants and auditors who attest to the millions of dollars spent on this research? You have not seen one scrap of evidence, not one bit of testimony to establish that SyCorAx actually did the work to develop these drugs."

The SyCorAx CEO, who had been lounging back in his chair throughout the trial was now hunched forward, whispering in Cabrini's ear, gesturing toward something written on a legal pad. Cabrini nodded, but without his characteristic bravado.

"I'll tell you what you have seen, what the entire case of SyCorAx rests on. SyCorAx's evidence consists of thousands of pages of computer code, reams of paper, hundreds of exhibits, detailing the complex chemical formulas of these drugs. This evidence is troubling indeed. No doubt it took an army of lawyers toiling day and night for months to generate this mountain of obfuscation. And I willingly admit to you that this evidence must have come from someone who had direct knowledge of those patents.

"When you consider this evidence, I ask you to remember what I said at the beginning of this trial in my opening statement. I challenged SyCorAx and its lawyers to explain how they got these secrets; I challenged them to produce someone who actually worked in SyCorAx's laboratory on the patents they claim are theirs. Why? Because without producing that witness, the only conclusion you can come to is that these formulas and all the details about Milano's patents were stolen. There is no dodging this fact. All SyCorAx and its lawyers had to do was to come up with just one witness, any witness, who could establish that he was the source of those secrets. But they couldn't. And they didn't.

"I want you to look at that empty witness stand at the front of this courtroom. That is all the evidence SyCorAx produced in response to my challenge, an empty chair. No witness, no testimony, no evidence. Don't you think if SyCorAx had someone, anyone, who could have proved me wrong, that person would have been SyCorAx's first witness? SyCorAx and its lawyers would have responded to my challenge, destroyed my defense, and proved their case.

"They didn't."

My lady in the top corner was now nodding conspicuously whenever I made a point. But she was only one of six. Some of the others were cutting their eyes toward Cabrini, trying to gauge his response to my argument, but he was too much a professional to let them know I had even drawn a nod, much less drawn blood.

"You are left with only one conclusion, that SyCorAx stole Milano's secrets. All those print outs—stolen. All those formulas—stolen. Now I don't have to prove how SyCorAx stole these secrets, how SyCorAx came in possession of something so protected that only Milano scientists had access to it. Only SyCorAx knows how it came in possession of these secrets, and so far it has refused to tell you. But I am confident what His Honor will tell you; His Honor will tell you that SyCorAx has to prove it got these secrets legitimately. SyCorAx has absolutely failed to do so. And with that failure, SyCorAx's case fails as well.

"So now the fate of Milano Corporation, the fate of millions who suffer from HIV, and the fate of others whose diseases have yet to find a cure, are up to you. I ask you to keep these patents out of the hands of SyCorAx, assure access to these drugs to all, and give hope to future generations that only Milano Corporation can bring. The health and welfare of millions of Americans cannot be entrusted to the Skinks and SyCorAxes of the world. I ask you to render your verdict for Milano Corporation. Thank you for your attention."

Cabrini's rebuttal was short and ineffective; the Court's charge, tedious and long. Yet the worst part of any trial for me is the jury's deliberation. Before the jury goes out, there is always something else I feel I can do for my case, call another witness, make another motion, advance another argument, but once the jury withdraws, it is out of my hands and into the hands of a group of strangers picked because they know absolutely nothing of the virtue of my cause. Many lawyers find it comforting when their work is finally over. It scares the hell out of me. And, in spite of all I had done to win, when the jury went out in the case of *SyCorAx, Ltd., v. Milano Corporation*, it was the same as always.

I chose to remain in the courtroom, hoping for an early verdict as everyone else departed. Legal lore has it that an early verdict is a defense verdict, though many a defense lawyer has been shocked by a quick and stunning award for the plaintiff. You just never know. A law-school colleague of mine who now does criminal defense work says that a long deliberation only means that the jury has called out for more donuts.

The quiet courtroom betrayed the intensity of the battle that had taken place here over the last several days. Papers were strewn over counsel tables; flip charts dangled on easels before the now-deserted jury box, numbers and graphs hurriedly scribbled over torn pages; banker's boxes of exhibits, computers, statute books, briefcases were all haphazardly lying about, no more need to maintain even the appearance of order.

The bailiff drifted in and out. A massive headache came on and settled behind my eyes. The courtroom clock audibly clicked off the seconds. Minutes, then an hour, then another passed. I dozed on and off in my chair.

A hard knock of a gavel and a geyser of adrenaline shot through me, instantly relieving me of my headache. The jury has come back. It had been a few minutes short of three hours. Too long for me.

"All rise."

I was the only one in the courtroom.

Judge Richards addressed me directly.

"Mr. McDaniel, I have been informed by the bailiff that the jury has reached a verdict. Have your client in the courtroom in thirty minutes. The clerk will notify the Plaintiff. We will be adjourned until four o'clock."

By ten till four the courtroom had sprung back to life, spectators, reporters in back, law clerks, court reporter, the bailiff down in front, and Enzo by my side, tight-jawed. Cabrini and the SyCorAx executives were relaxed, smiling. The judge's entry brought us all to our feet.

"Bailiff, bring in the jury."

At this point my chest was constricted and my breathing was short, but I did my best to radiate confidence.

"Has the jury reached a verdict?"

"Yes, it has, Your Honor." The foreperson was an elderly gentleman who sat in the front of the box. Every time I had spoken he had wrinkled his nose as if I gave off a bad smell. It was not a good sign. He had been elected by the other jurors to organize their deliberations and, in the end, to speak for them. I wondered what had happened to juror number three, the lady in the top corner of the box. Now when I tried to make eye contact with her she looked down. At that my knees got weak, and I held the back of my chair for support.

"Please hand the verdict form to the bailiff, and the bailiff will bring it to me."

"The verdict appears in order. The clerk will publish the verdict."

"The case of *SyCorAx, Ltd., v. Milano Corporation.* We the jury find for the Defendant on all counts."

Those were the sweetest words I had ever heard. And then I could hear little else other than the judge adjourning the case and Enzo instantly on his cell phone, no doubt calling his father half-way across the world to tell him the news. Cabrini and his crew slunk out without a word, Cabrini not even offering me the handshake due the victor, acting more like a peevish *futbol* star than an officer of the court.

All rules now relaxed in the decompression that ensued, I grabbed the foreperson before he left to ask what argument, what evidence, had carried the day. Lawyers are trained to believe that their every word and gesture in front of a jury has profound significance, that what they do and say determines their client's fortune, and in the most extreme situations, their life and death. I was certain he would tell me it was my brilliant closing that won it.

"Well, I have to tell ya, we just didn't believe SyCorAx or that other fella Cabrini. They were just too slick."

He paused as though he was letting me in on a secret and leaned close.

"But we sure had a hard time convincing one lady on the jury, a professor. She thought there was too much evidence in favor of SyCorAx. She finally agreed with the rest of us that we just couldn't believe 'em."

So much for Strange & Fowler's expensive jury research.

Perhaps perceiving some disappointment on my part, he volunteered that had Milano made a counterclaim against SyCorAx, several on the jury would have awarded Milano millions in damages for the indignity of having to respond to its outrageous charges. Then he shook his head.

"But I don't think the professor woulda gone along with that."

Two days after the verdict, my fortunes at the firm now secure, I drove out of a Porsche dealership with a new 911 Carrera, paid for in full by the bonus I got for winning the Milano case. Mom was comfortably residing at some fancy addiction center in the mountains, and I was heading down the coast, invited by William Fowler for a weekend at his home on Frederica Island. My victory gave me every reason to expect that he had called me to his beach house to offer partnership in the firm. But I had my doubts. I always had my doubts that someone like me, without the blue-blood background seemingly required of Strange & Fowler partners, could ever make the cut.

FOUR

R AIN WAS COMING DOWN SO HARD MY WINDSHIELD
wipers were useless. Navigating by the lights of the
Frederica Island guard house, just on the mainland
side of the bridge, I pulled under the portico, turned off
the radio that was blaring the final riffs of *Stairway to
Heaven*, and lowered my window. Cold water dripped on
my arm as I leaned out to address the guard, motionless
at his station.

"I'm visiting William Fowler."

The guard disappeared. Several cameras aimed and
focused from the ceiling; strobe lights flashed on the rear,
sides, and front of my car. The guard returned holding a
printed pass.

"May I see some identification?"

I produced my driver's license. The guard studied my
picture and my face, then handed me a pass. I placed it
on the dashboard and noted the license number, color,
make, model, and VIN of my 911 had all been gleaned
by the cameras and printed on the card. Contrary to
the Orwellian chill that the intrusive security measures
gave me, the guard's mood changed from icy to warm
once I was identified, and he welcomed me as though I
had just become a member of the club.

"Mr. McDaniel, my name is James. Mr. Fowler's expecting you. Turn right at Third Street. Fowler Cottage is at the end on the right. You let me know if there is anything I can do for you while you are here on the island."

"Cottage." The term fools the uninitiated. It's one of many signs that Frederica Island is a place to itself. It was no mistake that the G-8 Economic Summit was held here, with the President of the United States hosting the leaders of the world's richest nations in the cottages of Frederica Island, a few miles off the coast of Georgia. Frederica Island cottages are out of reach for all but a few. Even a small ocean-front home would cost millions to buy, if only one could. Cottages are passed down in prominent families for generations, the value of the island real estate going up each year as reliably as the interest on a trust fund.

I realized as soon as I arrived that I had left the shabby world I came from and had entered another of privileged perfection. From the mainland I crossed a series of bridges that span the still-pristine Marshes of Glynn, celebrated by the poet Sidney Lanier as "a world of marsh that borders a world of sea," separating the continent from the barrier islands. I turned onto a narrow two-lane causeway, which ran through a tunnel of grey-bearded live oaks and gnarled cedars leading over the tidelands. Three-hundred years ago this had been the site of the Battle of Bloody Marsh, where the British commander James Edward Oglethorpe, a regiment of Scottish Highlanders, and their native Muscogee allies had turned back the forces of the King of Spain, as though this island alone were worth the price of the blood and treasure of an empire. To this day the Scots' sacrifice is commemorated every evening on Frederica Island by a kilted bagpiper saluting the setting sun. Today the storm must have made that otherwise pleasant duty a miserable one.

I passed the guardhouse and crossed the cobblestone bridge over St. Simons estuary onto Frederica Island. The rain had slacked only a little as I turned onto Third. All that marked the entrance to Fowler's cottage was a brass plaque at the gate in a high brick wall that was almost completely covered in thick green foliage. The wall, coupled with heavy, hanging live-oak limbs, made the cottage nearly invisible from the narrow road. I pulled into the circular drive behind a three-story Tuscan villa—rough stone, wrought iron, and clay tile, huge terra cotta pots of citrus trees and tropical flowers.

Though my meeting with the senior partner of Strange & Fowler was supposed to be purely business, for me it was intensely personal. This meeting could transform my life.

I had toiled, unremitted, at Strange & Fowler since law school—successful by every measure—and now with the victory of the Milano trial only days behind me, I was seeking my reward. For me the exorbitant salary, a share of firm profits, and the prestige of partnership seemed the contemporary equivalent of being dubbed a knight of the realm. Yet, even with success, I strained to subdue my own peculiar doubts. I harbored the insecurity that poverty breeds, always trying to prove, if to none other than myself, that I was the equal of anyone whose birth had given them a status I felt I could never achieve. With all the outward assurance I was able to muster, at this moment I was nearly overwhelmed with uncertainty, the feeling that I was an impostor—not just unworthy, but a fraud soon to be discovered.

Fowler opened the door himself before I reached the porch. He greeted me with his arms wide, a broad grin, and a slap on the back, like I had just shown up at a frat party—and I was the one with the keg.

"Paul, come on in and get out of the rain! I can't have you catching pneumonia."

"Thank you, Sir. Some storm." I tried my best to shake the rain off my jacket onto the steps and not onto the Persian rug in the dimly lit entry hall, which was illuminated only by spotlights on the gallery of gilt-framed portraits lining the walls.

"I was afraid the weather was going to delay you. I should have known a little rain wasn't going to slow you down. Not in that new car of yours."

"Yes, Sir. A present to myself for winning the trial."

"Well deserved. Let's go to the study and have a drink. You like bourbon?"

"Whatever you're having is fine with me."

Fowler directed me to a room off the main entry hall and nodded to a wizened man, uniformed in grey and white, who was standing silent in the hallway nearby. He disappeared without a word.

The study was small and stuffed. Its walls were lined to the ceiling in books, mismatched and worn: some with tattered dust jackets and others with scuffed leather bindings; some lying sideways, others on top of each other; many with markers sticking from their pages; all arranged in no order. Books selected by their owner to be read, not purchased by some vapid decorator for effect. Scattered among the books were at least a dozen framed photographs. In the corner was a modest desk. A cracked leather sofa and two upholstered chairs were arranged around a low table stacked with more books and pictures.

One picture stood out. I picked it up. My drink appeared before me, golden liquid in cut crystal. I took a deep draft of the undiluted liquor and sank into the sofa, studying the photo.

"Yes, that is President Walker. My wife took that picture of him and me right here in this room. The Walkers were our guests during the Summit. While he was here I reminded him that our grandfathers had worked together on an unusual project some years ago. He confessed that he had only heard the full story after he became President."

What I knew about Prescott Walker from newspaper stories and Beauregard Fowler from firm lore was that they were about as different as two human beings could be. Walker was a Connecticut Yankee, Fowler the son of an unreconstructed Rebel. Fowler must have read the question on my face. He continued.

"They came from different worlds. Walker made his money on Wall Street, while my grandfather worked a cotton farm in South Georgia. With the little money my grandfather saved, he took a gamble on a company started by a druggist named Pemberton, one of his father's fellow Confederates. The company made a drink that Pemberton eventually perfected and called Coca-Cola. My grandfather owned twenty percent of the company. Despite the rage against anything Northern that was bred in my grandfather's breast, despite the disdain that the old money Walkers had for newly rich Southerners, by the time Fowler met Walker they found they had one very important thing in common: tremendous wealth. It was enough of a bond for the two of them to work together to save the sugar plantations in Cuba from Castro. Part of the plan was for my grandfather to help Walker get into the Senate, which he did just a year before Castro's first unsuccessful attempt to overthrow Batista. Fowler and Walker were able to keep Coca-Cola's Cuban plantations private, at least for a time, long enough for the company to find an alternative sweetener to cane sugar. So Coca-Cola continued to prosper, as did Walker, his Wall Street cronies, and his family, who, like my grandfather, were heavily invested in the company. The Walker and Fowler families have been linked ever since."

Fowler reached down to the table, picked up another silver-framed photo, and handed it to me. It was an aging snapshot of a thin, severe man in a dark suit seated at a desk, a demure servant girl stationed to the rear.

"This your grandfather?"

He nodded.

"Taken at that desk in the corner, soon after he built this cottage. When he passed away I inherited the cottage. I've changed almost nothing, not even Oliver, who began working here as a young man late in my grandfather's life. That's Oliver's mother behind my grandfather." Fowler acknowledged the man who had fetched our drinks, who stood at the ready just outside our door. Oliver made a slight bow.

"Paul, this cottage is a lot like Strange & Fowler. I inherited it, I have changed little, and I intend to pass it along just that way. I would do anything for the firm. I expect all of my partners to have the same devotion." He had been staring at his grandfather's picture, but he turned his gaze directly at me. "They say that if you scratch the skin of any one of Atlanta's founding institutions it will bleed Fowler blood." I knew the Fowler family was tied to every major institution in the city, and I was certain it was no coincidence.

"But we need new blood. That's where you come in. The firm needs to promote men like you, smart and accomplished and unafraid to take risks. That's why I personally reassigned the Milano case to you. And I watched how you handled yourself against Cabrini. Only a man with your combination of skill and confidence would have tried such a high-risk trial strategy."

"If it hadn't worked out, I would have been burned in effigy at the next firm picnic."

"But it did work out. You marshaled a stunning victory. Nothing great is achieved without great risk. Not even my grandfather's fortune was built without taking tremendous risks—risks that paid off handsomely, just like the risks you took in the trial, just like the risk I took in assigning you to handle the case."

Fowler usually didn't hand out praise unless it was to impress a client, and I didn't know how to respond. So I didn't. I glanced away from his gaze, and when I looked back Fowler seemed to be staring right through me.

"Paul, I want you to be a partner in Strange & Fowler. I have spoken to the Management Committee and they are in unanimous agreement. I have transferred one million dollars to an equity account established in your name." It was an effort for me to keep my jaw from dropping, my eyes wide in amazement.

The Equity Account. It sounds like a mere bookkeeping entry. But it represents a partner's share of the profits of the firm. And in the instance of Strange & Fowler, these profits are from a firm that generates over a billion dollars

in revenue annually. Even a small percentage of the profits on a billion dollars in revenue represents a very large
amount of money.

The Equity Account is the stuff of associates' dreams,
partners' anxieties, and the key to the firm's riches. I was
Ali Baba with his first glimpse of the cave, stunned at the
wealth arrayed before me. Partners were forbidden to talk
about their shares in an effort to prevent intra-firm rivalry,
but perceived inequities, slights, and favoritisms inevitably
resulted in waves of speculation among associates and
partners. But that was all it was, speculation. No longer for
me. That instant my ignorance turned into astonishment.

"This is only an advance. The final accounting of your
partnership profits will be made at the end of the year."
Fowler paused, his dark eyes boring into me. "Of course,
your share of profits is completely dependent on the
judgment of the Management Committee, based on performance. At your current rate you can count on profits
averaging in excess of two-million dollars a year. This year
they should be much more, as a result of the premium paid
by Milano for your victory. Congratulations."

Two-million dollars a year. This in addition to my salary.
I never had dared to assume my share of firm income
would be so much—maybe later, after years of devotion,
but not so much so soon.

I had rehearsed this moment in my mind hundreds of
times, the moment when all my efforts, my sacrifices, had
paid off, the moment in my life when my doubts should
be banished. But when the time came, I could barely bleat
a response.

"Thank you. I just—"

Fowler shook his head.

"This is no gift. You earned it. And I expect you to keep on earning it. With partnership comes great responsibility. I expect complete loyalty from you, as I do from every partner. And you should know that I am not willing to accept your loyalty, or that of anyone else for that matter, on blind faith. I'm willing to take risks. But I do so with my eyes open."

"Yes, Sir. I understand."

I truly understood, as did everyone at Strange & Fowler. Security was a firm fetish, Fowler's personal quirk.

The full extent of the internal security systems of the firm was revealed to few, and most of us were only enlightened concerning the measures that applied to our own areas of firm activity. There were rumors of clandestine overlapping systems that provided additional layers of security in the most sensitive areas, such as firm finance and intellectual property. As much as the firm's efforts were supposed to be secret, the results were often too evident to ignore.

On occasion attorneys vanished, glimpsed only as security officers whisked them from their offices, special property teams assembling their files and electronic devices for remote audit and removing their personal belongings for delivery to their astonished family. One day a valuable member of the team; the next, disgraced and defending criminal action. As intrusive as the island security had appeared when I arrived, it seemed primitive compared to that of Strange & Fowler. I suspected that William Fowler's own home would be at least as secure as the firm, and a glance around the study confirmed my suspicions as I observed several grey lenses, blinking red at every movement or sound they detected.

Mr. Fowler took a sip of his drink, and for the first time since we sat, he settled back into his chair, the business at hand now accomplished.

"Judge Richards is staying at the Abbey. We're meeting him in the morning down at the range to shoot a little skeet—you know how that man loves to shoot skeet. You can relax here in the afternoon while I excuse myself for a meeting. I'll be back in time for us to attend dinner with Anthony Milano. Anthony wants to thank you personally for what you have done for Milano Corporation. I understand his lovely niece Melissa will be in attendance as well. That last bit of information might interest a handsome, well-off young bachelor such as yourself."

I again tried not to look surprised—not about the information concerning Melissa Milano, but about Judge Richards. Few judges could afford to spend much time at the Abbey, Frederica Island's five-star resort hotel, where the daily fare for a room exceeds what a trial judge earns in a week. Judge Richards, who grew up on a one-mule farm in the north Georgia mountains, seemed one of the least likely to be able to bear the freight. Prior to becoming a judge, he had been a criminal defense lawyer, defending bootleggers and drug dealers, not a member of a big firm, who would have been able to draw significant cash for a run for the judiciary from affluent clients and partners investing in influence. Like many Georgia trial judges, it was the families of those he had kept out of jail and the hordes of others who identified with them who put him in office. He seldom received a campaign contribution exceeding the hundred-dollar threshold that required disclosure by the election ethics laws.

While I was curious how Judge Richards was able to stay at the Abbey and indulge his favorite activity at the Frederica Island skeet range, I wasn't concerned so much about his financial condition. I was thinking about myself. Being seen so soon after trial with the judge who had presided over the biggest victory of my life would not look good, especially not at a place so expensive and out of his league. But if William Fowler wasn't concerned about the appearance, then I couldn't be either. I would pass my first test of loyalty. So, instead of venturing an unwelcome comment about the propriety of socializing at the Abbey gun range with Judge Richards, I rose to the bait Mr. Fowler dangled in front of my nose.

"Melissa is beautiful, smart, and rich." I lifted my glass in a toast to Melissa and drained the last of the bourbon. "We connected a couple years ago at a symphony fundraiser. She had recently completed her Master's in Finance at the London School of Economics when she was tapped as Treasurer for the Capital Campaign, probably as much for her financial savvy as for the money her family brought to the table. The last I heard, she was engaged to an Argentine polo player who had just signed a hundred-million-dollar endorsement contract."

Fact was, I knew far more about Melissa Milano than I cared to let on. She had recently come to town and was getting her bearings. I had seen her only in passing at a few corporate meetings with Placido, but Melissa is not a woman easy to forget. So when I saw her at the symphony capital kickoff unescorted, I offered to show her around Atlanta. We went out many times, always casually, often to a Braves game, to a concert, or a restaurant, and I must admit that after a month of squiring Melissa around, I was as smitten as a schoolboy. But I was not the only one paying Melissa attention, and I was blindsided when I returned to Atlanta after a two-week trial in Charlotte to see a picture of her on the sports page hanging on the arm of a Hawks forward. Then there was the Argentine polo player. We never went out again.

I held no illusions about Melissa Milano. As gracious as she appeared, I realized she probably considered me more the hired help than a potential suitor. But a lot had changed in two years. I no longer was a highly paid wage slave, but now a partner in a powerful law firm, fresh off a highly public win on behalf of her family corporation. If I had another chance with Melissa, I wasn't going to blow it.

"That was a rumor about the polo player, probably concocted by the boy's agent. I can assure you Melissa is not engaged. Anyway, even a hundred-million dollars isn't a lot of money to the sole heir of Placido Milano. Thanks to you." Mr. Fowler's face betrayed the faintest of smiles. "Oliver will show you to your room. He'll see to it that you have everything you need. We'll breakfast at eight."

Oliver led me to a second-floor suite that overlooked the beach. Even as I turned in, the weather outside had not let up. I fell into a deep sleep to the sound of wind-driven rain against the windows and storm surge slamming the beach—with a grey lens focusing from the ceiling, blinking red with each breath I took.

FIVE

THE EARLY MORNING SUN STREAMED INTO MY ROOM well before breakfast. The storm had passed, and I drifted into consciousness and back out again, no clear demarcation between dreaming and reality, sleep and wakefulness. I decided to get up, find some coffee, and enjoy the morning before the heat became unbearable.

Oliver was way ahead of me, and the smell of fresh-brewed coffee led me to my first cup. Savoring the coffee and the serenity of the morning, I stepped onto the wisteria-shaded loggia that ran the length of the house and overlooked the ocean. I found a comfortable chair and began to get my bearings. Toward the ocean, a perfect green lawn terminated at a low brick retaining wall. Beyond it was a hundred yards of white sand and dunes, washed by the now-tranquil Atlantic and the sun, now a bright, orange ball just above the horizon. The shore curved outward to my right so that I could see the strand of homes along the beach, each one a bit further toward the rising sun than the one before, each one a unique vision of its owners' tastes and desires—a vision unencumbered by concerns of mere expense.

The ocean spread before me. Since my childhood, I have yearned to come home to it. There was no one to be seen for miles in either direction; I had the ocean all to myself. Now was my chance to get reconnected.

I jogged to the beach, kicked off my boat shoes, stripped off my T-shirt, waded past the waves breaking on the sandbar, and dove. I pushed myself down, farther, deeper, and opened my eyes. The ocean all around was a constant presence, a being. The sun shone through the green water, shafts of light illuminating the world around me, a place of quiet, peace. Sea creatures darted around me.

A face appeared, beautiful, young, feminine, unfamiliar, smiling, beckoning. I longed to stay, but could not; my lungs burned. I kicked and burst the surface breathing deep the salt air. The sun and salt burned my eyes. I searched the water for the source of my vision. I saw nothing.

I turned to the beach and surveyed the island from a hundred yards distant to anchor myself in reality. Though I could see much of the south end of the island, my view to the north was in part obscured by the brick wall that lined the Third Street side of the Fowler cottage. The wall ended at the edge of the lawn. There, one had an unobstructed view up and down the beach. I could see something just beyond the wall that piqued my interest, the appearance of something unusual on this well-established island: new construction. Seldom was anything new built at this end of the island because there were few places left to build. I waded back to the beach, climbed on the retaining wall, and peered into the neighboring lot.

It was an almost-completed home that looked much like a newer version of Fowler's cottage, a villa of stone, iron, tile, and terra cotta. A number of mature oaks had been planted around the cottage, where it was evident from the otherwise-uninterrupted tree line extending on either side that several had been uprooted for construction. The exterior was complete, and a team of workers swarmed in and out, intent on finishing their work. Unlike most construction sites, however, there were only muffled sounds of hammering and sawing, not the shrill whine of power saws and rhythmic pounding of pneumatic nail guns.

I looked at my watch and realized I had taken longer than expected. I sprinted back to the cottage, snatching and throwing on my shirt and shoes along the way, and entered the breakfast room off the loggia as Oliver produced two plates: one in front of an already-seated William Fowler, who was studying the newspaper, and one destined for me.

"I trust you slept well, Paul."

"I did. Just enjoying the morning. Time got away from me."

"That happens a lot here on the island. Have a seat."

Oliver placed my breakfast before me.

"I hope you like Eggs Benedict."

"My favorite."

Fowler returned to his paper for a moment as I cut into the perfection of a poached egg.

"So I see you discovered our new neighbor."

He caught me with a bite half-chewed, and I finished it before I spoke.

"Well, Sir, I was surprised to see new construction. I didn't think there were any parcels left on this part of the island."

"There aren't. Quite a story connected with that lot."

"I think I remember an article, something about a real estate developer getting in hot water for tearing down a cottage . . ."

"Right. There once was a lovely cottage on that spot owned by an elderly couple from Chicago. They were somehow connected with Wrigley's, I believe. When they passed away, the cottage remained in their estate, unused, for years. Without regular care it deteriorated.

"Along about that time there appeared on the island an Atlanta real-estate developer possessed of an extraordinary amount of money and little else. He had been rebuffed in several attempts to acquire one of the island's most desirable cottages. He found that the heirs of this estate were more interested in cash than in keeping a place they never had even seen, and he was able to purchase the cottage, but only at an exorbitant price. Once in possession of the cottage the developer proceeded to tear it down, and along with it uproot most of the two-hundred-year-old live oaks that shaded the property."

"That's it. But I thought he built something else there."

"You may be recalling the newspaper accounts of his razing the cottage and the huge modern monstrosity he built in its place. It was completely unsuited for the island. The Atlanta papers mockingly gave the developer several awards. He didn't get the joke. The island residents were incensed. It seemed to me he actually believed he was providing us poor benighted fools an education in architectural style. Well, he soon found he was unwelcome on Frederica Island. The brisk business he was doing in Atlanta came to a halt overnight, and his real-estate empire failed. His bankruptcy trustee could get only pennies on the dollar for that outrageous structure."

"So what happened to it?"

"One of my neighbors acquired the property, tore down the eyesore, and is building the tasteful cottage you discovered this morning. He discretely let it be known that it was available, and I am happy to say that we have a delightful new neighbor who just put a contract on the cottage."

"Who's that?"

"Judge Richards."

Fowler peered over his paper.

"I'm sure he'd be happy to give you a personal tour after skeet this morning. You should have plenty of time before our dinner with the Milanos."

We finished our breakfast in silence, Fowler devouring the newspaper, my mind racing to a hundred different conclusions.

Oliver drove us to the shooting club in a pristine, deep-black, forty-year-old Mercedes Cabriolet that had belonged to Mr. Fowler's father, top down, the ocean breeze cool. On the way we took an impromptu tour of the south end of the island, by the Beach Club and the Abbey and past a grove of ancient oaks said to have been established before the Declaration of Independence. The shooting club was off the island, across the estuary on a small hammock near the island causeway, the range sited across the marsh.

Judge Richards was already outside the field house with an attendant, assembling his shotgun himself. We walked over to greet the judge, and Oliver retrieved two gun cases from the trunk. I recognized the three golden circles and three golden arrows that serve as the mark of the five-hundred-year-old arms firm Beretta.

"William. Fine day for shooting."

"Judge, you know I'm happy to go shooting with you any day."

"Paul, I'm glad you could join us. I know William is proud of the work you did in the Milano trial. You were brilliant."

"Thanks, Judge."

"Ever seen one of these?" The judge broke his shotgun, checked the barrels, and handed it to me with the assurance of someone who had been around guns all his life. "Holland & Holland."

To be more precise, it was a Holland & Holland Royal Deluxe side-by-side 12-gauge shotgun with custom hand engraving, by the company that makes arms for the Kings and Queens of England. This shotgun cost about as much as my new car. I turned it, snapped the barrels closed, and sighted it across the marsh. A perfect drop, a magnificent gun, and a work of art. I broke the gun and handed it back.

"I've only seen those in locked gun cases."

"I'm sorry, Paul, but I only brought us a pair of Silver Pigeons. It seems the judge has us out gunned."

"Out gunned and out manned. Come on. I'll let you shoot it, once I beat you a few rounds."

Skeet shooting is a sport designed to ready one for shooting birds in the wild. But even in the South, there are few game birds left outside private hunting preserves, so most people don't get to do much more that shoot at clay targets, called pigeons, thrown to simulate the flight of birds. I usually shoot clays. I wasn't a very good shot, and I was pretty sure that not even a Holland & Holland would sharpen my eye.

Judge Richards took position first, signaling ready.

"Pull." The clay disk launched from a trap at the far end of the range, the judge's shotgun blasted a single round, and the target exploded into dust. The three of us alternated at eight positions around the semicircular range and fired 25 shots each. The first round Judge Richards hit 24, though I would have scored his only miss as a hit, since he clipped the clay, but it had failed to break. Fowler shot 20, and I, a dismal 16. I didn't get much better in the next two rounds, but the judge shot one perfect round of 25, and Fowler's best was 23.

"Good thing you're better in the courtroom than you shoot." Judge Richards handed me his gun. "Try a couple shots with this."

While it had been balanced to within an ounce and hand engraved by dedicated artisans, the judge's gun did little to improve my shooting, and I hit only three of five. By this time my shoulder ached, and I had almost lost what little patience I possessed. I had spent most of my adult life laboring in a steel-and-glass tower, not honing my hunting skills on a quail plantation. But after last night, I had reason to think that might change.

"Tell you what. You come out tomorrow morning, let me show you what you're doing wrong, and I'll have you shooting in the 20's before noon." I opened the barrel and handed the shotgun to Judge Richards. He broke it down and placed it in its walnut and brass case, waving off the attendant who approached with an oiled cloth to wipe down the gun.

"I'll take care of it myself as soon as we finish up here."

I watched Fowler break down his shotgun, wipe it, place it in the gun case, and hand it to Oliver. I did the same, trying to act like I knew what I was doing.

"Paul, Judge Richards has won his club championship every year he has entered. They now call it the Richards Cup. You couldn't have a better coach."

"I'm well aware of His Honor's reputation as a great shot. I'll certainly take you up on that, Judge."

"And I'll even let you use my gun."

45

Fowler changed the subject.

"Judge, I've got to go to a meeting this afternoon, but I told Paul you might be convinced to take him on a tour of your cottage. You think that might be arranged?"

"I'd be delighted. The crew has the afternoon off, and I have a meeting with the foreman to go over some finish items." He looked at his watch. "The decorators will start moving furniture at noon. I'll meet you there at two." I got the impression that this visit had been pre-arranged, that Fowler wanted to keep me occupied while he was at his afternoon meeting. With anyone else I would have taken this as an affront, but with him I understood it as his personal attention to his guests' needs.

After lunch served by Oliver on the loggia, I walked across Third and onto the judge's property through a chain-link gate with a sign that read "Construction Entrance." There was a moving van parked on the street with a half-dozen men carrying in furniture, with two women in skirts, heels, and pearls, clipboards in hand, monitoring their every step, hovering over each piece of furniture. I was a few minutes early, but the judge was already there, nose-to-nose with a man wearing a hard hat. The judge was chewing and spitting out his words; the worker only nodded. I stood at a distance until the judge concluded his business and motioned me over. He was shaking his head as the workman walked off. Most judges are used to having their every word obeyed; Judge Richards expected his obeyed immediately. It seemed that working with people who didn't know who he was—or worse, didn't seem to care—was frustrating him.

"As much money as I'm spending on this place, I expect everything done right. Hell, the foreman doesn't give a damn what I say. I'm going to have to get the contractor out here." He broke a smile for the first time. "Well, you didn't come here to hear me complain. Let me show you around." He led me toward the front of the building.

"The builder used traditional materials, stone, iron, and wood, throughout." Stone, iron, and wood. It sounded simple, even humble. But as we walked through the all-but-finished interior of Judge Richards's cottage, it became evident there was nothing simple or humble about it. The stone covering the floors was Italian marble, the iron work gracing the curved staircase was hand forged, and the wood framing the coffered ceilings was hewn cypress, from hundred-year-old logs recovered from Georgia river bottoms and prized for the worm holes that turned the beams into abstract works of art.

The judge was as giddy as a teenager showing off his first car, explaining the layout of each room, pointing out rare materials, hand-crafted details, custom appliances, antique furnishings now being positioned. We dodged movers as the decorators ordered them about.

After an hour I left Judge Richards standing in the first-floor game room that overlooked the Atlantic. He was questioning a carpenter about the precision of some of the dental molding finishing the fourteen-foot ceiling above a fireplace deep enough for a child to play hop-scotch in. The conversation was becoming heated, so I ducked out.

As I left, Judge Richards caught my eye, as if he wanted me to stay—even as he was still engaged with the work-man—as though he felt the need to keep me there. His body language betrayed the conflict, an impulse to pull me back into his conversation, countering his desire for candor with the craftsman. The cottage won out.

47

I smiled, waved, and walked back toward Fowler's. My head was spinning with questions about Judge Richard's new-found wealth. I resolved to do what I could to clear my mind, and instead of going back to Fowler Cottage, I walked under the canopy of trees toward the heart of the island. It was hot and steamy, and I didn't want to walk far, even in the shade. I headed toward the Abbey, only a few minutes away at a stroll. By the time I reached the front door I was drenched in sweat and welcomed a chance to sit in the hotel's bar, drink a beer, and cool off. Four liveried doormen stood at attention to open the doors, and they directed me to a room just off the main lobby. I had been here for a conference not long ago, but I hadn't had much opportunity to spend time in the hotel's bar. I perched on a softly upholstered stool in the dark and quiet and ordered a Samuel Adams draft.

How on earth could Judge Richards afford a Holland & Holland shotgun, much less buy a new cottage on Frederica Island? Was it a mere coincidence that his cottage was going up right next to Fowler's? And the judge must have inked the contract on the multi-million-dollar beach house not long after the dramatic change in his attitude toward my case. I could hear Fowler's words, "Nothing great is achieved without great risk."

Perhaps worse than any of these troubling thoughts was the realization that if any of this were what it seemed, my career-making win in the Milano case was little more than a cheap manipulation of a system in which I was an inconsequential pawn. I was too proud to accept that conclusion readily. Or maybe it wasn't pride I was feeling; maybe it was even baser than that. I had counted, over and over in my mind, what access to the Equity Account meant for me, how a couple million dollars annually would change my life and that of my family forever.

Was this what partnership, what loyalty to the firm, meant? In a few hours, had I transformed from one who at least espoused a belief in the principles of law, of concepts of good and evil, to one who was willing to see things excused by money, pardoned by power? I had wanted all my life to be one of the wealthy and privileged; now that I was one, was I willing to pay the price to stay? I resolved, for now, to see as little as possible and to say even less. After all, there could be perfectly honorable explanations for all that had happened: my victory, the result of my extraordinary legal skill; Judge Richards's new-found wealth, an unanticipated inheritance; and I after all indeed worthy of my exorbitant profit share—self-deception seemed an easier path than challenge.

My eyes took a few minutes to adjust to the dimness inside the bar. Once they did, I looked around and saw only a few other mid-afternoon patrons, but one caught my eye. It was the imposing presence of Hector Cabrini.

SyCorAx's lawyer radiated a Mediterranean heritage with a practiced smile that at once is disarming, but upon frequent repetition betrays insincerity; even so, it was all I could do during the trial to keep the women on the jury focused on the evidence and not on him. His physical attractiveness masked an aggressive manner he used to intimidate opposing lawyers and even judges. Cabrini was talking to an older dark-haired gentleman whom I did not recognize. The two leaned toward one another, both speaking so as not to be overheard, each intent on the other's words. The older man was wearing a tailored suit and silk tie even in the tropical heat. They were so concentrated on their conversation that neither of them noticed me.

I could not believe that even someone as shameless as Cabrini would show up here so soon after the beating he took in the Milano trial. His face and form were so well known, it wasn't as though he could show up anywhere and remain incognito. I expected him to have been on the first flight off to some five-star retreat as soon as the verdict came in, but not to this one.

It was a fair bet that with the high-flying status that shares in Milano Corporation had once attained—and regained after the trial—that many of the financially sophisticated investors on this island held stock in Milano Corporation, and the prevailing attitude here would be decidedly sympathetic to the Milano family. Cabrini was as welcome on Frederica Island as the developer who had bought the cottage next to the Fowlers. It was a good thing Melissa and her uncle weren't here yet.

I resisted the strong temptation to walk up to Cabrini and to gloat a bit in front of his companion. Whoever he was, if he was willing to be seen in public with Cabrini, he wasn't innocent. Instead I slid around the other side of the bar, kept my head down, drank my beer, and left.

I had resolved nothing. I spent the remainder of the afternoon trying to enjoy the view of the ocean from Fowler Cottage in a failed attempt to banish the doubts from my mind. So far, the Equity Account was holding them off.

When Fowler returned, he announced we would be dining with the Milanos at the Abbey.

"Anthony does not maintain a cottage on the island. He has a villa on the Amalfi Coast where he now lives most of the year. He's arranged for us to dine this evening in the Summit Room." The Summit Room of the Abbey was dominated by the table at which the leaders of nations had pulled the levers of the world economy at the G-8 conference, and it was only used for very special events. "If you didn't bring your tuxedo, Oliver can fit you with one." I was well aware of the Abbey's dress code from my previous visits, and I came prepared, not wishing to embarrass myself or my host.

But I smiled to myself for the irony of it all. It was just a dozen years ago when I had left Thornwood. Tonight I was having dinner with an heiress where presidents and prime ministers had plotted the course of the world.

After graduating high school and walking out the gates of Thornwood Orphanage, I worked my way through Georgia State and landed a scholarship to Emory Law. I studied every waking hour for three years, was on the Editorial Board of the Law Review, and finished in the top five of a class of two-hundred-and-fifty Ivy League-educated rich kids.

My resume got me inside the heavy oak doors of Strange & Fowler, but it was my Horatio Alger story the partners took to. They hired me, ostensibly touting my academic accomplishments, but I knew it was mainly for my background that tempered the otherwise overly-privileged image of the firm: an orphan could become an associate at a firm populated with the beneficiaries of multi-generational trust funds. I was more than happy to play the part and tried not to let their motivation concern me. My salary the first year was more than my bourbon-befuddled father had earned in his entire alcohol-shortened life.

As Fowler and I walked into the Abbey, it was the prospect of an evening with Melissa that got my blood going, though I did look forward to meeting her famous uncle. My eyes were instantly drawn to Melissa as I entered the Abbey lobby. She wore a long low-cut black sheath dress that vividly demonstrated how Italian women inspire exotic sports cars. Melissa was more Ferrari than Lamborghini, more grace than flash.

Melissa held out her hand.

"Paul. It's wonderful to see you again. May I introduce to you my uncle, Anthony Milano?" She indicated a dark-haired gentleman, who had not noticed my arrival and was involved in a quiet discussion off to the side with the maître d'.

At the mention of his name, he turned. "Paul, I am Anthony Milano. I am very pleased finally to meet you."

Anthony Milano was the man in the bar that afternoon in discussion with Hector Cabrini.

SIX

"THANK YOU." THAT WAS THE BEST I COULD DO, disoriented by the realization that Anthony had been in cordial conversation with someone who had been his enemy through six years of scorched-earth litigation. Anthony seemed to find the silence to be evidence of my humility; I was fortunate he took that characteristic to be a virtue.

"Come now, you must regale us with all the tales of your brilliance, which I have heard so much of! And do not be so modest. I know your victory on our behalf came at great personal sacrifice. Though we can never fully repay you, we can certainly express our appreciation. Can't we, Melissa?"

"Of course."

Melissa, oblivious to the turmoil that her uncle's appearance had caused, flashed a disarming smile, and with it I put Anthony's meeting out of my mind for the moment.

The maître d' escorted our party down the hall to a pair of paneled wooden doors that he opened with ceremony. We entered the Summit Room. In the center was a round table, local oak inlaid with the flags of countries that had attended the meeting. The table was adequate for eight, but it now was set with every imaginable plate, crystal, and silver for four. The walls were wainscoted with the same wood as the table, iron chandeliers hung from the coffered ceiling, and a deep Persian rug covered the floor, giving the room the appearance of a royal hall in a medieval castle. The maître d' left, and four white-coated and -gloved waiters glided in, took cocktail orders, reappeared with our drinks on silver salvers, and vanished.

Anthony, now leaning against a carved limestone mantle, took charge of the gathering. He gestured expansively and without concern for the ancient Chinese vase inches from him.

"William, I want to thank you and your new partner—congratulations, Paul, William just told me the news—for the triumph of Milano over SyCorAx in the courtroom. We are most grateful for an extraordinary victory. I, therefore, propose a toast. To Strange & Fowler, to William Fowler, to his partner Paul McDaniel, and to Milano Corporation: May we all continue to prosper. Salute!"

I raised my glass, glanced around, and caught Melissa's eye. She smiled the kind of smile beautiful women have perfected to disarm the skeptical and charm the gullible. After a few sips of my martini, I felt myself slipping from the first group and falling into the latter.

When dinner was served, we sat around the massive table at the points of the compass, not close enough for any pair to break off in a separate discussion from the others, so that all four of us bantered throughout the evening. Both Anthony and Melissa appeared engrossed in my detailing, at the prompting of my partner, of the chess match that was the Milano trial. William was effusive in his praise, not so much for my benefit, but for the benefit of the Milanos.

"The case was challenging enough, but Paul's most brilliant maneuver was to parry an unfavorable Supreme Court decision that came out just weeks before the trial and still launch the thrust that proved to be SyCorAx's final undoing."

I was not often to be embarrassed by compliments, but, nevertheless, I had tried to tamp down William's remarks, if only to maintain my credibility with the clients. Even so, I did not waste the opportunity for a little showmanship for Melissa's benefit.

"It was such an unexpected turn that Judge Richards called both sides into his chambers, postponed the trial, and pushed to settle. With the backing of Anthony and Placido, I insisted we press on. Judge Richards was against it. Cabrini was gleeful. But I had a plan:

"In my opening statement, I dared SyCorAx's lawyers to explain how the corporation came in possession of Milano's secrets. They never did."

Anthony glanced at William, eyebrows raised in a look of true bewilderment.

"So what was your plan if SyCorAx came up with a witness who knew, surely you—"

"There wasn't one."

"In Italy we say that is '*avere I coglioni*,' which, given our mixed company, I will translate loosely as 'very courageous.'"

Melissa laughed, "Uncle, you know I speak Italian."

"Well then, you can translate it for yourself." Anthony gave a wry smile. "I'm sure Mr. McDaniel gets the context."

More than once I had related the key points in the case to partners, friends, and the press, and after repeating, yet one more time, the more dramatic turns in the trial, my enthusiasm for re-telling the courtroom battle waned and my interest turned to the Milanos. After a few bottles of Brunello di Montalcino were passed around the table, each taking long pauses at Anthony's glass, William encouraged Anthony to talk about their fathers' business relationship. It didn't take much to get the two of them telling war stories, how they assisted their fathers preparing for trials up and down the Atlantic seaboard, spending long nights on New York-to-Atlanta trains. Their relationship was based on the successful efforts of Strange & Fowler in keeping Northern unions out of Southern mills. The firm's work was the key to the Milano's paying low wages and reaping high profits. The elder Milano and Fowler were largely responsible for keeping hundreds of thousands of Southern millworkers in abject poverty for generations.

My family was one of those stuck in the mass of humanity that fed Milano's mills. But in less than a generation, the McDaniels had moved from mill workers to legal champions of the mill owners. I wondered how much of a move it was. As Milano and Fowler spoke, never mentioning the hardship their successes caused countless others, I was struck by how the wealthy consider the poor. I was certain they had no idea both my parents were lives sacrificed at the altar of Milano mills, and I was even more certain they didn't care.

But the truth of the matter was that my father died in an accident of his own making. As was his custom on Monday mornings, he showed up drunk to his shift at the Laurens Milano Mill, not yet having time to sober up after a weekend of drinking. It wasn't that anyone cared. His job tending the loom required little mental acuity, only the willingness—so as not to idle the line—to mend thread and replace bobbins while gears continued to spin and levers flew within inches of fingers, hands, and arms. That morning, his arm caught in a chain drive that lifted him from the floor and flayed all the flesh from his elbow to his wrist. He bled to death before they could get the machine stopped.

My mother fared little better. The scant amount she got to compensate her for the loss of her husband was sufficient only to bury him and to fund her own month-long drunk. They fired her before she returned to work. She tried to sober up and get another job, and she did so for a time, but the longest she ever stayed employed after the accident was about six months. As soon as she got a few dollars in her pocket, she would start drinking again and lose her job, only to sober up once more when her money ran out.

In the brief intervals when she was working and sober, things at home were tolerable. I had food, and my clothes were clean and mended. But when she was drinking, I was on my own. By the time I got to sixth grade, I was self-conscious that my clothes were dirty and torn, that I had no money to do anything. Tired of the taunts, one day I just stopped going to school. About a week later the school social worker showed up at our house, found my mother passed out on the couch, no food in the refrigerator, and me playing in the dirt in the back yard. The next day I was shipped off to Thornwood Orphanage, an institution supported by the Presbyterian Church and run by a cadre of severe retired ministers and ancient widowed matrons.

There I discovered, with the stability afforded by three meals a day, a warm bed at night, and the discipline of required study, that I was a gifted student. And it did not take much insight to come to the conclusion that if I were to escape the tarantella of poverty and poor employment prospects that had plagued generations of my family, education was my only hope. I was no longer the indifferent student, but now the earnest scholar bent on going to college.

Seven years after graduating valedictorian of my high school, I walked through the doors of Strange & Fowler, the top recruit of its associate class.

I shook myself from my introspection. Anthony was going on about his father, the first Enzo Milano, the founder of the firm, an Italian immigrant who brought his clothing trade to New York City. According to Anthony, the family began by selling clothing manufactured by others, but soon was manufacturing its own. It didn't take his father long to recognize the benefit that resulted from making his own fabrics in the South. He purchased textile mills in small towns in South Carolina and Georgia. One of them was the mill in Laurens, South Carolina, where my parents had worked.

"Placido and I inherited the family business from Enzo. I was interested in everything business related, while Placido was the studious one, who loved his books and the laboratory our father built for him in the basement of our home." Anthony looked down as if recalling a long-forgotten event, chuckled a bit, then continued. "Our mother was frequently appalled at the smells that came up from that basement—but mostly our father just looked on with bemusement. I remember once the two of us got ahold of some nitroglicerine—I can't recall how—and blew out an entire wall of the basement! We *did* get in trouble for that one. But we had some great times!"

Anthony kept the far-away look on his face for another instant, but then re-focused.

"I ended up going to Harvard business school and Placido went to MIT. It was the first time the two of us had ever been apart."

It had long been evident to me that the brothers had been groomed by their father to lead Milano Corporation. Unlike the case in so many such planned family successions, the brothers hadn't disappointed him.

"Once we took over Milano, we decided to bring all of the family's businesses under one corporate structure. I became CEO, while Placido focused on research and development. It was through acquisitions and spin-offs that Milano Corporation came to concentrate on pharmaceuticals. And it was through Placido's talent that Milano's laboratories became world dominant in the field. And, thanks to you, Paul, we will remain so. You probably know, as a result of all the recent press, Milano Corporation is now concentrating its research efforts in the field of artificial intelligence. We expect to have the same success in this area as in the pharmaceutical industry."

At a pause in Anthony's storytelling, I took a chance to move the conversation in Melissa's direction. I asked a question I thought she might have as much interest in as her uncle.

"That's a big leap—from drugs to AI—will Placido head up the transition?"

Instead of opening up the conversation, talking ceased at my remark. Melissa and Anthony looked away. I must have wandered past a line that had been obscured to me but clear to everyone else. Fowler was making a study of folding his napkin in his lap. I was in terra incognita, on my own.

"I'm sorry, I had no business asking." I looked from Melissa to Anthony, searching their faces for some sign of reassurance. Anthony broke the silence.

"No, it's not that. You have earned our complete confidence."

With that Fowler looked at me as a death-row priest might look at a criminal reprieved just moments before his execution.

"You see, Melissa's father, my brother Placido, has been missing since the trial ended. We have been unable to get in touch with him. We didn't want to make his absence public, and we didn't want to burden you with the information. We fear if the news gets out it will cause Milano stock to plummet once again. Not to mention the pain and anguish that his disappearance causes Melissa and myself." He patted her hand.

"My father and I usually speak every day. Since my mother's passing it has fallen on me to manage his finances and investments—he's notorious for being indifferent to money and business, and focuses only on his research. I haven't heard from him in days. I can't tell you how concerned I am. My uncle and I are pursuing every avenue, but I just . . ."

Anthony reached for Melissa's hand again as she fought back tears.

"I'm confident we will find my brother wherever he may be and bring him back safely. He has done this before, disappearing for a couple days at a time, only for us to find that he was off somewhere 'thinking.' What makes us so concerned is that he has now been gone for almost a week and hasn't even checked in with Melissa."

Anthony's aspect became grave as he watched Melissa

trying to regain her composure. His glance returned to me, his undershot eyes and arched brow signaling we had gone far enough in that line of discussion, and that I should not pursue the issue further. For the moment, I waited for someone else to take up the conversation. Before silence could overtake us entirely, Fowler steered the conversation to other topics. After a few unsuccessful starts it seemed that my gaff was behind us, and our party was soon enough focused on lighter matters, all of us laughing again at Fowler's understated humor.

Melissa, appearing eager to move to lighter topics, showed a gratifying interest in my career and success at Strange & Fowler, giving me the chance to talk about something other than the recent trial. She did a good job, acting as though she was not merely being polite, and it gave me the opportunity to satisfy some of my curiosity. I asked how she finally decided to live in Atlanta, something that was still up in the air when we last spoke.

"So, once I graduated from LSE, I was determined to set up my own investment bank with the help of my father and my uncle. After looking at several locations I landed on Atlanta as the best fit for my firm. But managing my father's finances and investments became so time consuming that I came to concentrate almost exclusively on that, and I have not taken on any other clients. After all, he has taken very good care of me, and now that he needs me, I can return the favor. Our arrangement has worked out perfectly."

"Well, not so perfectly." Anthony paused, reached unsteadily for the open bottle of wine that he kept at his elbow, sloshed the remainder in his glass, and leaned toward me as though he were revealing a family secret. "Melissa has worked so hard on family matters that she has neglected her own happiness."

Melissa grabbed my arm to refocus my attention away from her uncle, who was now downing the last of the wine.

"What my uncle means is he thinks it is high time I find a nice Catholic boy and get married." Melissa made a coy little smile in Anthony's direction. "I'm surprised that the evening has proceeded this far without it coming up."

"It's not just me. Your father thinks so as well. He told me so himself."

In one way both Melissa and I had arrived at a similar point in our lives from different poles of the planet. We were young, professionally successful, and financially well-off. Yet we had each achieved success at significant personal sacrifice, single, without any current romantic relationship. For me it was a remarkable stroke of luck.

"Yes, a good Italian girl, still single past her thirtieth birthday." Melissa leaned closer toward me. "They think there's something wrong with me."

There sure wasn't anything wrong with Melissa from what I could tell. It was probably a combination of the success of the evening, Melissa's striking looks, and her attentiveness, but I felt my feelings for her stirring once again. Or maybe I had just had too much wine.

From that point, the formality of the dinner discussion relaxed. The other three became more comfortable and began sharing more intimate details of their lives. Yet I was ever aware that I was in a room with three very wealthy people, people who had known nothing but luxury and advantage their entire lives, and I wasn't about to start blathering about growing up in an orphanage. I was content to focus discussions on my more recent past.

We were all in good spirits when we finished our

espresso. Anthony signaled the end of the evening.

"It has been delightful to be with you, but I regret that we must go. I can no longer stay up as late as I did in my youth." We stood, and I walked with Melissa to the lobby. William and Anthony were hanging back, engaged in some conversation which it was evident they did not want us to hear. I used the opportunity to speak privately with Melissa for the first time.

Melissa's apparent interest in me and expressed appreciation for what I had accomplished on behalf of her family had dispelled my reticence. That and the wine. I decided to take a shot.

"You don't have to turn in as early as your uncle. No need to end the evening yet. I know a few spots off the island we can go."

Melissa glanced over her shoulder at her uncle and then to me, turning her back to William and Anthony.

"I need to talk to you. I have to wait until my uncle is asleep. I'll try to be on the beach in front of your cottage in an hour."

Whatever I thought of myself and whatever I may have had in mind, it was clear Melissa still viewed me as a Milano family retainer, someone to assist when the need arose, not someone to spend an evening with. I nodded.

Anthony appeared behind Melissa. The vision of his afternoon meeting with Cabrini, which I had banished from my mind for the last few hours, now came rushing back.

"Melissa, we must go. Good evening, Mr. McDaniel. Thanks again for all you have done. I look forward to our continued relationship." Melissa did not betray a look or gesture in my direction as she and her uncle disappeared from the lobby.

William clapped me on the shoulder.

"So, how'd things go with Melissa?"

I didn't think William was suspicious or fishing for some information about Melissa's surreptitious contact.

"It was a wonderful evening. Thank you. I hope I'll be able to see her again before she goes back to Italy with her uncle."

"I'm sure you will. They aren't planning to leave for a few days. Well, let's head back to the cottage and have a nightcap before we turn in, shall we?"

Forty-five minutes later I was shucking my tux and pulling on a pair of well-worn jeans and a T-shirt. I went to the kitchen, grabbed a bottle of mineral water from the refrigerator, and went out the door from the breakfast room to the loggia. I sat for several minutes in one of the lounge chairs on the porch and sipped the water as though I were just out enjoying the night air. I waited to see if anyone had seen or heard me and had decided to investigate. When no one did, I walked down to the beach, sat in the sand at the high-water mark, and waited.

SEVEN

T HE NIGHT WAS MOONLESS. HOME OWNERS ALONG
the beach are discouraged from keeping security
lights on, to avoid disorienting the loggerhead tur-
tles that crawl onto the dunes at night to lay their eggs. The
effect was almost complete darkness. My eyes adjusted,
and as they did, I became aware of innumerable stars, pin
pricks of light against the black night sky, which were providing the only illumination. The ocean had tamed from
the night before, waves breaking on bars a hundred yards
off shore, lapping the dunes, the salt smell sweet. Waiting,
listening, my mind turned to lines from Mathew Arnold's
Dover Beach: "The sea is calm tonight. . . . Listen! you hear
the grating roar / Of pebbles which the waves draw back,
and fling, . . . With tremulous cadence slow, and bring /
The eternal note of sadness in."

Melissa appeared from the darkness. She, too, had
changed, into tight jeans and a baggy sweatshirt. Her perfect legs peeked out from the sweatshirt, which hid just
about everything else. Just me and a beautiful girl on a
deserted beach. Melissa grasped my hand. I thought for
a moment my prospects had improved.

"Paul. I'm so glad you're here. You've helped my family
so much. I hope you can help me now." Relieved of the

immediacy of her uncle's presence, Melissa appeared more vulnerable. And, alone with her on the beach, I was more willing to stifle any feeling that I was being used once again by the Milano family and instead to entertain the belief that I was just coming to the aid of a beautiful woman.

"So, tell me what . . ."

"My father isn't missing. He's hiding. He's hiding from Anthony. He doesn't trust Anthony, but my father hasn't told me why, or at least he hasn't told me everything, just enough to know that I shouldn't trust Anthony either. He's—"

"Whoa. Slow down. You know where your father is?"

"Yes."

"And you've talked to him?"

"Yes."

"And he told you he's hiding from Anthony, and you are not to trust him?"

"Yes."

"So, why are you with Anthony?"

"Anthony says it's his duty to watch over me in the absence of my father. I indulge his little fantasy. He's really trying to keep tabs on me, hoping to find my father. I don't want him to suspect that I know where he is. Anyway, my father thinks it's a good idea for me to stay close to Anthony to watch him, though for what, I don't know."

"So, all that back there, the tears, the struggle for composure, all that was an act?"

"My uncle is looking for some clue that I know where my father is, so I have to shed a few tears now and then, otherwise he'll be even more suspicious."

"Things can't be that bad."

"It's far worse than you can imagine. Anthony somehow has taken my father's entire interest in Milano Corporation." Melissa was silent for a few seconds to allow the full effect of her statement to register. If this was so, Anthony had acquired Placido's stock, which was worth billions. And Melissa was no longer potentially one of the richest women in the world. Just another smart, beautiful, single, woman.

"Do you have any idea how?"

"He told me it had something to do with the lawsuit."

"Nothing I did in the lawsuit could've had anything to do with Placido losing his shares in the corporation." I surprised myself with the defensiveness of my response. A suspicion of guilty complicity was already stirring beneath the surface of my conscience.

"Not you, the lawsuit. My father said it had something to do with the lawsuit, and he thinks Anthony had a hand in it somehow. But we can't figure out how."

"The first person I'd go to is Ariel. She's Placido's assistant, she's been involved in the lawsuit since the beginning, and she knows everything there is to know about Milano Corporation. I'd ask . . ."

"You've never met Ariel, have you?"

"No, just—"

"We can't risk bringing Ariel into this, at least not now, not without Placido's blessing—she might have been compromised by Anthony. So you are my last hope. I am sure you know Anthony purposely kept me ignorant of the details of the case."

"So that's why Enzo was pressed into service at the trial instead of you—even though he has no knowledge of business, and you have a graduate degree in finance." I had wondered.

"And I have been closely involved with my father throughout the development of the patents that were central to the case. But I was completely shut out of the litigation."

My suspicions, suppressed for much of the evening, now grabbed my consciousness, the thought of Anthony and Cabrini in the bar together this afternoon, chatting like a pair of old buddies. That meeting, Judge Richards' new found wealth, and my disproportionate partnership share, all conspicuous incongruities.

"But the lawsuit had nothing to do with Placido's ownership of stock in the corporation. I'm missing something."

"It may have been mere coincidence, but just before the lawsuit was filed my father had some significant financial difficulty as a result of what can only be called an obsession with rare books. You may be aware that my father is a famously avid collector. What you probably don't know is the lengths he would go to to acquire his objects. And being in charge of his finances, I am all too familiar with what he spends on books."

"I've seen his name in connection with some very expensive items at auction."

"You should know his library contains some of the most magnificent manuscripts in the world: Shakespeare's First Folio, a notebook of Leonardo DaVinci, a Gutenberg Bible, an early copy of the Declaration of Independence, and hundreds of beautifully illuminated medieval manuscripts, books of hours, incunabula, and codices. Through the years he has bought thousands of rare books at auctions and private sales all over the world. It became an obsession with him, and even someone with my father's wealth had to borrow money at times to keep up his habit."

"Not a surprise there—last I heard one of Leonardo's notebooks went for over $30 million. I don't think even your father has that much cash lying around."

"He borrowed the money and pledged his stock in Milano Corporation to secure the loans. While the stock value was high, it was sufficient to cover the loans, but when it went down as a result of the lawsuit, the bankers told him he had to come up with more money or lose his books. Somehow he kept his library, but he lost ownership in the corporation. I just don't know how Anthony manipulated the situation so that he ended up with my father's shares."

"Well, things are coming together. I have an idea."

Melissa looked both puzzled and suspicious at once. "Surely you and your law firm didn't have anything to do with Anthony stealing Milano Corporation from my father?"

"We may have been his instrument. I think I know what happened."

"I'd sure like to hear it."

"One of the first things I worked on when I started at Strange & Fowler was a Shareholders' Agreement for your uncle and father. Since these instruments are long, tedious, and boring, the task of writing the document often goes to a very junior associate, someone who ghost writes for a senior partner. The partner charges the client exorbitant rates for what is represented as his work. It was William Fowler who looked after your uncle and father while I labored on the document for weeks in a windowless cubical in the Strange & Fowler library.

"The primary concern in a corporation like Milano is that the control of a significant number of shares and, thus, control of the corporation, remains in family hands. I remember I provided in the agreement that if either your father or your uncle passed away or were in danger of losing his shares, then the other was given the right to purchase the shares for cash at market value—not an unusual provision in such an agreement.

"When the lawsuit depressed the value of Milano shares, the banks called for more security. They probably wanted Placido to sell some of his books, but when he refused they threatened to take the shares. That threat triggered the Shareholders' Agreement, and Anthony snapped up your father's shares in Milano Corporation for pennies on the dollar. The banks didn't care to have the shares, or the books; they just wanted money. And when the stock went back up after I won the suit, your uncle multiplied his fortune by thousands of times."

Melissa's jaw was no longer clenched in anger, now her eyes were wide, her mouth open in a caricature of disbelief.

"I just don't understand how . . ."

"Your father could have sold his books and avoided it all."

"He'd never do that. He's spent a lifetime collecting treasures that are irreplaceable. He once told me he could always make more money, but he could never make another First Folio."

Few things unite the fratricidal brotherhood of lawyers, but it is fair to say that most are bibliophiles at heart. Law school, with three years in a law library, will do that to you. For me, I had found the law library to be the quiet refuge I needed. In the company of books that held the recorded wisdom of centuries, I could believe that my hard work and study would be rewarded. I understood Placido's addiction.

"Wise men have embraced poverty, and rich men have courted bankruptcy over their desire to possess great books. Universal symbols of creativity, knowledge, power. Once they build their libraries they'd just as soon stare down the gates of hell before they'd relinquish even a single manuscript. The only way significant libraries ever come on the market is when the collector's unenlightened heirs part with them for mere cash after their benefactor's death. It's a good thing you can't take it with you, otherwise heaven would be stacked floor to ceiling with old books. Although, come to think of it, that may well be what heaven is like."

Melissa smiled and her hand brushed mine. The touch seemed timed and calculated, but it nevertheless sent a jolt through me, like a school boy holding hands with his girlfriend for the first time. I was still grasping at the illusion that Melissa could be interested in me for more than legal advice, and I realized that that hope left me vulnerable to Melissa's blatant manipulation. But I didn't care. I held ever tighter to the illusion. With effort I brought my thoughts back to Anthony Milano. And with even greater effort I moved my hand away from hers, for no other reason than just to keep my focus.

"What I fear is that your uncle is guilty of far more than taking advantage of your father when he was down. He may have orchestrated the entire scheme. And I may have been his stooge."

"I'm not following you . . ."

"You recognize the name 'Hector Cabrini?'"

"I know he is the lawyer for SyCorAx."

"That's all you need to know. As the lawyer for SyCorAx, he came painfully close to stripping Milano of the patents it had developed."

"But you won the case."

"So get ready for this: Hector Cabrini was having a drink with Anthony in the Abbey bar this afternoon. And they didn't look like they were getting ready to duel to the death."

"That's unbelievable. My uncle acted incensed with the lawsuit, and he was convinced that no decent attorney would bring such a case. The way my uncle talked, he wouldn't have been caught dead with anyone associated with SyCorAx, and under no circumstance with any of its lawyers."

"Well, caught he was. And he was very much alive. I saw him myself. He's right about the SyCorAx lawyers; no decent lawyer would have filed that lawsuit, and Hector Cabrini is no decent lawyer."

Melissa shook her head.

"That just can't be."

"And here's another bit of interesting news . . ."

It passed through my mind that I should let Melissa know about the Equity Account, my disproportionate share of firm profits, appearing now to be more of a payoff for my silence than a reward for my services.

So, was I going to tell Melissa she had reason to suspect me, too? That my total loyalty was purchased by Strange & Fowler for the price of a few million dollars a year, the equivalent of what Melissa Milano probably spent annually on her private jet? I looked into her eyes.

I decided not to.

"The judge who presided over the Milano trial has recently come into a *very* large amount of money. And I mean a very large amount of money, enough to buy a multimillion-dollar beach house and to drop a hundred thousand dollars on a shotgun. All this from a man who, before he came on the bench, could barely have scraped up enough money to pay cash for a used double-wide."

"So, what are you saying? That my uncle helped SyCorAx sue Milano? I can't imagine such a thing. What if SyCorAx won? It just doesn't make sense."

"It makes perfect sense. And it explains a lot of things. Anthony must've been aware of your father's weakness and, seeing an opportunity to take advantage of it, contrived a lawsuit to drive the price of the shares down. When the value of the stock inevitably plummeted, it triggered the Shareholders' Agreement. By the time your uncle exercised the option to purchase the shares, they were trading at close to penny status.

"SyCorAx came from nowhere with a hard drive full of patent secrets and with an extremely aggressive law firm behind it. It takes a lot of money to fund a patent-infringement case, particularly when it's brought by Hector Cabrini, and those secrets had to come from somewhere. I'm betting your uncle was the source of both.

"But the trick was, once Anthony got the lawsuit going, he had to assure that Milano couldn't lose. He did this by withholding key evidence from SyCorAx's lawyers. But your uncle was blind-sided by the Supreme Court decision just like I was, and it threatened to undo everything. He took care of that problem at the last minute by putting a lot of grease on the wheels of justice, or in this instance, cash in the pockets of Judge Richards.

"Somehow Anthony had to make sure a recklessly brash young lawyer was in charge of the case, someone who would try to win the suit outright, instead of a steady old hand who would play it safe and wisely try to mitigate the damages."

I couldn't repress a shudder at the thought of Billingsley's death. I had finally come to accept his suicide. The autopsy report found a near-toxic level of oxycodone in his blood. Billingsley was so drugged he hardly would have been able to drag himself to the top of the office tower and throw himself off. His widow, when she was finally able to talk about it, said he had been troubled for weeks about something at the office—no doubt the Milano case. Had Anthony just taken advantage of Billingsley's unfortunate death, or was there a more sinister explanation? I couldn't bring myself to believe that Fowler could have been complicit in a partner's murder, and I pushed the possibility out of my mind.

"But once the value of the shares went back up, the costs Anthony incurred in paying off attorneys, bribing judges, arranging for unlikely promotions—possibly even a murder—were miniscule compared to the gains he realized. Not to mention the value your uncle has secured for himself by achieving complete control of Milano Corporation and the marketing of the patents it developed."

"It is almost as bad as if SyCorAx had won."

"SyCorAx did exactly what Anthony wanted." It was only then that the full realization of what I had been saying took effect. I shook my head and laughed.

"What's so funny?"

I shrugged.

"I'm not the hot-shot lawyer I want you to think I am. At least I was good enough not to blow a victory that was handed to me." The homily on risk taking Fowler served me last night came rushing back once more. "And I suspect Fowler has known about this all along. He's probably been right in the middle of it."

"This is too much to take in."

"Yeah. I agree. Both William and Anthony would have known that it was foolish to bring the two of us together, that your father is smart enough to have figured out what had happened and would have told you. It wouldn't take too much imagination to think you might try to enlist my help and together we would know enough to bring them both down. We're not thinking this through."

"You're missing one more very important piece of information."

"I don't know if I'm up for any more surprises. What?"

"Anthony thinks my father is dead."

"Why?"

"He arranged for his murder."

"But I thought Placido and Anthony were extremely close; what about the two childhood buddies playing pranks in the basement? Is all that just corporate spin?"

In the years I had done legal work for Milano Corporation, I had been indoctrinated into the corporate mythology of the inseperable brothers. It was a narrative crafted to humanize the image of a financial leviathan, and one I drew from at trial to soften the hard edges of Milano Corporation. I had had no doubt the story was embellished, like so much else developed by public relations firms for their corporate clients, but after tonight's revelations, I was fast coming to the conclusion that whatever small truth may lay in the family lore, it hid much larger deceptions. But the extent of the deceit still escaped me.

"They were close, at least until my father got the foolish notion that he was going to save the world and license some of the firm's patents, the ones that figure prominently in HIV research, for next to nothing. The problem was the patents were not Placido's to bestow; they were created at the cost of millions by the corporation, and Anthony was not about to let my father give away what could prove to be a corporate gold mine."

I couldn't tell from Melissa's tone whether she identified more with Placido's altruism or Anthony's greed.

"So, what do you think? Did Anthony devise the lawsuit to save Milano Corporation from Placido's philanthropic intentions or to grab all the potential profits from the patents for himself?"

"What does it matter? Anthony bribed my father's chef to poison him. My father suspected the plan and foiled it, then disappeared before they could confirm whether he had succumbed to the poison. Without a body to show for his efforts, Anthony has strong suspicions that Placido is still alive. So right now my father is in hiding to keep his brother from killing him, and I am serving as a hostage to keep Placido from publicly revealing Anthony's intentions and as bait to reel Placido in to his demise. I have shared my family's dirty secrets with you in the hope that you might help me figure a way out of it all. Is that too much to ask?"

With that Melissa's composure melted. She buried her face in the folds of her sweatshirt, and her shoulders shuddered. Melissa's sudden despair left me at a loss as to what to do or say. I slid closer. It was a few moments before her sobs slowed, stopped, and she raised her head. Even in the darkness I could see the tears that streaked her cheeks.

"I'm sorry. You have done everything Milano Corporation has asked of you. I have no business requesting you to risk getting personally involved in our family affairs. I just don't know what to do." Melissa let out a deep breath and leaned on my shoulder.

I was as baffled as she, maybe more so, since I had Fowler's apparent complicity with Anthony and my conflicting loyalties to the firm and my profession to deal with. I had little experience comforting distressed heiresses, nor did it occur to me that Melissa's tears on the beach might be of the same sincerity as those shed at dinner, then an act for the sake of Anthony, now, to soften any reluctance I had left.

With all my social insecurity, I had great confidence in my intellectual ability. But without more sure-footed social instincts, my over-active imagination frequently got me into trouble. This time I felt I may be jumping into something I could not get out of. But jump I did.

"Well, I know one way to stop Anthony from killing your father, from doing away with you, and from keeping all of Milano Corporation for himself."

Melissa looked up, doubt and hope mingled in her expression.

"You and I find your father and go public with Anthony's scheme."

I knew as soon as I said it, it was a foolish gamble. I had worked all my life to get where I was with the firm, and all I had to do to count my share of the Equity Account for the rest of my life was walk away from the Milano family problems and let Anthony and Placido work out their disputes themselves. Melissa would be fine even without her father's share of the corporation; after all, she was an investment banker in her own right. At worst she could sell just one of her father's magnificent volumes and live well the rest of her life.

But I couldn't walk away and leave Melissa to suffer whatever fate Anthony had planned. And I wasn't willing to give up a chance to be with Melissa. My old feelings for her were stirred, but there was more to it, a challenge really. With Melissa I had a chance to prove I was, in fact, worthy. So I threw everything I had worked for to the wind, all to be with a beautiful woman. I wasn't the first man to do so.

With that Melissa kissed me, a long, soft kiss, tinged with the salt of her tears. Then the evening took a different turn.

EIGHT

WAS UP WATCHING THE SUNRISE FROM THE DUNES THE next morning, and I got in to Fowler Cottage well after first light. My eyes must have betrayed my lack of sleep when I appeared for breakfast.

"How did you sleep, Paul?" Fowler inquired, peering over the edge of his newspaper, a forced heaviness behind the questioning in his voice.

"Couldn't sleep. Took a long walk on the beach."

Fowler laid his newspaper on the table. The lines in his face looked deeper, more pronounced, eyes red-rimmed and weary, as though he, too, had been up much of the night.

"I've just received some shocking news. Early this morning Judge Richards was found dead in his room at the Abbey. A shotgun wound. He was cleaning his gun when it went off. The blast woke almost everyone in the hotel. It was either suicide or an accidental discharge. The authorities are investigating." Fowler was watching me, measuring my response.

"What? He couldn't have . . ."

I was already struggling for control of my emotions after a night of disclosure in which I was forced to confront the thought that the greatest success of my career was but a small part of a cynical manipulation of the world's financial markets by Fowler on behalf of a client so ruthless he would attempt to murder his own brother. I was now well beyond tact.

". . . No. Not suicide. I can't imagine it. Not him. Not another." My face was distorted by incredulity, and my words continued to tumble out. "Just yesterday afternoon, he couldn't have been happier showing me his cottage. He was looking forward to moving in. Accidental discharge? No. He handled a shotgun like he was born with one."

"Paul, I understand your shock. But more often than not it's the people most familiar with guns who have accidents." Fowler was still maintaining the façade, still trying to keep control, but the tension in his voice betrayed the effort.

"Not the judge. He wouldn't try to clean a loaded shotgun. And why would he, just before we were to go out shooting this morning? He would have cleaned and oiled it yesterday, after using it—which, as I remember, is exactly what he told the attendant he was going to do. This makes no sense. None."

"Look, Paul, I'm as distressed as you. I suggest we let the Glynn County authorities perform their investigation and we accept their conclusions. I'm confident they'll come to a prompt and proper resolution." Fowler's tone was tense. He was used to having his judgments obeyed, and he made no attempt to hide his displeasure at my questioning. Fowler's eyes bore into me. My loyalty was in doubt.

I now had no reason to believe anything this man told me. I was convinced it was well within his ability to make sure the authorities rule the matter an unfortunate accident or tragic suicide and not something more sinister.

But I realized in order to keep safe, if not to maintain the pleasure of my ostensible patron, it was essential that I not continue to betray my skepticism. After all, where was I heading with this? No suicide. No accident. Was I willing to say I thought the judge was murdered? And what about Billingsley? I had to tone down my initial outrage and attempt to appear more circumspect. I let out a deep sigh to signal I had backed down from my overly emotional response and shook my head in a feigned display of resignation.

"I can't imagine anyone like Judge Richards killing himself. He seemed so enthusiastic about life and was so happy to be on the island. It could only have been a tragic accident. He prized that shotgun so, he must have been cleaning it one more time to admire it. It's such a shock. I just can't . . ."

Fowler appeared skeptical, hesitated, then as if to indicate his acceptance of my apparent change of heart, his tone softened as he continued to carry on his part of the charade.

"The sheriff asked me to accompany him to inform Mrs. Richards, so I must leave shortly. I'm sure there will be a number of details that will have to be attended to. I know you'll want to be going soon, and I probably won't be back by the time you do. Please have a safe trip. I regret your weekend had to end so badly."

My host had surrendered all subtlety. It was clear he wanted me gone.

"Thank you for your hospitality. I'll make it a point to get an update from you when you return to Atlanta."

I choked down my breakfast in silence. I went upstairs, packed, and by the time I came back downstairs, Fowler and Oliver were gone. I stood for a moment in the entry hall, bag in hand, looking through the study and out the heavy-beamed window to the cobbled plaza below, listening to the quiet of the house.

Since I had left Melissa early that morning, I had been thinking only of her. We had ambled the beach, climbed the dunes, confiding, conspiring, until just before dawn when she had to return to avoid detection by her ever-watchful uncle. I walked Melissa back to the Abbey before first light, and we kissed, long and slow, before she disappeared inside the lobby. We had planned to meet for lunch after my outing with the judge to continue our plotting. If I was being manipulated by Melissa, I was enjoying it.

Then came Fowler's incredible revelation at breakfast. With the death of the judge, my suspicions of Melissa's uncle and ostensible guardian now went beyond mere corporate corruption and attempted murder to cold-blooded execution. It horrified me to bring the logic to its obvious conclusion: If Anthony was willing to kill a judge to cover his bribery and to kill his brother to claim his shares in the corporation, what would he be willing to do to Melissa, Placido's only heir, the only one left in a position to challenge his dominion over Milano?

I threw my bag in the back seat of the car. I stopped myself before I climbed in. I went back inside the house, grabbed one of Fowler's shotguns and a box of shells, stashed them in the back seat under my bag, and headed straight to the Abbey.

"We have no one by the name of Milano registered." The clerk, sweat beading his upper lip, tap, tap, tapping a chewed pencil on the desk, peered over my shoulder at a detective interrogating the manager and then back at me.

"No. No one by that name." Police vehicles, blue lights flashing, jammed the valet stand, officers flooded the lobby, questioning staff and visitors. The Milanos couldn't have been checked out for more than an hour; Melissa hadn't returned much earlier than that. I had a chance of catching them at the airport. Even if you were Anthony Milano, it takes time to get your jet in the air, and this departure had all the earmarks of a hasty and unplanned retreat. I knew Melissa had no prior warning that she'd be leaving, since we'd made arrangements to meet again for lunch.

I jumped back in the Porsche and flew down the main road toward the airport, passing most of the morning commuters in the opposite lane. I sped to the hanger that housed the Milano jet, hoping to catch Melissa and Anthony before they took off. I hadn't yet determined what I'd do if I were successful.

The Frederica Island airport is like everything else about the island: different. It's not even on Frederica Island, but rather on St. Simons, the island to the south—though it's not more than ten minutes away from Fowler Cottage. The airport was once commercial, served by daily flights from Atlanta. Soon the private jets out-numbered the ones from the commercial carriers, and today the only way to fly to Frederica Island is on your own plane. This requirement doesn't seem to be an inconvenience for the island residents. Anthony Milano's Gulfstream G650 wasn't the only one parked on the tarmac this week, though the Milano Corporation logo on the tail made it the most recognizable. I careened onto the airport road just in time to hear the jet blast and to see that logo rise high above the live oaks of the Frederica Island lodge and disappear as the Milano jet banked sharply on its flight over the Atlantic, taking Melissa out of my life as abruptly as she had appeared.

Being a lawyer has many benefits. One, not so evident, is that a lawyer's mind is filled with obscure legal data which often comes in handy at the most opportune times, such as the knowledge that flight plans of private jets are public information, a fact that popped into my head as the Milano jet became but a speck in the sky. My check with the tower confirmed that Milano had filed a flight plan directly to Naples, the closest airport to Anthony's villa that could safely handle his jet.

At a top speed of Mach .90, the Gulfstream G650 is one of the fastest civil aircraft in the world. It can travel non-stop from Frederica Island to Naples in less than 8 hours without breaking a sweat. In little more than the time I could drive from Frederica Island to Atlanta and unpack my bag, Melissa would already be climbing the rugged hills of the Italian coast in her uncle's Lamborghini to his villa in Positano. Even during Melissa's flight, she would be in cell phone contact, although I knew I couldn't safely call her until I was confident she was out of her uncle's sight.

Still, I had more to do here. I had to find out for sure if there was more to Judge Richards' death, if it was more than a suicide or accident. It still was not beyond possibility that Judge Richards killed himself either out of guilt or for fear of being exposed, but if Judge Richards was murdered, then Melissa was in far more danger than I wanted to think about.

While Frederica Island has its own private police force, it isn't a separately incorporated municipality, and it must rely on Glynn County and the port city of Brunswick, the county seat, for most of its other governmental services. In

spite of the wealth of the islands, the less affluent residents
of Brunswick control the politics of the county by dint
of sheer numbers. Other than the facts that it's located
on the Atlantic and surrounded by some rich neighbors,
Brunswick is much like any other county seat in South
Georgia. One of the common fixtures in these towns is
the coroner.

Coroners in Georgia, those who are charged under state
law with pronouncing death, are elected officials. Coroners
gather those who died of suspicious circumstances and
give opinions on cause of mortality. They usually work
part time and are not required to have any formal medical
training. The Office of Coroner is but one of many endear-
ing legal quirks left over from Georgia's antebellum era,
when there were few professionally trained doctors. And,
for some reason not so readily apparent, those elected to
the Office of Coroner often have colorful nicknames like
"Boo," "Shug," and "Peabo." As I pulled up to the place
of business of "Wimp" Boyd, Glynn County Coroner, an
ambulance was idling in front of the loading dock, its
crew keeping cool in the air-conditioned cab, awaiting
yet another call.

I found Wimp cleaning up from bringing in another
unfortunate. He had the professional appearance of a part-
time shade-tree mechanic whose full-time job was drinking
beer. And he wasn't unsure of his conclusion about the
judge's cause of death in the slightest.

"Clear case of dumb-ass. Blew the top of his damn fool
head right off. Hell, those people at the Abbey already
had movers, cleaners, and painters outside the door 'fore
I could even get the body out good. They gonna have a
time, though. There was hair and brains all over that wall,

85

what was left of it." He finished wiping his hands on a bloody rag and tossed it in a stainless steel sink. "What else you wanna know?"

"The judge and I went skeet shooting yesterday afternoon. We were supposed to go shooting again today. I can't imagine that he would have waited until this morning to clean his gun."

"That's what it looked like he was doin' to me. Sittin' on a sofa with the gun on the floor 'tween his legs. Shoulda knowd there was two shells in the chamber. Sure wasn't suicide though. Seen a lot a that. Somebody wants to kill hisself puts the gun in his mouth. Ain't never seen anyone point a shotgun at his own head and pull the trigger— mighty hard to do, after all. Was an accident all right."

"Will you make an official report?"

"Yup. Public Record. You can get a copy of it if you want."

"Thank you for your time."

"Sorry it didn't work out with you and the judge, but the way it looks to me, you'd been taking your life in your hands goin' shootin' with him."

None of this made sense, but I had nowhere to go with my suspicions. As I walked back on the loading dock, one of the drivers was sitting on his heels outside the ambulance having a smoke. As I passed him, he rose, crushed the butt under foot, and spoke.

"Sorry 'bout the judge. You a friend a his?"

"Yes, sir."

"Well, I sure hope they find who did it."

"Did what?"

"Shot him. Wimp didn't tell you? Found him in his pajamas laying in his bed with his head blown off. Sure as hell was no accident. Whoever did it must want to get caught. Shotgun was right beside him, wasn't even wiped clean. Wimp got it in his truck."

A jolt of realization pulsed through me as I recalled the judge taking his shotgun from my hands and gently placing it in the gun case, waiving off the attendant who offered to clean the gun. It was likely there were only two sets of prints on that shotgun: his and mine.

By the time I got back to Fowler Cottage, Fowler had returned. He didn't answer the door. I let myself in. I walked down the hallway and glanced into the darkened study. There he sat, staring at the door, poised for a challenge, no longer the affable law partner, his eyes shining with malevolence in the darkness. His look stopped me short before I entered the room.

"Wimp told me you were on your way. What I paid him to assure the judge's cause of death is officially an accident was apparently insufficient to secure the silence of his assistants. I chastised him for the indiscretion of his ambulance driver. I'm sure he will be dealt with severely. My only surprise is that you made it back so quickly. That new Porsche is rather fast. You are predictable Mr. McDaniel, you and your poor-boy earnestness."

Fowler stood, and I took a couple steps into the cramped room toward him, remaining just out of his reach.

"What the hell is going on? You think I—"

"Oh, you know very well what's going on. You and that Milano girl. You both got it figured out last night, didn't you? Anthony and I were able to manipulate the results of the Milano trial and get the shares of the corporation in his hands with hardly a wrinkle in our plan. And I had every reason to believe you would take your undeserved share in the partnership and keep your mouth shut even if you figured out what happened. But I did not count on Melissa's considerable charms and her ability to convince you to throw it all away for an illusory chance to be with her. I am always amazed how beautiful women can make brilliant men act stupid, and you're just another in a long line."

His taunting had the desired effect: I clinched my fists, ready to pummel him. Fowler looked down at my hands, then locked on my eyes; he didn't flinch.

"Melissa didn't—"

"Melissa is a liar. But now I'm afraid you'll never have the chance to find out just how thoroughly she deceived you. All she really wants is the shares of the corporation to be returned to her father so that they can be hers when he dies, preferably sooner rather than later. And she figures you are the only one reckless enough to take on Anthony Milano and risk all on her behalf. You probably should've studied *Don Quixote* a bit more closely; in the end things don't go well for the chivalrous knight."

"How . . . how did you find out what . . ."

"Don't act so surprised. You don't really think you could spend any time in this house where the President of the United States once stayed and make a move, say a word, or even think a thought without my knowing about it, do you? This cottage is wired as tight as the White House. As soon as you went out last night, James alerted me from the guard house that you had walked out the kitchen door and were sitting on the loggia. He sent a live video feed to my cell phone. He even told me you were drinking San Pellegrino. When you went to the sand and out of range of the surveillance cameras to meet Melissa, the microphones lining the beach picked up every word of your conversation.

James sent the audio to me as well. Hell, I thought you were going to get lucky. Both you and that girl would have been better off doing that instead of talking all night, which is what I was forced to listen to until dawn."

Fowler's intimate knowledge of my evening with Melissa turned my pugnacity into loathing; I could barely spit out my disgust.

"So you had Judge Richards killed as soon as his utility for you and Anthony passed?" I shook my head. "You didn't even let the poor bastard spend the night in his beach house."

"You shouldn't feel sorry for Judge Richards. He died as the result of acute hubris. One would have thought ten million dollars from the coffers of Strange & Fowler would've been sufficient to keep him happy for the rest of his life, and it would have, had he just been discrete. But he had to show it off, buy a beach house and a hundred-thousand-dollar shotgun. Hell, even you suspected something was amiss. Does everyone who grows up poor have to prove they made it by buying outlandish trinkets and bringing unwanted attention to themselves? Like that Porsche of yours. And who, in their right mind, buys a hundred-thousand-dollar shotgun, even if they have the money? So I'm afraid that Judge Richards had to learn just how dangerous such a weapon is. There are some very dedicated people in Strange & Fowler's security arm, and they've been able to accomplish their task without bringing attention to me or to the firm; that is, until your snooping resulted in a chance encounter with the coroner's ambulance driver."

"So everything's come unraveled because someone had to smoke a cigarette."

"The reason is of no consequence. Now Anthony and I risk having our entire plan exposed by you and Melissa, something I don't intend to endure. I can only guess how Milano is going to deal with Melissa, but I sure as hell know what I'm going to do with you."

Fowler closed the gap between us in two steps, pulled a dark pistol from inside his jacket, and pointed it at my heart. I looked around the room for the security camera and saw a small grey lens near the ceiling over Fowler's shoulder.

"Oh, don't worry. I disabled the cameras and the microphones in the study. And the camera in the kitchen as well. Just before I shot Oliver to make sure there were no other witnesses. But the sound monitors worked perfectly, as I expected. Security called immediately. I told them I eliminated a raccoon that had gotten into the kitchen through an open window. When they call back I'll tell them you were holding a gun to my head when they first called, and the next shot dispatched you."

I made a move to the door.

Fowler grabbed my arm and shoved the gun in my chest.

"You're going nowhere."

"You can't get away with killing me."

"Of course I can. I'll tell the cops you became enraged when I confronted you about being out of the cottage at the Abbey this morning—about the time the judge was shot, a fact the doorman will conveniently confirm. And your prints on the shotgun will establish your guilt. I'm sure Wimp will revise the cause of death from accident to murder just as soon as I point out his error. You determined that your desperate attempt to prevent the judge from betraying your bribery scheme had come undone, and after you killed the judge, you tried to kill me to seal the final leak. Oliver nobly gave his life to protect me."

Fowler smirked.

"You're just another brilliant young lawyer gone bad."

I wasn't going to die this way. I grabbed the gun, still hot from the shot that killed Oliver, and bent it hard away from myself. Though a former athlete, Fowler was no match in strength to someone forty years younger. The gun kept turning, turning away from me toward Fowler, my hand around his, my finger groping for the trigger. In an instant the gun was only inches from Fowler's chest.

"*You are so damn predictable.*" The gun went off. The shock momentarily stunned me. Fowler's hand went limp. I had no idea whether it was my finger or his that found the trigger, or even if the gun had gone off as we both struggled for it. He fell toward me, then crumpled to the floor. I still held the gun in my hand. When I realized it, I dropped the pistol to the floor beside the body. Blood and powder residue were on my hands, and a fine red spray covered the rest of me. I ran from the room, looking for Oliver, sprinting to the kitchen, turning the corner to the pantry, finding him lying in a puddle of his own blood. There was a dark hole in his forehead.

The phone rang. Security. If Fowler didn't answer they would be here in seconds. Surely he wasn't dead. I ran back into the study. I touched his neck to find a pulse. There was none. But my own heart was about to pound out of my chest. And the phone kept ringing.

I picked up the gun. I realized my prints were now on two weapons involved in three deaths on the island within the span of a few hours. I would soon be the prime suspect in three murders. I could hear sirens in the distance. Standing there with the gun in my hand, I knew there was one sure way out: I could turn the gun on myself. Was that what Fowler had done? Was that what he meant just hours ago when he told me in this very room that he'd do anything for the firm? Was this to be the ultimate test of my loyalty? Had Fowler staged his own death to look like a murder to avoid the inquiry that his suicide would bring—that would destroy the firm? Or had he used me as the agent of his death so that he wouldn't have to endure the fall that loomed before him? Is that what he'd meant by telling me I was so damn predictable?

One thing was sure. For Fowler there would be no arrest, no interrogation, no trial, no jail, no humiliation, no pain. And by leaving the gun in my hand as his last act, Fowler gave me the option, no—*he challenged me, he dared me*—to follow him, and by my death to wrap up this Shakespearean tragedy with a pile of bodies in the study, and so leave Strange & Fowler inviolate.

But I'd endured far too much to quit now, to take the easy way out, to admit defeat, to hand victory to the spirits I wrestled daily: to acknowledge that I really wasn't worthy. And there was Melissa. Last night with Melissa gave me the hope I had a chance with her. And whatever Fowler may have thought, whatever he may have said, I wasn't going to give that up, and without me now, I knew Melissa had no chance in the hands of her maniacal uncle.

I threw down the gun and ran in full flight out the door to my car, abandoning all pretense that I could prove my innocence to the Frederica Island Security Force. If this new German sports car was worth anything, I could elude the cops in their minivans at least until I got off the island, and then I might have a chance to lose myself in the backwoods of South Georgia and come up with a plan. I passed two patrol cars speeding in the opposite direction, heading directly toward Fowler Cottage, as I screamed down Frederica Island Drive toward the causeway. If they were going to catch me, they were going to have to have something that could outrun a 911.

NINE

I CUT HARD TOWARD THE BRIDGE, WHICH WAS NOT YET blocked, the only way off the island. Fowler had allowed that this strategic choke-point had been equipped for the Summit with a tank-proof carbon-steel barrier that could be raised hydraulically in seconds from beneath the cobblestone in the event that an emergency required the isolation of the island from the mainland. Once raised and locked in position, he had boasted, nothing—not even an M-1 Abrams tank—could cross that bridge. I had to get past the barrier before security reached Fowler's Cottage, decided they had a murderer on the island, and radioed the guard house to trigger the barricade.

As soon as I hit the base of the bridge on the island side, I saw steel posts rising from the pavement, yet only inches extended from the road-bed. Downshifting hard, I aimed the wheels between the teeth and redlined the engine, feeling the jolt of tires against metal, hearing the screech of the carbon-fiber rear bumper rip from the back of the car. I splintered the wooden arm extended from the guard house, which was sufficient to slow only the law-abiding, sending pieces flying into the doorway where the guard stood talking on his radio. Panic distorted his face, and he pawed at the side arm strapped to his hip, then straightened, but by then the 911 was screaming across the causeway.

The steely teeth of the barrier, now extending toward their full height, glinted in the sun through my rearview mirror, a piece of my bumper still tumbling down the road on the other side, its clatter drowned out by the engine's roar. I could only hope the tank-trap had missed ripping out something vital. A bumper I could do without. If an oil line were severed, it would disable my car in a few seconds, but the engine winding at 6,000 rpm showed no evidence of damage. Now the barrier behind me would work in my favor, slowing the pursuit of the island cops, and with any luck I'd have a few minutes head start on the Glynn County Sheriff. Even as I blew down the winding marsh roads toward the coast at over 90, the locals didn't give me much notice. I was just another of the innumerable coked-up, over-privileged brats who ply these ways in exotic sports cars, hurtling toward an early demise.

My immediate goal was to make it to the Sidney Lanier Bridge, spanning the Brunswick River, a paradox of mass and delicacy. Soaring nearly five-hundred feet, the bridge stretched a mile and a half, dominating the flat coastal landscape even twenty miles inland. The graceful arcs prescribed by its cables and piers seemed to float above the tranquil waters of the harbor. From its height, one could see the roads leading in and out of the islands to the east and glimpse the vast South Georgia wilderness to the west. I would find my bearings, get a look at anyone forming a pursuit, and make a decision as to which direction I'd flee. The thought flashed across my otherwise terror-stricken mind that the old Sidney Lanier Bridge, the dangerous, narrow, rusted structure that the current artful form had replaced a few years ago, was the site of the getaway in *Smokey and the Bandit*. Unlike the movie, there'd be no heroic escape for me, just the ignominy of flight from a sure murder charge.

Running like a damn felon! What the hell was I thinking? Why was I throwing away everything I had struggled so hard to achieve in a foolish flight from an obviously staged crime-scene? I should turn around now, turn myself in, explain what happened, depend on the good judgment of the police officers, on the wisdom and integrity of the justice system, a justice system I'd dedicated my life to serving.

But that was the catch, wasn't it; that was precisely the problem: I knew the system all too well. I knew that police rush to the easiest solutions, that judges incline toward the conclusions of law enforcement, and that courts dispense not justice but resolutions—the quicker the better. Once caught in the avalanche of justice gone bad, I would be buried alive, like any other poor unfortunate overwhelmed by the weight of the system, nowhere to turn, no one to listen.

No, I knew too much about the justice system, and I didn't want my fate decided there, not now—now that I knew the ease with which Strange & Fowler had manipulated the system for Milano and could as easily manipulate it against me. I would escape, find a place to hide, and figure out my next move as far from here as possible.

The barrier island causeway intersects the Coastal Highway at the city limits of Brunswick, and I took the turn to the south, barreling toward the bridge that loomed before me. I was still in second gear, near redline, topping 70, when I crested the bridge, and my stomach took leave of me for a second. The view was majestic and perfect in all directions. Toward the east, I could see no flashing lights on the island causeways, nothing to give me concern. Before me, to the south, lay open highway. To the west the hundreds of thousands of acres of swamp and forest which make up South Georgia stretched uninterrupted for two hundred miles—from I-95 hugging the coast toward Jacksonville, to I-75 winding through the middle of the state on its way to Tampa. Between the two interstate highways lay the vast swamps of the Okefenokee, untouched forests, few towns. The rest were fish camps on slow black rivers and hunting lodges in deep pine woods. Here a man could disappear. Here was where Jefferson Davis was headed as Richmond, the northern stronghold of the Confederacy, collapsed around him. He was captured in Irwinville, just sixty miles north of the Okefenokee. Had Davis made it, he may never have been caught, and the Civil War would have raged on as a guerrilla campaign led from the swamps of South Georgia. Some folks believe it still does.

At the base of the bridge, the Coastal Highway makes a dramatic turn inland, crossing under I-95 before going south again. Once across the interstate, I could pick up the road to Waycross, which was less than an hour distant, perched at the north end of the Okefenokee. That path would lead me to the highway heading directly to the swamp through Nahunta. The road was used primarily by logging trucks hauling pulp wood to the paper mills on the coast. I could open up the Porsche, make time, look for a path cutting cross country, and find a place to hide.

I still had my cell phone, which I knew could be tracked. I wanted to use it one last time to send a message to warn

Melissa. I pulled into a Waffle House near the entrance ramp to the interstate, texted Melissa, "Anthony knows," and ducked into the men's room. I left my cell phone on the sink, confident that in a few minutes someone would pick it up, and with any luck, head down I-95 and take the cops with them. I envisioned some petty thief cruising down the interstate, chatting on his new phone, pulled over by a half-dozen patrol cars and thrown to the ground by a squad of armed officers. By then I should be deep in the woods. I could only hope my unwitting accomplice would have little trouble demonstrating that he's not me, not wanted for murder, and merely a phone thief.

My chief concern was FLETC, the Federal Law Enforcement Training Center, a few-thousand acres of top-secret facility just to the west of Brunswick, a place where the FBI, DEA, ATF, Secret Service, and Homeland Security trained, where several-dozen black military helicopters and hundreds of federal troopers stood ready to assist local law enforcement. I figured I had less than an hour to get lost before the choppers took to the air.

It doesn't take long to get into the wilderness in South Georgia. The Satilla River, a vast unspoiled waterway teeming with prehistoric gators, catfish the size of johnboats, wild pigs big enough to inspire tales of Hogzilla, and so many rattlesnakes the locals have annual roundups, cuts across the Waycross Highway just before Nahunta on its way to the Brunswick Harbor and the Atlantic Ocean. There are so many nutrients drained by the Satilla that the mouth of the river at St. Simons Sound is one of the largest breeding grounds for hammerhead sharks in the world. Any track through the underbrush near the Satilla would likely take me to an isolated hunting lodge or fish camp on the banks of the river, a place where I could hide, regroup, figure out my next move.

I had been flying down the road at well over 100 for 15 minutes, passing a dozen logging trucks on the long, flat straights, closing in on the Satilla, allowing with each passing minute for a flicker of hope to catch and grow in my heart that I might find refuge, when I felt it. I felt it even before I heard it, the rhythmic visceral pounding of a helicopter, maybe more than one, moving in my direction, low and fast. I shot off the road into a hammock of live oaks, burying the car deep under the low-hanging branches. In seconds two Black Hawks swept fifty feet above the dense canopy, following the highway, moving west. I stayed motionless for several minutes after watching them fly out of sight, having made no indication of detecting me.

By my reckoning the Satilla should be ahead only a few miles, making its wide bend south from above Nahunta on its way to the Brunswick River. Once across it, I would look for any track into the forest marking the way to a shelter on the river, most likely deserted, used only in season by a privileged few who had access by dint of wealth, descent, or both. There I could hole up, consider options, make plans, find what I need to get by. I could live off the land, catch fish, shoot deer. Hell, I might never leave.

Pushing my Porsche harder than I had ever driven before, I hit 125, as fast as I trusted my reflexes. Even then, if a slow-moving logging truck pulled on to the highway a quarter-mile ahead, I would be going too fast for me to end up as anything more than a large greasy spot on his trailer. The temperature gauge showed the engine was over-heating, the air-dam previously enclosed by the now-missing bumper, leaking. But I had to get into the woods soon; I pressed on.

The Satilla appeared, wide, flat, dark, languid, draining thousands of square miles of deep forest. I took the first trail off to the right, no more than two tire tracks, into the woods. It wasn't even a couple minutes before I felt the next wave of choppers flying over, but by now I was well into the wilderness on a trail double-sheltered by over-arching branches of live oak and wax myrtle. Safe for the moment, I needed somewhere to hide the car and stop moving.

It was three long miles of crawling down the road, trying not to tear out the undercarriage of the Porsche on the rocks and logs that littered the trail, trying to keep the engine from seizing while laboring at low rpms, before I saw what I was looking for: a low-slung, unpainted, tin-roofed building with deep screened porches wrapping it on all sides. To the left was a barn, divided, open, wide enough to drive my Porsche into. Which is just what I did and then turned off the engine.

It took only seconds for me to realize the absolute, perfect, quiet of the place, a peace I had disturbed by my raucous entrance. Once the engine was off, a complete silence enveloped me, punctuated by my rapidly pounding heart. I took a few deep breaths and tried to calm myself. I was safe, at least for the moment, and I needed to let my mind accept this peace before I pressed on.

The darkness inside the barn contrasted with the bright sunlight outside, and it took my eyes a moment to adjust. I stepped outside the car and looked around. This was not an animal barn but an equipment shed, with a tractor, bush-hog, disk harrow, broadcast seeder for managing food plots, and—of more interest to me—a four-wheeler, far more efficient and much less conspicuous for moving cross country than a Porsche, and the keys were conveniently in the ignition. I turned back to my car to take stock. Other than the jeans and T-shirt I had on, I had no clothes that would be of use out here—unless, of course, I happened upon a black-tie affair and could wear my tux. I was happy I had had the foresight—or dumb luck—when I left Fowler's cottage to toss one of the Beretta shotguns and box of shells in the back seat, along with my ubiquitous lap top. I decided to look around, dug in the back seat, and grabbed the shotgun.

In my limited experience, I have found that the sound of a round being chambered in a pump action shotgun has a way of getting one's attention. That and two black barrels pointed toward your chest, which now appeared at the entrance to the barn, not twenty feet from me. The shotgun, aimed directly me, seemed as big as a howitzer.

"Don't touch the gun. Step back from the car, hands in the air. One wrong move and you'll be buried out back next to my bird dog, and no one will ever know you were here." The voice, disembodied, came from around the corner; its owner had yet to show himself.

"Keep your hands up. Move to where I can see you good." And now I could see him. Athletic, medium height, ball cap over large mirrored, aviator sun glasses, trimmed grey beard, camo shirt, faded jeans, heavy boots. Just like every other man within a hundred miles, except there was no trace of the beer gut that usually graced the form of middle-aged men from these parts, only wiry muscle.

"Who you runnin' from?"

"I'd feel a lot more like talking if you'd be so kind as to point the gun in some other direction."

He lowered the gun. "I can hit three quail on the rise with one shot. Unless you can move faster than that, I wouldn't try anything."

"Can I put my hands down?"

"No."

"Now, who you runnin' from? I saw them Black Hawks. They don't put those in the air to track shoplifters. You a terrorist?"

I saw nothing to be gained by lying. If he was going to turn me in, I stood my best chance with the feds, not with the locals in cahoots with Fowler.

"Some might think so. The FBI and every other federal agency are probably looking for me."

"Why?"

"Well, for starters, they think I shot a judge."

"Did you?"

"No."

"So why the hell you runnin'?"

"I don't trust them. I was trying to get someplace where I could figure out my next move."

"And how did you just happen to end up here?"

"Your road is the first one after the river. I couldn't keep going on the highway or I'd a been caught. Looks like I was anyway."

He bent over and spit on the ground. "Feds. Hate them bastards. I sure as hell ain't going to turn you in to them. Least not yet. Name's Bill Grey, GBI retired. Most people call me Agent Grey."

I went from thinking I was going to be shot, to thinking I was caught, to thinking I was rescued, all in a few seconds. Words failed me. I just stared.

"So who is it I have the pleasure to meet?"

"Agent Grey, I'm Paul McDaniel. You're not . . ."

"Look, after working for thirty years in the GBI I only learned to hate the feds, bunch of arrogant bastards. The rest of 'em are idiots. I might let you hide here in the barn while I figure out what to do with you, but I'm going to take your gun and your keys. Don't want you thinking you can sneak up and shoot me like you shot that judge and run out of here."

"I didn't shoot the judge."

"No one ever did. You got any other weapons?"

"No."

"I want you to stand with your back to me, legs apart, hands on that wall, and I'm going to pat you down, just to check. We're going to need to develop a little trust."

Holding the shotgun in one hand, he patted me down with the other and lifted my wallet from my back pocket.

"I have some cash in my backpack if that's what you're looking for."

"I'm not looking for money, Mr. McDaniel, I'm looking to see if you are who you say you are. I see a driver's license issued to a Paul William McDaniel with a picture that looks a little like you and Georgia State Bar card with your name on it. Shoulda figured you a lawyer with that fancy car." He stuck my wallet back in my pocket. "You can turn around and put your hands down, but don't make any quick movements."

Agent Grey sat down on a plank laid over two short stacks of concrete blocks up against one wall of the barn. The shotgun was still at his side, but no longer pointed at me, and no longer with his finger on the trigger. He saw me look at the shotgun.

"I can pick it up faster than you can get to me. Now

you're going to tell me just how you got all those Black Hawks stirred up."

"There's a lot to it."

"I ain't in no hurry. Like I said, we're going to need to develop a little trust. You can turn that bucket over and sit down if you want. Ain't nobody gonna come lookin' for you here, least not for a while."

Agent Grey spit on the ground again and focused on me. I began with my going to work for Strange & Fowler, where all my problems started. And I finished with the murder of Judge Richards, the execution of Oliver, the death of Fowler, and the uncertain fate of Melissa. I held back a little about Melissa. Even now, just a few hours since I last saw her, my headlong rush to rescue her from her uncle felt rash and impulsive. I needed time to think before bringing someone else into my confidence.

"That's a lot to swallow."

"It's the truth."

"I 'spect it is. No one could make all that up, least ways no one in his right damn mind."

We had closed the barn and moved to the porch in case some fly-over got too curious and decided to take a closer look. Agent Grey had set his shotgun in the corner, and we both sat on rocking chairs under ceiling fans, which kept a cool breeze stirring all afternoon. A pleasant evening chill had settled in. For a few moments, talking to Agent Grey about the firm, the trial, and Melissa, I relaxed, allowing the solitude of the place to envelop me, forgetting I was a fugitive from a triple-murder charge, hunted by every law enforcement agency in the State. In these moments, through multi-paned floor-to-ceiling windows, I could see a comfortable, well-appointed lodge, with pine floors, walls, and ceilings, a deep-leather sofa and over-stuffed chairs, trophy-buck and lunker-bass lining the walls. Beyond the clearing of the house and barn lay trackless forests, tangled swamps, torpid rivers.

"Nice place."

"Lodge was my father's. I inherited it from him, as he did from his father. Most of the land around here was my grandfather's farm. He sold all but a couple hundred acres to the paper company. The paper company used to clear-cut everything but our property 'bout once every twenty years. Now Canadian logs are so cheap it's easier to buy from them than it is to get up in here with all their logging equipment. They haven't cut up here since I was a boy."

"You live here full time?"

"Now I do. Was a time when I didn't. That was 'fore I got shot by a psycho holed up in an elementary school with thirty kids and a school teacher. I 'bout had the guy holding the kids talked out of it when his partner snuck around behind me. FBI was 'sposed to be watching my back. GBI gave me a commendation and made me retire. I moved out here."

"You got a family?"

He looked in my eyes, then away, shaking his head, his look betraying a deep sorrow, a sorrow I felt best left further undisturbed. He turned back to me, the pain still in his eyes.

"So what you gonna do now?"

That was the question I had yet to answer, had not even begun to answer, my entire being focused for the last few hours on escaping. Having found temporary refuge, I was at a loss as to my next step. I needed time to think.

"How long can I stay here?"

"Not long, maybe a day, two at most. Probably take that long 'fore a cruiser comes nosing up the trail to check out the place. There's a bunk in the barn. You can hide out in there. In case anyone shows up looking for you, I'll at least have a straight-faced excuse for not knowing you were here if they find you. I spend most of my time in the woods and on the river." He tossed me my keys. "You can have your car back, but it's not going to do you much good—every cop in the country is looking for it now. By the way, if you get any ideas about heading out on that four-wheeler, it's booby trapped. You try to crank it, all your troubles will be over."

"Anything else I need to know?"

"Don't try coming in the house. Bubba wouldn't like it."

"Bubba?"

"Rottweiler. Electronic security systems don't work out here."

I remembered having seen a chain-link dog-run on the side of the lodge when I drove up, but no dog.

"I haven't even heard him bark."

"You won't hear him. And you won't see him until he has a big hunk of your ass in his teeth."

Agent Grey rose and started to head inside.

"I'm gonna fry some fish and cook some grits for supper. Interested?"

Only then did I realize I hadn't eaten since my breakfast with Fowler and Oliver long hours ago. The mere thought of food made my empty stomach growl. While I sat in the rocking chair on the porch, Agent Grey soon had two black cast-iron kettles fired up on a gas cooker in the yard, fish frying in one, grits bubbling in the other. The fish, filleted crappie caught this morning, breaded in cornmeal, Cajun-seasoned, deep-flash-fried in peanut oil, was served with buttery grits doctored with plenty of salt and pepper, and it tasted better to me than meals I have had at many a four-star restaurant.

"Agent Grey, thank you for what you're doing. I know you can get in a lot of trouble for this."

"I ain't getting in any trouble over you. I never knew you was here."

"Thanks anyway. I'm tired. I'm heading to the barn."

The barn was now my refuge and my prison, my security from the helicopters and cruisers that had crisscrossed the swamp searching for me, but also a cell I dare not escape for fear of certain capture. That night I lay on the dusty mattress, listening to the squirrels and mice run the rafters and gnaw bags full of seed. I imagined the seed was meant both for feed plots and to cultivate habitat for deer and quail, the game that Agent Grey would hunt in season. I wondered where I would be by the fall, the leaves in the swamp turned golden, when the game, fattened on grain which now lay as seed in the barn, would be frying in Agent Grey's blackened skillet. Fall was too long a time to consider; too many things could happen for me ever to think that far along. Tomorrow was as far as I dared go.

It was always two and three in the morning when my own mind tormented me, the looming deadlines, the hand-to-hand combat that litigation had become, the fears of loss and of failure taking palpable form, but nothing I had yet experienced matched the terror that overwhelmed me that night. Vast armies of troopers were arrayed, even at that hour, bent on my capture, equipped with all the power and intelligence the state can field against its citizens. I was nothing and had nothing in the face of all that the government could bring to bear. Yet I had to survive, if for no reason other than for Melissa. Maybe I was deceived, and maybe what Fowler said about her was true, but I chose to believe Melissa over a dead man who had killed himself and at least two others to keep his corporate crimes from being discovered. Having made my choice, I had to play it out. It was only the thought of Melissa—now thousands of miles away, sheltered in her own refuge, captured in her own prison—which kept me from walking out of that barn and flagging down the first state trooper I saw.

TEN

T HE GRAYING OF DARKNESS JUST BEFORE DAWN FIL-
tered through the upper windows of the barn, then
brightened and woke me, for the time sparing me
further torment. Morning brings hope, fresh thoughts,
and new plans, no matter how dark, how dismal, the night.
My mood rose with the sun. Now I lay thinking, my mind
teeming, racing.

I had to get into the firm email system, to find out what
my partners were saying, to see if anyone were trying to
contact me, to gauge what was known publicly. If someone
were trying to contact me, it might give me a chance to
plant some disinformation concerning my whereabouts. I
held out some hope that I hadn't been tagged with Judge
Richard's death, a fact which would significantly simplify
matters, for if it were just my word against that of a dead
man, I might consider turning myself in and taking my
chances with the DA.

I needed access to the Internet. From there I could get
into the firm's email system and into my email account
without attracting suspicion. Though the firm's security
was severe, and it touted the faultless confidentiality of its
systems to its clients, many of its lawyers were less than
attentive to security measures. I know several passcodes

belonging to other attorneys, and it wasn't unusual for an associate to check a senior lawyer's email and even monitor it for him. Hell, some of the older lawyers didn't even know how to use a computer. The firm's paranoid clients would pass out if they knew that anyone from a secretary on up could access their most delicate company secrets, take them home, and laugh about them with their friends over drinks. Like the time when a paralegal in the white-collar crimes section—euphemistically known as the "Special Operations Unit" so as not to scare off potential clients—downloaded a Fortune 500 CEO's personal porn collection, including pictures of him and his mistress, and displayed it at a party. Security systems only go so far.

Once the lawyers of Strange & Fowler got the news of my imminent demise, there would be dozens of firm hackers—chief among them my "loyal" partners, my "dedicated" associates—from the merely curious to the thoroughly malicious, plundering my email. Each one would be searching for the gem that would further his own career, jumping on any opportunity to stand on my shoulders and push his own head above water, pouncing on any unprotected leads to increase his revenue share. In this regard, a major law firm is no different from law school, the closest thing to swimming naked with great whites one can do on dry land. With all the activity in my account, I would be just an unidentifiable face in the crowd, working someone else's passcode.

The problem was finding some way to access the Internet in the middle of the woods. I had my doubts whether Agent Grey even had a computer, much less Internet access, but he was a start. Maybe he knew someone who did. As soon as I saw light in the lodge, I tapped on the screen door, wary of arousing Bubba. Agent Grey met me at the door, coffee mug in hand.

"Internet? Sure. I've got a dish in a pine tree locked on to a satellite feed I've hacked into. No one can even trace the signal."

"You're kidding me, right?"

"You don't think I'm some dumb-ass redneck do you? Hell, how do you 'spect I get along out in the woods? I cross-trained in electronic surveillance while at the GBI. My undergraduate degree is from Georgia Tech."

"Your undergraduate degree?"

"I've got a master's degree in psychology from Vanderbilt. That's why the GBI used me in hostage negotiations." Agent Grey betrayed a slight smile. "Have some coffee and a biscuit and I'll get you hooked up."

After two cups of strong coffee and a couple hot, buttered biscuits, Agent Grey took me inside and opened a pair of doors that appeared to be a hall closet, but instead revealed a small room with a desk, server, large flat screen monitor, and laser printer—all the latest equipment, newer even than what I had at the firm. Agent Grey rattled off some computer-geek talk about how fast and good it all was, but as far as I was concerned, he might as well have been speaking in tongues. I looked around the lodge.

"So where's Bubba?"

"Out back."

I turned my attention to the computer.

"You sure this can't be traced?

"Hell, I've hacked into the FBI from here. No one knew it happened."

Relieved, I pulled up a chair, grabbed the mouse, circled it once, and the desk top appeared.

"So how do I get on? Any special protocol?"

"Just click on the browser."

The Google homepage popped up immediately. Agent Grey drifted away, leaving me to my investigations. I typed a few lines of instructions, and within seconds I was connected. A press release on William Fowler's significant life and unanticipated death was posted at the firm's home page.

ATLANTA, GEORGIA. FOR IMMEDIATE RELEASE.

William Fowler, 72, son of the founding partner of the firm Strange & Fowler, was found dead at his cottage on Frederica Island this morning. He is survived by his wife, Sarah, three children, all of whom are attorneys, and six grandchildren.

Mr. Fowler was well-known for his civic accomplishments. . . .

I SCROLLED DOWN. The press release mentioned a private graveside and memorial service at St. Phillips Cathedral. But there was no cause of death, no mention of the judge, no mention of Oliver. And there was no mention of me, only that "Fowler had spent the evening before dining at his favorite restaurant in the Abbey with friends from the worlds of business, law, and the arts." I looked further for a separate press release, something that might mention the judge or Oliver or me. Nothing. I got into my email account using the password of an associate whom I had authorized to monitor my account during a recent trial. Though there was still an email account with my name, there was nothing in it. I had not one single email in my inbox or deleted files, though I received, sent, and deleted hundreds a day; by now I expected it to be close to overflowing. Someone had performed a security erase on my account and was diverting all my emails to another user. My email account was nothing but electronic bait. All my other accounts were shut down.

I had to find out what the official word at the firm was about me, whether they were still trying to keep my name out of the discussion of the three deaths, or if they'd already elected to let me hang for them. But I had one backdoor left to the firm.

Tracey.

Tracey is the once drug-addicted first child of my secretary, Lillian, the result of a teen-aged indiscretion. Lillian had never married Tracey's father. At the firm Lillian presented the image of the perfect mother of the perfect family, and she did everything to keep it that way. Husband a middle-manager for BellSouth, two children, boy and girl, in seventh and eighth grades in the public schools, soccer, baseball, softball, church, scouts. No mention of an illegitimate child, and never was such a thing suspected. She was always proper, never out of control, except one day.

Lillian came into my office and closed the door, crying. My immediate thought was there had been a death in her family. But she told me her daughter Tracey had been arrested, a daughter no one outside her family knew about, a child she had while in high school. Lillian's parents had raised Tracey. Always defiant, now she'd been arrested for possession. Lillian feared that if it got out there would be trouble for her at the firm. There was already trouble at home.

Without telling anyone where I was going or what I was doing, I was on the next plane to Dallas. I called a law-school classmate who was the chief prosecutor where

Tracey was arrested. I was able to get her first-offender treatment on the condition that she'd attend a twelve-step program. Tracey was one of their successes. After a year, I got her a job with a friend in a small firm outside Dallas. I'd stayed in touch with Tracey, befriending, encouraging, counseling her. Now she'd step in front of a bullet for me with a smile on her face. So would her mother.

Tracey's great utility at this point in my life was the fact that no one at the firm knew of her other than Lillian and me. I could risk a call to Tracey, have her call her mother, then call me back. It was worth talking to Grey about.

"I have a couple of drop phones you can use to call her, but use each phone only once, no more. For their sakes make sure they don't use your name; at least it will give them some deniability. Tell Tracey not to contact her mother on a firm line under any circumstance. I'll leave the phones in the truck so you can steal them. There's no cell phone reception here. You'll have to walk down toward the road 'bout a mile before you can pick up the cell tower in Nahunta, but stay in the woods in case someone comes nosing around. When you finish with them, pull the batteries and throw the phones into the river."

Keeping off the trail toward the river, I picked my way through brush, over downed trees, on the lookout for sunning snakes, dozing gators. By the time I picked up a cell tower, I was close enough to the road to hear the occasional logging truck. I buried myself deeper in the woods to make my calls.

Tracey's cell rang several times. I imagined her, hearing her cell ring, seeing a strange number on the screen, debating whether she should answer. Please pick up.

"Hello."

"Tracey, don't hang up. I hope you recognize my voice. I can't use my name and you can't either."

"Well, this is a little strange, but I think so. You've got just a few seconds to assure me you are who I think you are or I'm hanging up."

"I helped you a few years ago with a small legal matter."

"O.K. So why are we talking in code?"

I told her only that I had a problem with the firm, was concerned about security, and needed her to contact her mother to find out if anyone at the firm was looking for me. We hung up. I waited for her to call back on the other phone.

Sitting still in a primordial swamp even for a few minutes makes you the target of all manner of creatures. I was fending off a swarm of mosquitoes, hoping I had not attracted the attention of something more immediately lethal, when the other cell rang.

"No one in the firm has any information about you, and the fact that you're not there hasn't been noticed. Everyone is so shocked about Fowler's death. The managing partner has told Lillian to direct all questions about you to him. You're not in trouble, are you? You know I could—"

I cut Tracey off. The last thing I wanted her to do was to start aiding a potential felon. She had enough to overcome on her own.

"Nothing else? No other contacts?"

"One other. Lillian said your mother left the rehab facility and showed up at your office yesterday. Says she's got a lease on a trailer but has a week to come up with next month's rent or she's going to be on the street again. Your mom needs a utility deposit, too; needs a thousand dollars."

Mom.

Before I got my job at Strange & Fowler and had a steady income, Mom had made her last disastrous reappearance in my life on the day of my graduation from high school. Somehow my mother made her way to Thornwood, a well-meaning matron finding Mom, telling her I was graduating at the top of my class and had won a scholarship to college. It turns out her interest in my graduation had nothing to do with pride in my accomplishments.

She stumbled into the auditorium just as I was starting my valedictory speech. At first I didn't recognize her—hair matted, dress immodestly askew, loud and awkward, red-faced, finding a seat in the back, pointing toward the podium.

One significant irony about Thornwood Orphanage was that most of the kids there weren't orphans. Like me, the majority were sent there because their parents were unfit. So we were often dealing with a peculiar form of embarrassment: an unfortunate parent who, by merely being alive, kept you from being an orphan, from being someone who could create themselves, from being free of their past. My mother was that person to me. But, unlike other parents of children at Thornwood, she never tried to make contact with me in all the years I was there, never a birthday card, Christmas present, or visit. By the time she showed up the day of my graduation, I had willed her dead. I was an orphan.

Yet there she was. Her entry had caused a stir, and those around her were noticing, watching, pointing, snickering.

I stumbled, caught myself, began again. Nothing could break the lock her eyes had on me. I tried to look away, though the auditorium was so small that she was always in my line of sight. I finished, cutting my speech paragraphs short—paragraphs I had labored over as though they were sure to impart true wisdom—now realizing something countless valedictorians before me have realized: No one cares what you say so long as it's over soon. When I finished, I tried to pass through the flow of other students' friends and families; I sought to leave without being identified with her, being seen with her; I just wanted out. But there she was.

"Leave me alone."

"Paul, please, I just want to talk to you, for just a minute."

"You forgot me. I forgot you."

"Paul, I'm about to be evicted. I need some money."

"I don't have any money."

"They told me you won a five-thousand-dollar scholarship."

"But that's for me to go to college."

"I need to borrow it. I promise to pay you back. You'll get your money before you go to college in the fall. You got to help your Mom."

I loaned her the money. She disappeared. All my efforts to find her and get my scholarship money back in time for school were unavailing. She never paid me back. I had to work an extra job my freshman year just to make up for the money she took.

I didn't see her again for years. On occasion I'd wonder about her, how she was, whether we could have some kind of relationship, whether I should seek her out. Every time I decided against it, determining it was best not to find her, afraid somehow of what she'd be, perhaps a picture of my own destiny, my future played out for me.

The next time I heard from her was a call from building security the day I went to work for Strange & Fowler.

"Mr. McDaniel, we have a . . . a lady down here at the loading dock saying she's your Mom . . . she's . . . well, she's in rough shape, and I don't know—"

"I'll be right down."

The security guards were understanding, seeing my embarrassment, and offered that they wouldn't mention it to anyone.

Now I had seven days before Mom showed back up at the firm, all her belongings stuffed in a bag, looking for her rich son to take care of her once again. I couldn't count on her not being discovered a second time. And if she was discovered, she would be the perfect pawn to be used against me, evidence of not only my heartlessness but more importantly, my deception of the firm. Seven days to get absolved of three murders and avert another disaster.

"Tracey, thanks. Don't tell anyone we talked."

"Anything you say."

It appeared that the firm was keeping quiet about me, at least for now, keeping its options open. I needed to get to the lodge and check whatever information was publicly available.

Back at Grey's computer, I pulled up the *Brunswick Ledger*, the local newspaper that covered Frederica Island. Other than a reprint of the Fowler press release, word for word, there was no mention of suicide, murder, or an investigation into the cause of death. Nothing. Nor did the website of the local television channel have anything about a triple murder on Frederica Island. The cause of the judge's death, which was by now old news, was still listed as "accidental discharge." The death of Oliver was apparently not worth notice. The firm's mighty PR arm had flexed its muscle, protecting me for no other reason than any suspicion cast in my direction would look bad for the firm, at least until it could effect a proper separation. The way things looked now, they had their pick of excuses.

I was considering what all this meant when a message popped up on Grey's computer addressed to me. So much for Grey's untraceable Internet connection. I was shocked but curious. It looked like an email, but it didn't have any indication who sent it. I clicked on it.

Mr. McDaniel,

Melissa tells me you can be trusted beyond just being our corporate attorney. Your recent actions, seeking to rescue her from Anthony and warning her of his knowledge—at great physical peril to yourself—confirms her confidence. I too have great confidence in you. I am in communication with Melissa, and she is in significant danger. If you wish to help her, you need only indicate to the affirmative in response to this communication. It cannot be printed or traced, and it will completely erase itself momentarily. If you respond positively, I will be in touch.

Placido

AGENT GREY HAD gone outside. This message seemed like such an obvious ruse I almost laughed out loud, but the idea that my pursuers were baiting a trap with Melissa sent a shot of fear through me. They would know about my message to Melissa if they found my phone, something pretty likely by now. But how would they know about Placido? As far as the world knew, Placido might be dead. Agent Grey was confident this computer could not be traced, yet almost as soon as I logged on, a message appeared for me. I took the chance. I typed, "Yes," and the message disappeared. I got up and turned toward the door, just about to call out to Agent Grey, when I heard a car door slam and the crackle of a two-way radio. There was a Georgia State Patrol cruiser parked in the yard, with a trooper leaning out the driver's side window, talking to Grey.

I pulled the door of the computer room toward me and peered around the edge and out the open window. I could hear everything. Agent Grey and the trooper knew each other.

"Agent Grey, we're looking for a lawyer in his thirties who might know something about a man they found dead on Frederica Island. Seen anyone come through here, might have been driving a Porsche?"

"Henry, I spent most of the week on the river, so I wouldn't have much chance to see anyone even if they'd come through here. But how the hell you think someone could get a Porsche up that road? I'm surprised you could get that cruiser up here."

"Chief saw some suspicious tire tracks at the turn off and thought I should investigate."

"Bet whoever it was half tore out his engine at the first wash and turned around."

"Probably right. Mind if I look around a bit? Need to get the Chief off my back."

"Suit yourself."

The trooper walked toward the barn. "Can you open the door for me?"

"You know I keep the barn booby trapped. It'll take thirty minutes to take it down and thirty to set it back up."

"How long's it been that way?"

"Since I last went in it two weeks ago."

"Well, you mind if I take a look in the house?"

"Go ahead."

The trooper took several steps toward the lodge.

There was nowhere for me to go. I pulled the doors closed on myself, but if the trooper opened them, he'd be staring me in the face. I heard the trooper's boots hit the porch and pause as he opened the door. I considered staying put; I considered stepping out and turning myself in; I considered running out the back door and taking my chances with Bubba and the trooper, and there I ran out of options.

"You got company?" Through the crack between the doors, I eyed the trooper looking at the two plates and cups from our breakfast.

"Rebecca."

The Trooper stopped, backed away from the door as he would have had he spied a rattlesnake coiled on the threshold.

"Well, I'll just let her be for now. Thanks for letting me check around. If you see anything suspicious give me a call."

"Sure will, Henry. You be careful." The trooper stopped and shook Agent Grey's hand, and with that he got into his cruiser, turned it around, and left.

My heart was pounding in my ears so hard I thought my head would pop off. I needed to sit down. When Agent Grey came in, I was sitting in a chair with my head in my hands, fighting a wave of nausea.

"He got here sooner than I thought, but now that he's been, he won't be back for a while. They got plenty of other places to check out to keep them busy."

"What made him turn around?"

"Rebecca. A girl from Nahunta. I let her hunt and fish on my land. When she does, she comes by and keeps me company for a few days. Last time she was here, Henry came up to the lodge as he usually does and walked in without knocking. Caught Rebecca in her skivvies. She whupped his ass. From then on he's knocked, and he'll never come in the lodge when Rebecca's here."

"Next time you see Rebecca, you thank her for me."

"You can thank her yourself. She's coming tonight."

ELEVEN

"DON'T YOU WANT ME TO STAY OUT OF SIGHT while your company is here?"

"Hell, no. Rebecca will get a kick out having supper with an outlaw. I already told her about you, and she's catching a few extra fish for the occasion." My face must've betrayed my thoughts, and Agent Grey read them as if I'd said them aloud. "She's as trustworthy as they come."

"But aren't I putting her in danger if I'm caught?"

"Not unless you tell them we holed you up. Far as I'm concerned, we've never seen you."

"I plan to be out of here soon." I felt my heartbeat slowing, my blood pressure easing a bit. I told Agent Grey of the results of my search of the firm's website and the message from Placido.

"Sure sounds like a trap to me, but there's no way anyone can trace you to this computer. We still have to be careful and not give them any information. Someone is probably monitoring your email. What he said in the message about your trying to rescue her and warning her could easily have come from other sources. The cops probably picked up your cell phone and found the text message. If he tries to contact you again, we'll demand some proof from him that he could've gotten only from Melissa. In the mean time I want to check out this message and see if I can find out where it came from."

But after thirty minutes of searching his computer without results, Agent Grey gave up trying to find it.

"However he sent the message, it's something I've never seen before. There's no trace of a message from 'Placido' anywhere on the hard drive or on the back up, and I automatically back up the system every few seconds. It's as though it never happened. Whoever or whatever is responsible for it has some mighty powerful surveillance gear that I've never seen before."

I spent the rest of the afternoon brainstorming with Agent Grey on how I might escape the swamps of South Georgia, save Placido, rescue Melissa, and prove my innocence—a significant challenge even for an experienced GBI agent. For the moment I was hanging on Placido's promise of subsequent contact, and though Agent Grey didn't say it, I knew it needed to come soon or I'd have to leave the relative safety of the lodge without any prospects of making contact again. But Grey was not silent about what he thought I should do with Melissa.

"You need to get your own situation resolved before you try to rescue some damsel in distress. From what you've told me, she has assets you can hardly imagine. She'll be just fine without your help. And you sure aren't going to be any help to her from a jail cell. Aside from that, you might be assuming a lot more about this relationship with Melissa than is actually there. After all, you just spent less than 24 hours with her. Melissa may be a perfectly nice lady, but she also could be the kind of woman who has no problem encouraging a man to risk everything to help her out of a fix with no intention of sticking around to say, 'Thanks.'"

"I know she—"

"Look, you don't know her well enough to say one way or the other. Just make sure you don't get so committed to one course of action that you don't have a way out if things don't go as planned. In the military they call it an 'exit strategy.' You need one."

But I was already committed. And I couldn't see any other course open to me. Not that I was thinking of leaving Melissa to fend for herself with her murderous uncle. I listened to Grey's advice without further comment.

I didn't bother to discuss with Grey the complication that Mom presented or what I intended to do about her, either. If she didn't get her thousand bucks soon, she would show back up at the office, increasing the chance that someone at the firm would figure out who she is and would try to use her against me. Even if I cleared myself of everything else, it would not be out of the question for some cynical partner to contend that I had misrepresented myself to the firm and concealed the existence of my homeless, alcoholic mother to make myself look better, when all the while I was a heartless son who wouldn't come to her aid.

The real problem with this picture is it was true.

When I came down to the loading dock that first day at work, I didn't recognize her, at least not until I saw her eyes.

"Look, if I give you some money will you go away?" I grabbed for some cash, realizing as I opened my wallet that I had spent more for it than the poor woman in front of me had spent for every tatter she was wearing. Still, my heart was hard. I had accomplished what I had without her, in spite of what she had done, and I owed her nothing. "Here, I have two hundred in cash. It's yours. Just don't come back here."

"I need more than that. I'm being evicted. I need six hundred."

"You have to go. If you agree not to come back, I'll call you. Just tell me your number; you must have a phone."

"They took my phone."

I pulled a card from my wallet.

"Borrow a phone. My number is on my card. Call me on my cell. Don't call the office. Don't come back here." I folded the money around the card, handed it to her, and walked away.

But she did come back. And I was relieved when she did. I'd spent the night reliving my relationship with my mother, casting blame on her for what she had done, then wallowing in guilt for what I hadn't done. Before the sun rose, I had resolved to do what I could to help her.

When she showed up the next morning, I took her around the corner to a breakfast spot. She was ravenous, smelled bad, and made no attempt to hide the fact that she wanted money for alcohol.

"There are nice people at churches around town who will give me a place to stay and something to eat. But they won't give me money, and they won't buy me booze. You need to help me now that you work for that fancy law firm."

This encounter restarted our relationship and revived my mother's cyclical acquaintance with sobriety. After some cajoling, some threatening, I convinced her to check into a residential addiction facility that I'd pay for in full. It was the nicest place she had ever lived.

The program was known for its success with the most inveterate drunks. She stayed a couple months, cleaned up, got sober, and appeared to be on the road to recovery until she slipped out one day and didn't go back. When I next saw her she looked the same as she did the first time she showed up at the firm.

The most effective weapon I had at my call was the threat to have Mom committed for a psychiatric evaluation, and then while there I could get a court to grant me guardianship powers over her. On several occasions I used that threat to get her back into rehab. But I never really wanted to do it, not to her, not to me. To make my mother my ward would be humiliating to her in the extreme. It would signal that I had lost faith in her recovery. And for the rest of her life her well-being would no longer be her responsibility, but mine. I held out the hope that she'd be able to turn herself around. So I got her into yet another rehab facility. And another, and another. Between them she'd disappear for weeks, months, at a time, always coming back, desperate for money. Each time I weighed whether it was the right thing to give it to her. Most of the time I decided it wasn't, but I'd give it to her anyway. But this time I couldn't, at least not now. I was sure that getting her a check would set off alarms with law enforcement; a credit-card number was out of the question, and I didn't see how I could get her cash.

No one at the firm other than Lillian knew about Mom; Tracey was her secret; Mom, mine. All anyone at the firm knew was that I had grown up in an orphanage. I left them to their own assumptions concerning my parents. No one, it seems, would believe that you could grow up in an orphanage and still have a mother. But it was a long story, too long for anyone in the firm to want to hear. Now having encouraged the belief among the partners at Strange & Fowler that I'm a true orphan—with all the romantic imagery that plight entails and with no alcoholic parents left to embarrass me or the firm—appeared a monumental indiscretion that, even absent any role in the incidents on Frederica Island, could result in my undoing.

Given everything else I was facing, the problem presented by Mom's imminent homelessness seemed less significant. Had she not been a threat to unravel my life at the firm, I could more easily dismiss her problems from my mind as she'd done mine from hers. But this time the memory of her eyes haunted me, as did every other wrong turn I'd made in my life, all heaped in my lap as Grey and I tried to figure a way out. The sun was setting. We had yet to land on a plan when Rebecca appeared.

She pulled up in the yard on what was formerly a camo-green four-wheeler, now half black, covered to the wheel-wells with ooze from running the bottoms near the river. Two coolers shared the rear deck with a tackle box and three rods, each set up with different reels, bait-caster, spinner, fly.

Neither voluptuous nor skinny, the best way to describe Rebecca is athletic, solid but not heavy, thin but not willowy, feminine and strong. I could see why the trooper backed away from another confrontation with Rebecca, but even though she was in a fish-smeared T-shirt and ragged jeans, I could tell it would be well worth an ass-whipping to see her in her skivvies. She pulled off the full-visor helmet, revealing a pleasant sun-tanned face scattered with freckles, not a hint of makeup covering lines that radiated from the corners of her eyes and mouth. It was the face of someone who smiled easily and often. Her hair was short, ash blond, streaked with gray. She looked only a bit older than me, but years younger than Agent Grey. She lit up as soon as she saw him on the porch.

"Grey! And you must be Paul, the desperate outlaw!" She yelled, like we were all old friends, unhooking the bungee cords that held the coolers. "Got a mess of fish and a cooler full of beer."

Agent Grey turned to me. "Paul, meet Rebecca, the perfect woman: she's beautiful; she fishes; she brings beer."

"Men are pretty damn simple. I don't know why other women have so much trouble with 'em."

Grey shrugged. "Domestic relations would be far more amiable all the way around if more women showed up with beer."

"And if you men got your asses off the porch and gave me a hand with these coolers."

"What you catch?"

"I was in the mood for a little fly fishing. Found a bed of bluegills and wore 'em out."

Grey grabbed one of the coolers and lifted the lid.

"Sure did—looks like a couple dozen nice ones, 'bout a pound each. Perfect eatin' size."

"You two clean 'em, I'll cook 'em."

Even large bream are too thin to filet, so the best way to cook them is to cut off the heads and tails, gut and scale them, and batter and fry them, with skin, bones, and all. Most of the rib bones dissolve, and sweet meat just falls off the backbone. Agent Grey and I were soon at work with filet knives while Rebecca got the fish cooker fired up, all of us well hydrated with cold beer. Before it got good and dark, we each had a plate piled with Rebecca's catch. Fish, hushpuppies, cheap beer, good company. If I weren't in the fix I was in, I would never leave. Even under the present circumstances, these seemed like pretty good reasons to stay as long as possible.

After supper, we sat on the porch in the darkness under the fans, satiated, a brilliant full moon casting shadows in the yard, the click and smack of insects, drawn by the lingering scent of dinner, slamming the screen. A couple six packs of beer had loosened even Grey's tongue, and he was soon telling us stories of moonshiners and pot growers, and even his most famous quarry, Derrick Randolph, who had eluded Grey in one of the largest manhunts in history until hunger drove the fugitive from his Appalachian hide out.

Rebecca told tales of growing up on the Satilla every bit as entertaining as Grey's, and I soon realized many of her relatives were some of the very moonshiners and pot growers that Grey stalked. There was a curious respect on both sides, seldom resulting in violence or even prosecutions. The GBI would tear down one still, and the moonshiners would build one further in the swamp. The GBI would cut down one pot patch; the growers planted another. Grey and Rebecca had evidently reached a truce: Grey no longer concerned with her family business, Rebecca not afraid of giving comfort to the enemy.

I told Rebecca of my encounter with the trooper, how I was saved from discovery by her fearsome reputation, that I was saved from bolting more by the fear of tangling with Bubba than having to deal with the trooper. Rebecca burst into unrestrained laughter, so much so I realized there was more to the story than I was privy to. Agent Grey was in on the joke, too, and I was out. When the laughter slowed,

Rebecca was only able to squeak.

"Bubba! You used that old dog story on him? Is Bubba still a Doberman?"

"Oh, hell no, Bubba's a Rottweiler! Figured Paul here would be more concerned with a dog that could bite through a two-by-four than one that could run down a deer. Told 'im Bubba's so sneaky that he'd be latched onto his ass before he'd even see him."

The two dissolved into laughter again. By now I was a bit impatient with being the butt of the joke.

"So there's no Bubba?"

"Hell, no. He uses that story on everyone who comes out here just to keep them out of the house. He probably told you the barn is booby trapped, too, didn't he?"

"No, he told the trooper that. He told me the four-wheeler is." I laughed at myself. "What's the dog run for?"

"That's for my bird dogs. They're off in Waynesville being trained for quail season. If they got a hold of ya, they'd lick ya all over."

"So, what about all that trust you were talking about?"

"Guess you just earned it."

The three of us, the wounded agent, the back-woods prom-queen, the disgraced lawyer, each craving solitude, each seeking the warmth, the trust, of another—for that brief moment, whatever we were looking for, we found. We joked and laughed and told stories and laughed some more, until I begged off to my bunk in the barn, leaving Agent Grey and Rebecca to themselves, hoping to keep my spirits at bay till morning.

It was not to be.

"Paul." Rebecca had slipped into the barn and was sitting on the edge of my bed in gym shorts and T-shirt and evidently nothing else, a vision that made me think I was still dreaming. "Placido's trying to get in touch with you again. Grey logged on to the computer to check the tides for our fishing trip. You gotta see this."

"What time is it?"

"A little past two."

"Placido needs a better sense of timing."

Grey was staring across the room when I walked into the lodge a few seconds later, still shaking sleep from my head.

"I have no idea how . . ."

What I saw looked like the scene from the first *Star Wars* movie at the point when a hologram of Princess Leia appears to Obi-Wan Kenobi and Luke Skywalker projected from R2-D2—only in this case, the image was projected from Grey's computer, and the quality of the hologram was so good that it looked as though two other people had entered the room. Placido appeared sitting at a desk. Melissa was opposite him, though from her surroundings she was not originating from the same location.

"Paul! Thank God you're safe! My father told me how you barely escaped Fowler's killing spree. I'm so grateful to your friends who've helped you." Melissa's voice quivered.

"Melissa. I was worried I might never hear from you again. It's great to see you . . . even under these circumstances." I did my best to sound positive, but I was almost overwhelmed to see her still alive. She looked much the same as she did when I last saw her, only she had exchanged her baggy sweatshirt for an over-sized T-shirt. She recovered her composure and got down to business.

"This message should relieve any concerns you may have that my father's contact is legitimate. Instead of flying to Italy as planned, Anthony brought me to the family island in the Bahamas where he can keep me isolated. Right now, he's left the island for business in Miami, and he's put me in the charge of the island caretaker. He knows there's no way for me to get off the island, so I pretty much have the run of the place. I'm sending this message from the empty jet hanger on the far end of the island.

"Anthony now suspects my father's still alive and I'm in contact with him, but I don't think he knows how. He's holding me as bait, hoping to draw Placido out. My father can't risk trying to rescue me; if he's caught, Anthony will kill him, then kill me. Paul, we are counting on your offer of help. Anthony won't be looking for you."

"Mr. McDaniel, Anthony will hold Melissa as long as it takes in his effort to get to me. Once he's killed me, he'll have no further use for Melissa, and he'll kill her. That is his ultimate goal; then there will be no one to challenge his control of Milano Corporation."

"Paul, I need you. I need your help. I don't want to die on this island." With that Melissa's poise failed her and tears welled in her eyes. "I'm sorry. I just . . ."

"Mr. McDaniel, if you're willing to help, meet me in the morning two days from now at the Cape Florida Lighthouse. I also want you to know I believe I have access to some information that might well prove your innocence. I think we can help each other."

I looked to Grey.

"To get there I'm going to need some wheels and plausible cover. You think you can help me out?"

Grey nodded.

"I think we can work something out for Paul to get down there. Once he's there, he'll be on his own. I'm too far along giving aid to a fugitive to help further."

"Understood, Mr. Grey."

Grey raised his eyebrows. "I have just one question: How are you doing this? I have a fair knowledge of computers, but this is something I've ever seen before."

"Mr. Grey, allow me to introduce you to Ariel, my assistant." A face, then a figure appeared, superimposed over Placido's image, beautiful, young, feminine, familiar: It was the face I'd glimpsed diving in the Atlantic off Frederica Island, the face of Oz to Placido's Wizard, whose actions for now remained behind the curtain. Ariel looked straight at me and smiled.

"Ariel operates the most elegant and sophisticated means of communication ever developed. Ariel is what is often referred to as artificial intelligence, though I think you'll find her capabilities far beyond mere artifice. What Ariel accomplishes is nothing short of magical."

I gawked.

"Surprised, Paul? Sorry I blew you off during our brief-writing marathon, but Placido wasn't ready to bring you in on our secret. Now you're one of the family." Ariel smiled at me again, disarming, her tone, her features, her gestures, perfectly human.

"You said you thought you were a lot like me, but you're—"

"Dedicated, intelligent, hardworking—"

Grey couldn't help but break in. "Modest."

Placido shook his head. "Mr. Grey, a lot of thought goes into deciding what attributes may be useful in an AI program. I haven't found modesty to be one of them."

There was no defensiveness in Placido's voice, just clinical precision from the mind of Ariel's creator.

Ariel seemed as knowledgeable of her own development and as disinterested in discussing it as Placido. "Mr. Grey, once we have resolved our present circumstance, I will be delighted to give you a full briefing of my capabilities, that is, if it pleases Placido."

"Of course, Ariel, of course. But for now, I want you to do everything possible to assist Mr. McDaniel."

"I shall."

I couldn't imagine how a high-powered word processor and super-slick video conferencer—as beautiful as she was—could help me rescue Melissa, a prisoner on an island a thousand miles away, but I was willing to throw my hat in with Placido to figure it out. As Ariel's image faded, I swear she winked at me.

"Melissa, you know I'm going to do all I can to help."

"Thank you, Paul. Thank you."

My decision to help Melissa had already been made. Looking back, I wondered when the die had been irrevocably cast. Was it when I decided to flee Fowler's den rather than surrender to the island police? Was it when I made the offer to help Melissa find Placido? Or was it when I agreed to meet her on the beach? Or even earlier, that evening when I became so hopelessly infatuated with Melissa? Whenever that decision had been made, at this moment there was no doubt in my mind that I would not only risk my career, but risk my life, to rescue Melissa. And now with Ariel's offer of help I felt even more emboldened.

Grey was resigned to the inevitability of my desire to help Melissa, as foolish as he may've thought it was. So he and I landed on a plan, at least one that'd get me to the lighthouse; after that, as he said, I was on my own. I'd drive my Porsche up the river road and abandon it in the woods. We agreed that I'd steal Grey's truck and his old wallet. Grey had more than one expertly crafted extra set of IDs, and I chose an Alabama driver's license with a picture of a younger Agent Grey sporting short-cropped beard and gray hair. Rebecca worked her own magic on my hair and on the scruffy stubble that'd been growing since Fowler's, and I got outfitted with some of Grey's old clothes. From a distance I could pass as Grey, but I didn't know how much close scrutiny my disguise could stand.

Agent Grey and Rebecca were headed for a week-long fishing trip to the Slow River Fish Camp where he had a cabin on the Altamaha. He'd find the Porsche and report the truck and wallet missing when he got back. Or maybe he wouldn't.

Late the next afternoon, I was heading down I-95 in Agent Grey's ancient pickup truck, a short gray beard, gray hair under a ball cap, mirrored aviator glasses, and an old wallet of Grey's in my pocket. The shotgun lay on the floorboard, backpack with my laptop beside me. It was about an eight-hour trip if I drove straight through, but I'd have to make a few stops for food and fuel, so with some additional time for contingencies, I figured I'd drive all night and pull up at the lighthouse by early morning with some time left for reconnoitering.

TWELVE

T HE COP GOT A CLEAR SHOT AT ME AS I CRESTED THE
hill, the only rise for miles along the flat South
Georgia landscape. He was parked on the shoulder,
radar gun aimed up the south-bound lane of I-95, just
before the Florida line, no exit close. Since getting on the
interstate, I had kept uncharacteristically under the speed
limit, chugging along in the slow lane, cars flying past,
doing my best not to attract attention, heart pounding
every time I would see a patrol car cruise up behind me,
then shoot by, like sharks searching for the scent of death
in the water. But I knew that I had only so much time to
make it all the way to Miami, and I picked up the pace,
soon cruising over the speed limit, in the flow of traffic
with the rest of the lawbreakers.

Even though this cop had plenty of speeders to pick
from, I felt a shot of adrenaline as soon as I saw him, one
that changed to a blood rush when he jumped into his
cruiser and hit the blue lights, speeding onto the highway,
pulling past traffic, in hot pursuit. He was after some other
quarry, I told myself; he wouldn't have picked me out
from the crowd; he was after someone else, and I kept
telling myself that as I saw him in my rearview, glancing
up, trying not to stare, getting closer, closing fast, on my

bumper. He hit the siren. My heart hammered against my ribs and my eyes blurred.

I pulled over slowly, taking every moment I could to think out my situation. It'd been little more than an hour since I left Grey's lodge. It was unlikely that someone had spotted my ditched Porsche and made the connection between it and Grey's missing F-150. This had to be a routine traffic stop, part of the endless hassling of the poor by the powerful, the cop pulling over some red-neck in a beat-down pickup truck, rather than chance an encounter with a heavily armed drug dealer—or worse, a politician or a judge—in a shiny S-Class Mercedes flashing down the fast lane. Unless Grey set me up and ratted me out. The possibility that Grey had yet one more surprise seemed remote—remote, but not out of the question. All I could do was try to keep calm and see how this would play out, and keeping calm seemed almost impossible. Hell, I was having a hard time just keeping control of my bladder.

The officer moseyed up, looking in the bed of the truck, taking note of the dented tackle box and the few old fishing rods I'd found in the barn and tossed in the truck as props: suspected murderers didn't go on fishing trips, I thought. He rounded the cab, his eyes fixed briefly on the Berretta on the floorboard, and it was far too late that I thought how out of place an engraved-steel shotgun looked in a rusted-out truck, how it contrasted with the salt-corroded reels and sun-splintered rods in the truck bed, how fugitives are caught by failure to attend to that one telling detail.

I handed over my license and registration. He looked in at me and back down at the license, studying the picture, and back up again.

"Mind taking off those glasses and cap?" In the days I'd been on the run I'd not shaved. Rebecca trimmed my hair and beard, dying them Agent Grey's shade of gray. With a ball cap and aviator sun glasses Grey and I could pass for twins. Trouble was, the picture on his license was taken without cap or glasses, and we certainly weren't twins.

"Sure." Pulling off my cap and glasses. "I hope I ain't as ugly as that picture makes me out ta be."

The cop had said nothing about the picture. I was already sounding defensive, and he squinted at me all the harder.

It was only now, and for the first time, I wished my law-school experience had given me some exposure to police procedure. Rather than learning how to help the poor and defenseless in a criminal law clinic, rather than spending hours at some metal-desk store-front down by the projects, interviewing crack-addled criminals, attending countless arraignments, sipping stale coffee, inhaling the stench of wasting bodies and wasted lives, I had spent my academic career in the rarified atmosphere of the law library, ensconced in the overstuffed leather chairs of the third floor, studying the intricacies of the corporate form, becoming useful to the rich and powerful. It seemed like a good idea at the time, but my superior knowledge of advanced corporate finance provided no advantage on the shoulder of I-95, running from what stood to be a sure triple-murder charge. Though I was a top graduate from one of the nation's finest law schools, the only practical information about criminal procedure I had came from TV shows, and that told me cops were trained to listen, let people talk, ramble on, giving more information than necessary, saying something stupid. This was the point when nerves caused the guilty to jabber. I'd already violated the common wisdom. I resolved to keep my mouth shut, managed a faint smile, and hoped I didn't do something else to give myself away.

It seemed like a hundred hammering heartbeats before the cop nodded. I pulled the cap on my head, hooked the glasses behind my ears, helmet and shield for the coming battle.

"Goin' fishin'?"

"Yep."

"Where 'bout?"

"Close in."

"What for?"

"Speckled trout. Maybe some redfish."

"Damn, boy, you ain't gonna catch any reds on those rigs you got. Them reels no good, and the line looks ten years old. A bull red'll snap that rod in half." He leaned in hard. "You sure as hell ain't goin' fishin', least ways not with that junk."

I swallowed before I responded. My thin attempt at cover was now a liability. "Gonna pick up some new tackle 'fore I go out."

The cop shook his head.

"You got any shells for that fancy shotgun of yours?"

I pointed. "In the glove compartment."

"You keep your hands on the steering wheel."

"Yes sir."

"I got you on the radar gun going 80 in a 70."

I put my head down and held the steering wheel. I could tell this guy was looking for an excuse to handcuff me in the back of his patrol car, and I wasn't going to give it to him. I didn't respond.

The officer went back to his cruiser without another word. The next few minutes I struggled to remain outwardly calm as my stomach knotted and sweat poured down my chest. I left my window rolled down so the perspiration that beaded on my forehead looked more of a response to the tropical air rather than the heat of suspicion.

In the side mirror I saw him step out of the car, pop the strap on his holster, and radio something back to his dispatcher. He watched my hands as he approached the truck, his hand on his revolver.

This was it. In moments the shoulder would be swarming with heavily armed law-enforcement officers, I'd be hand cuffed, stuffed into the back of a patrol car, and hauled off to jail. A week ago I'd been speeding down this same highway in my shiny new Porsche on top of the world. Now the world was soon to be on top of me. I put my head down, held the steering wheel, and took in a deep breath.

"Agent Grey, I'm sorry about the delay. My radar gun read 60 not 80. My mistake. You are free to go." I managed a nod and a faint smile. He walked away.

Agent Grey. So he figured out who I was supposed to be. My story checked out. I sure as hell wasn't going 60. He was giving me a pass. I let out a long breath, tried to steady my nerves as a great rush of relief washed over me. I reached down to crank the truck, hand trembling. I looked up to check the traffic.

The officer was standing right at my window. I couldn't help but flinch.

"Sorry to startle you, Agent Grey. I meant to tell you that was some work you did on the Derrick Randolph case. I'm a great admirer. You should've told me who you were when I pulled you over. But I have a question for you. Since the case is over, I hope you won't mind telling me."

I kept my hands on the steering wheel to keep them from shaking. I'd almost made it, but now my cover was blown. The cop suspected me, and he was going to ask me some highly technical procedural question that I wouldn't even understand. I braced.

"Say, how long was 'at boy eatin' outa that dumpster?"

I almost laughed out loud, but I contained my elation. No technical question here, just basic human curiosity.

"From the looks of him it'd been quite a while. But he was eatin' better out of that dumpster than he ever had during the two years he was in the woods."

"Hell, I thought he was more of a country boy than that. I figured once he was in the woods he'd never come out."

I just smiled.

"Well, you have a good day. An' good luck fishin'. If you're ever headed down to Live Oak Island, you can get your gear at Beer-N-Bugs Bait Shack. 'At's my brother's place."

"I'll make it a point. Thanks."

Before the officer could get back to his cruiser, my truck was in the flow of traffic. I hadn't even gotten out of Georgia, and I'd already been stopped. While I had met that challenge, I knew every cop in the nation could now access the information that "Agent Grey" and his pickup truck were spotted heading south on I-95 at Georgia mile marker 2 on Tuesday evening. I'd soon cross the Georgia-Florida line. If the real Agent Grey didn't give me more lead time, then the noose could be tightened around the north end of the Florida peninsula, and I would have nowhere to go. At least I now knew he hadn't turned me in. Not yet.

From Amelia Island, marking the far-north point, to Biscayne Bay, framing the sparkling skyline of Miami, the state of Florida is one long, boring drive: flat as a road-kill squirrel, straight as a jungle runway, with few turns in any direction. If I weren't scared out of my mind, I might've fallen asleep at the wheel. Even when I managed to settle my nerves a bit, I was in no danger of dozing off. I was too attuned to the shaking of the steering wheel, vibrating to the tune of the misaligned wheels and unbalanced tires, and the coughing and wheezing of the engine, sick from some semitropical disease contracted while lying months untouched in Agent Grey's shed. I feared each gasp would be the truck's last, leaving me stranded and conspicuous on the side of the highway. No, I wasn't likely to fall asleep at the wheel. So the Florida landscape stretched on interminably, mile after mile, the waters of the Atlantic, wave upon wave, the Florida Interstate Torture. At times I felt it would've been better had the cop seen through my cover and hauled me off to jail.

THIRTEEN

F LORIDA'S FLAT TERRAIN PRESENTED AT LEAST ONE advantage as the truck and I labored down the interstate: I could see trouble coming a long way off, and with vigilance I might be able to avoid it. I slowed as I approached the infrequent exits and searched the distance for blue lights. Past an exit I'd be boxed in unless I could cut across the median, bringing even more unwanted attention to myself.

After about a hundred and fifty miles or so of this monotony, the interstate took a jog toward the coast a few miles past Exit 244, and then the roadway straightened, and an overpass blocked my view. On the other side of the overpass I saw a blaze of blue and red flashing lights in the distance. I looked for a cut-through to the northbound lane, but the median narrowed, and a steel guardrail had replaced the dense growths of pine and live oak that had forested the center for hundreds of miles. I was still far enough away that it was unlikely the cops would notice my bolting through the median, but the guardrail extended unbroken to the next exit. I found my heart pounding, my options fading. As I closed on the tangle of official vehicles ahead, my fear grew to panic. The highway was shut down, cops diverting traffic from the interstate. It was a road block.

My disguise satisfied the last cop who stopped Agent Grey miles north on I-95. If this was a road block to catch me, it meant only one thing: Grey had ratted me out. The choke point miles ahead; I pulled to the shoulder to slow my slamming heart and consider my options.

The right side of the southbound lane was enveloped in woods. A swampy ditch and a farm fence, which looked too stout for my truck to take on, blocked any attempt to pull off in hopes of finding a track through the forest. There were often paths cut by deer hunters on four-wheelers or by cops hiding in the trees stalking their own prey, but for the last couple miles none appeared, and there weren't any close by.

Unless I wanted to drive into the teeth of the road block and risk certain capture, I'd have to leave the truck behind and set out on foot. I could circle back to the right and walk the entire way, or I could cross the median and hitchhike. Either way, I had to get back up the highway to the previous exit, where I'd try to catch a ride heading cross country and around the roadblock. I figured I'd still have plenty of time to meet up with Placido, but if I were delayed I didn't know how long he'd wait for me. It was light still, so I decided to walk through the woods and attract as little attention as possible.

I grabbed my backpack and swung from the cab. The shotgun was lying on the floorboard. If I were going to head through the woods, a shotgun would be handy. I climbed back in the truck, grabbed the gun and broke it down. The stock was a snug fit inside the backpack along with a box of shells, but the barrel stuck out the top.

I left the cab again and tossed my pack on my shoulder. I was surveying my route just as a car traveling in my direction pulled from the interstate and came to a stop right behind my truck. It was a 1950s black stretch Cadillac, the name of a funeral home not completely scratched off a rear window, long hood, tall fins, slab doors, shock absorbers gone, it bounced on its springs several seconds before coming to rest. The driver's side door squeaked open, and a pomaded gentleman unwound from behind the wheel.

"Reverend Barnabus Duffle of the Cow Creek Full Bible Baptist Church of Jesus Christ Our Lord and Savior. Saw you had some trouble, friend, and thought I'd might stop. Truck broke down?"

"Engine cut out. Wouldn't crank back up."

"Well, maybe I can help. What you say your name is?"

"Bill Grey."

"What you think's the problem?"

"Can't say as I know. I was going to leave it here to find help."

"Well, I guess help just found you. I try to stop for folks broke down on the highway. Meet some mighty interesting people. Guess I just met another one." The Reverend pointed at the shotgun barrel sticking out of my pack. "You a hunter?"

"Do a little bird hunting."

"My day job is taxidermy, case you ever need it. You kill 'em, I fill 'em." He handed me a crumpled card with his tag line over the name Barney Duffle. "Got some samples of my work in the back of the hearse. On my way to drop off a buck head, if you'd like to take a look. Hearse sure comes in handy for both jobs. One time, when I had an eight-foot gator in the back that my brother-in-law tagged, I got a call to pick up one of my church members who had just died at a nursing home. Both fit just fine."

My mind was spinning, thinking how I might use Reverend Duffle to get through the road block. So far, the best I could come up with was to play dead and lie in the back. I asked to see his work to buy time to think this through.

"Now this's what I call a six-and-a-half-point buck."

He showed me a mouse-colored deer head with one complete antler and the stub of another.

"Woulda been a twelve-pointer, had someone not blow'd half his rack off." He pushed the deer head out of the way. "Since you're a bird hunter, I bet you'll really like this." Reverend Duffle pulled out something that looked like a rooster on a stick. "A red-tailed hawk—now I know you're gonna tell me ya can't shoot a hawk. This one's road kill. One of my deacons brought it to me. Turned out real nice."

"Ah, yeah."

I saw several largemouth bass that looked like freeze-dried catfish, and a rattlesnake that was so emaciated that there wasn't enough of him to make a good belt. After showing me all the examples of his work, Reverend Duffle closed the mile-wide tailgate of the hearse. I was stuck with a part-time preacher and wild-animal embalmer on the side of the road, and I was afraid I was about to have hands laid on me. I decided to take the offensive.

"So, Reverend, what you think's going on up the road?"

"I heard there's been a bad accident. Chemical spill. They've closed the south-bound lane of the interstate 'tween Oak Hill and Mims. You gotta take Exit 231, go to Oak Hill and pick up US 1 to Mims, there you can get back on the interstate heading south."

Reverend Duffle announced the chemical spill like it was bad news, and I suppose it was for just about everyone else, but while the Reverend didn't know it, he had done just what he'd set out to do. He saved me right there on the side of the road.

"I can take ya back to the Church. We got some fried chicken left over from prayer meetin' if you're hungry."

"Thanks, but I need to be getting on the road. I'm gonna try to crank the truck one more time. Maybe it just needed to cool down a bit. If it doesn't start this time, you think you could drop me off at a service station?"

"Sure thing. If you can get it started you probably oughta get it checked out in Oak Hill before you head back on the interstate. There's a couple service stations there. If it won't crank, I can take you to the next exit. You oughta carry that backpack with you, but you don't need to worry about those rods you got in the back. I don't think anyone'll try to steal those."

What was it with my fishing gear? I thought the ruse was pretty clever. So far no one thought I was really going fishing. Maybe I ought to toss those rods and tackle box and try to avoid further derision. They seemed only to attract unwanted attention.

Grey's truck cooperated in the charade, making it difficult to crank back up, so difficult that I began to worry that I might actually have to hitch a ride to the service station, but just then the engine caught and turned over, blue smoke engulfing the hearse adding to the effect. I stepped out of the cab, threw my backpack in the seat, jumped back in, and waived to the preacher, still perched on the side of the road.

Through the detour, I crossed over the interstate toward Oak Hill, and in five miles pulled into the only restaurant that seemed to be open. Buddy's Burgers was a local hamburger joint that from the outside appeared unable to pass an honest sanitation inspection, and upon entering removed all doubt. But this was Buddy's lucky day. Most of the travelers inconvenienced by the detour seemed to have the same idea I had: regroup, figure out the shortest way to get back on the interstate, and grab some food in the process. I tossed my backpack on the bench at a booth. Buddy was at the grill flipping burgers as fast as he could, dispensing travel advice in the process.

"So you turn out the parking lot to the right, go to the next intersection—that's US 1—take a right, and in about ten miles you'll run into the town of Mims. Hit State Road 46, go right again, that'll take you to the interstate in about a mile."

I ordered what I thought would be the safest thing on the menu: burger, fries, and sweet tea. I figured he sold enough burgers for the meat to be fresh and enough fries for the grease not to be rancid, and no one in the South messes up sweet tea. Before my order arrived, I unzipped my backpack and pulled out my laptop, just to check out Buddy's directions. When I looked up, someone had slid into my booth in front of me even before I had a chance to open my computer.

She looked mid-twenties, skinny, long wavy blond hair that hadn't been washed in a while, sunken cheeks, too much eye makeup, long fake nails that she skittered across the Formica top of the table.

"So, you just get off the interstate?"

I didn't want to be rude to one of the locals, but this encounter had all the indications of a hustle. Why else would a young girl come up to a strange old man in a burger joint? Instead of speaking I nodded. I tried very hard not to look encouraging. I hoped she might go away on her own.

"You want some company?"

"No. My wife wouldn't like that."

"I didn't see any wife in that truck of yours."

"She's lying down. Not feeling good."

"Ain't nobody in there. I looked."

"So, what you want?"

"I'm looking to make some money."

"Sorry. Can't help. Don't have enough for myself." I hoped my scruffy appearance would be all the convincing she needed that I was a waste of her time and she might move on.

"You don't understand. I need money bad." She tapped her nails faster and flipped her hair from one side of her head and back, glanced over at Buddy dispensing more advice, for now oblivious to the freelancer shaking down his customers. I shoved my laptop into my backpack and pushed to the edge of the booth. She grabbed my arm.

"Look. I ain't had nothing to eat for two days."

"If I get you a burger, will that help?"

She looked away, nodded.

I went up to Buddy, ordered her the same thing I had, and paid. When I turned to go back to the booth, she was gone. So was my backpack.

I flew out the front door, saw no one in either direction, heard steps sprinting toward the rear, turned the corner and saw her toss the backpack over a wooden fence and scale it with a grab and a kick. It took me a second longer to get over, and by then she'd turned the corner into a neighborhood. If I didn't catch her, she'd disappear in a few seconds. From where I stood, I could see across two back lots to the fronting street. If I cut through the back lots, I could get to the road a hundred yards ahead of where she turned, and I took a chance that her flight would take her there. I sprinted through privet hedges, under clothes lines, past swing sets, and broke onto the street. There was no one to be seen in any direction.

I tracked back toward the house where she'd made her turn, looking down driveways and over fences. No sign. There were dozens of bungalows on the street, with small fenced lots, an infinite number of hiding places. I kept to the street, moving toward where I'd last seen her.

She saw me first, broke, and dashed through the adjoining yard, backpack still in hand, over the fence and through the next yard. I ran the street, keeping her in sight through side yards and walkways, looking for a point to cut her off.

She sprinted behind a garage, through an open gate, and into the next lot when luck turned in my direction, and she got cornered by a pit bull doing guard duty. She tossed the pack again, climbed the fence, but before she could get over, the dog caught the leg of her jeans. By the time she pulled free, I was on the other side. We both dove for the backpack. She got her hand on a shoulder strap, jerked it from me, and bounded in the direction of the road. I tackled her before she was out of the yard, the pack tumbling free. I jumped for it.

She rolled and swiped a box cutter from her jeans, sprang to her feet, lunged and slashed. I shoved the backpack in front of me. She missed twice, then launched again, and ripped across the nylon, cutting across my left hand. The pain shooting through my arm, I could no longer hold on, and I dropped the backpack at my feet. I yanked the gun barrel from the pack and swung it at her. She ducked and slashed at my chest. I brought the barrel down, knocking the knife from her hand, and it fell at my feet. I stomped the box cutter under Grey's boot. She kicked my shin to get my foot off the knife. I pressed down harder with one foot and swung the barrel at her head. She fell back. I snatched up the box cutter, the blade still open, moved toward her.

Out of options, she turned and fled. I let her go.

The damage to my backpack was minimal, a four-inch slash; the shotgun suffered a gouge in the barrel, but the harm was only cosmetic. My hand was bleeding, the worst of it a gash in my index finger, a flap of skin peeled back, and I grabbed a T-shirt from my pack and wrapped it around my hand to staunch the blood. I was more fearful of the beating the computer had taken, though I decided not to take the time to check it out where I stood. I figured I had to get back to the truck before my assailant returned with reinforcements or alarmed neighbors called the police. I set out at a jog toward Buddy's.

My heart rate had just about dropped to normal when I got back to my truck and tossed my backpack safe in the seat. Buddy emerged from his shop.

"You still want that burger?"

Buddy was good for a burger to go and some first aid for my wound. Said he'd never seen the girl before, probably just off the interstate looking for someone to shake down. When he took a look at my cut, he said the blood made it look worse than it was. Turns out Buddy was an EMT before he started his restaurant, and just about everyone in town stopped by if they needed help. The wound cleaned, I was ready to set out, gauze taped around my finger. I followed a steady line of traffic along the detour back to the interstate. An hour after being saved by Reverend Duffle, robbed by a roadside hustler, and reassembled by Buddy, I was again heading down I-95 to Miami, about two hours behind schedule.

FOURTEEN

WAS TO MEET PLACIDO AT THE CAPE FLORIDA
Lighthouse. It was a place iconic in my childhood, a
story I'd shared with Melissa during our only night
together—a night that threatened to fade into the past
even as I struggled to hold on to its memory, a night that
motivated me to press on, to do all I could to get back to
her. No doubt it was she who suggested to Placido that we
meet at the lighthouse, a place where, as a boy, my mother
would take me, one of the few fond memories of her I'd
managed to salvage from the wreckage of my childhood.

The island road ended about halfway down the key, and
Mom and I would hike to the beach through a forest of
tall Australian pines. They blocked all outside sound, and
entering the forest was like entering a sanctuary. All we
could hear was the soughing of the wind, the whispering
of an unseen congregation. Beyond the emerald forest, a
beach so white and an ocean so blue that I used to take
two jars, one for sand and one for sea, hoping to capture
their essence and keep them forever.

We usually had the beach to ourselves. Mom would
spread a blanket under the shade of a palm tree. Her wide-
brimmed hat, gaudy with a ribbon tied around the crown,
her face relaxed and eyes bright as she watched me while

I swam or hunted for shells. It became our ritual to walk to the ruins of the old Cape Florida lighthouse at the end of the key before we headed home. Seminoles had built a bonfire at the base of the lighthouse to burn out the keeper, whom they thought was signaling settlers to come take their land. The lighthouse was not repaired. The watchtower where the beacon once shone was bent and twisted by the flames and corroded by more than a century of exposure to the salt air, and nothing was left on the inside. If you gathered your courage, you could squeeze through a crack in the jammed door to look up the darkened brick to the sunlight above.

That was when Dad worked in the booming construction industry in South Florida. All this was before—before Dad took Mom and me to South Carolina in search of work when the boom was over. Before they found jobs at one of Milano's mills. Before our lives spiraled downward from there.

The little town of Laurens was a far cry from Miami, where even without money there was a lot to do. When we got to South Carolina, both of my parents concentrated their efforts on staying drunk as much as possible, so even before Dad died and Mom gave up, I'd pretty much raised myself. And it had been that way ever since, with the fortunate intervention of Thornwood. If anyone could say that it was a stroke of luck to be sent off to an orphanage, I was the one.

It was closing in on two o'clock in the morning, I'd been on the road about seven hours and covered about three hundred miles, but I still had more than a hundred and fifty to get to Key Biscayne. By this point, I'd memorized every squeak and cough, every rattle and bang, of the truck's ancient drive train. Now I was hearing a different sort of rumble. At first I thought it was my imagination—after all, I hadn't slept, and I was spinning on high doses of caffeine I picked up from every Starbucks I passed. But after time, I realized this was indeed something new. I tried to ignore it, hoping it would get better or go away. It didn't, and it only got worse. I resolved to pull off the next promising exit and check it out.

The exit for Fellsmere showed several service stations which were lit up and appeared to be open. I pulled into one that had a 24-hour food mart, stopped at a pump, went inside, and handed the attendant $40.00 for gas. I'd been traveling on cash, certain that any use of a credit card or ATM would set off alarms, and I now only had enough for about one more fill up and some food. I was going to count on Placido when we met, but I had to get there first.

It didn't take a master mechanic to figure out what was making the rumbling sound: the tread on the right front was almost separated from the rest of the tire and looked to be only a few miles from a complete blow out. The time spent in the woods at Grey's had contributed to serious dry rot all the way around, but that tire was the worst. I hoped I could limp the rest of the way on the others, but I'd have to replace the front one. I looked under the truck for the spare. There was none.

It took a few seconds for the desperation of my situation to sink in. It was 2:00 a.m. I was still about three hours from Miami, and I was expected to meet Placido in the morning. If I had to wait until a tire store opened at nine to get my tire fixed, Placido would likely have given up on me before I got there. Besides that, if what I needed was a new tire, I had no money to buy one, and I dared not use my credit card.

There had to be some repair shop open 24-hours close by the interstate. The best way to find it was on my laptop, which I pulled out of my backpack for the first time since it had almost been stolen from me. I didn't even know if it would work after all the rough treatment it had gotten. But the service station touted free WiFi, so I decided to give it a shot.

I opened my computer, powered up, and Ariel's face appeared.

"Your disguise works well. I didn't recognize you until I did a retina scan. Your computer has taken a beating in the last few hours. It was hard for me to tell what was happening. Did you have an accident?"

"Someone tried to steal my backpack along with everything I have, including my computer. There was a foot chase and a knife fight." I held my hand up to the screen. "Got slashed with a box cutter. I'm lucky to have gotten it back. But right now, I have an even bigger problem." I explained.

"I can let Placido know you will be delayed. Two miles from here is a tire store that opens at eight in the morning. They have all sizes of tires in stock. I have scheduled you for their first appointment. You can get an entire new set of tires, be on the road by nine, and meet Placido at the lighthouse by noon."

"Ariel, that all sounds good, but I have no money to pay for a new set of tires. I can't use a credit card, I can't use my bank card at an ATM, and I have to use cash. Unless you can convince the people at the tire store to give me the tires for free, we still have a problem."

"Paul, cash is never a problem. There is an ATM in the food mart in the service station. Just walk up to it and smile in the camera."

"And who said computers don't have a sense of humor. Sorry, I'm afraid my good looks won't work."

"Paul, you do not understand. All you have to do is walk up to the ATM, look in the camera so I know you are there, and I will give you some cash."

I walked in and went to the ATM and smiled. Nothing happened. The attendant was looking at me funny. Then the cash dispenser whirred and $1,000.00 in twenties popped out. I took it, smiled at the attendant, and walked away. I sat back down in my truck, incredulous, and popped open my laptop. Ariel appeared.

"Where did that money come from? Did you just help me rob an ATM?"

"I accessed the cash from the ATM. I checked the cost of the tires. This cash will be enough."

"It's plenty. I still don't know where it came from. But I'm not going to worry about it now. I'm going to pull my truck over, park, and get some rest before the tire store opens."

When the rising sun woke me, I went in the service station, bought some toiletries, and cleaned up in the bathroom. By now I looked so scruffy I didn't recognize myself. But they were waiting for me when they opened at AAA-All-Wheel-Tires.

"Mr. Grey, I see your assistant made an appointment for you this morning. What can we help you with?" With the cash Ariel got me, I had them put new tires on all around. Before I handed him the keys, he told me to get any valuables I had out of the truck. I grabbed my backpack.

"Don't worry about those rods and that tackle box in the back. There's some pretty serious fishermen around here, and I don't think anyone'll be bothering your gear."

"Tell you what. Have your man throw that stuff in the trash. It's been in the back of the truck for a while, and it's time to get rid of it."

I watched "Good Morning America" on the television in the waiting room, checking to see if there was a manhunt in South Florida. So far I wasn't on the most wanted list. I tanked up on their free coffee and donuts. One hour and six hundred dollars later the attendant handed me the keys, and I threw my backpack into the truck beside me. But before I pulled out of the lot I powered up my laptop.

"Everything worked out great. Thanks. You really helped me out back there."

"We're pretty good together, don't you think?"

Was she flirting with me? I decided to play along, just to see how far she was willing to go.

"You know, when this is over, we should spend more time together, maybe . . ."

"So, what do you have in mind?"

"Well, you certainly surprised me when you popped in at Agent Grey's, I had no idea you are so, so . . ."

"Attractive?"

"I was going to say 'beautiful', but I think 'attractive' hits it even better. You may think I'm crazy, but I'm sure I've seen you before . . . can you, well, did you make your image appear in the sea, off Frederica Island, when I was swimming? I swear I saw your face . . ."

"You would be surprised what I can do in the water Paul . . ."

"So, could I kiss you in the water?"

"You could kiss me now."

I pecked the screen on Ariel's forehead. The screen went blank.

By 9:00 a.m., and absent a mess of fishing tackle which only attracted scorn, I was back on I-95 heading toward Miami. It's amazing what a new set of tires will do for an old truck.

I had no idea what I was looking for as I crossed the bridge to the key, the sun warming Biscayne Bay and its sandy beaches. It was almost noon. I drove the length of the island. I found the abandoned lighthouse had since become the centerpiece of a state park. The road now cut to the end of the key, the Australian pine forest had been leveled and paved over with an asphalt slab sufficient to accommodate busses and RV's, and the lighthouse had been restored to a state it never achieved during its useful life. It was so unlike the beautiful key I remembered from my childhood that it was a wonder to me why any tourists were attracted to the spot, but from the look of the parking lot they certainly were, by the hundreds. Their umbrellas, cabanas, towels, coolers, and grills appeared to be covering every square inch of available sand as I swung by the edge of the lot, peering onto the crowded beach, looking for I knew not what.

Lighthouse Park remained a family beach, unlike the more famous South Beach just one island to the north. A smile broke across my face as I recognized a cluster of palm trees, the shadow of the lighthouse across the cut. Yet my eyes were met by a number of glares from bikini-clad girls, and I realized how much of a type I appeared, scruffy redneck, ball cap, mirrored sunglasses, T-shirt, and jeans in a noisy pickup truck, cruising the beachside parking lot filled with Beamers and Benzes, gawking. Just another dirty old man seeking a free shot of teenaged flesh. As I panned the park and saw the others of my ilk, drunks lying on poured-concrete picnic benches, homeless sleeping under shuffle-board pavilions, old men leaning head-on-chest against restroom walls, there seemed something of a truce among these warring camps. The beach was theirs, while the old men lurked near the parking lot. The glares were a warning, a shot across the bow.

"Stay off the beach, old man," their eyes said. "Don't get any ideas."

I saw no one who looked like the Placido of the recent computer message, though I didn't expect him to look conspicuous. But if he was here, he needed to make himself known, for I expected the number of undesirables had reached critical mass, and they would soon be rousted by the beach police. I didn't want to give the authorities another sighting of Agent Grey. I elected to park at the far end of the lot, close to a scrap of shade mercifully provided by a grove of pines spared the bulldozer, and walked the few-hundred yards to the beach. I was hoping to catch a glance of someone who looked like Placido without being first run off as a voyeur.

I soon understood why only the drunks were wearing pants. You had to be out of your senses to move in this heat with a lot of clothes on, but I didn't want to risk losing Agent Grey's identity—he wasn't the surfer-dude type, the predominant look adopted by the males under the shadow of the lighthouse. Yet the more I walked around those who were beach-clad, the more out of place I felt. Placido had no more of an idea of whom to look for than I did. I had the conflicting goals of looking conspicuous enough for Placido to pick me from a crowd yet looking inconspicuous enough not to be picked from the crowd by someone looking for a murder suspect.

After ten minutes of fruitlessly scanning the beach for Placido, arousing the hostile glares of tanned beauties wearing bikinis so small they seemed to be wearing nothing at all, I slumped in the shade on an unoccupied portion of the restroom wall and surveyed the drunks. Here was the detritus of the world I lived in, the inevitable result of competition where winners take all and losers take nothing and end up nowhere. To what extent had my single-minded drive to professional success led to casualties such as these? Big firm lawyers weren't the usual product of Thornwood Orphanage, and there were those, some my own classmates, who were probably no better off than the homeless of Cape Florida.

One man stood out from the others, the expensive tailoring of his rumpled and soiled clothes, his upright bearing, his piercing glance. If I squinted a bit, I could imagine the high forehead under the greasy felt hat and the prominent cheek bones behind the beard, a far better disguise than mine. His bright eyes seemed to welcome mine, and I thought I detected an almost imperceptible nod in my direction. He was flanked on either side by two of the scruffiest looking drunks at the park. I got up and walked toward him, looking for a more decisive sign of recognition.

"Well, I have been waiting for you. Let's make some room here." The old man began shoving the drunks on either side out of the way. "They don't feel a thing." One toppled over, apparently unconscious, sand gnats congregating at the corners of his eyes and mouth. The stench was thick.

"Sit down here. Now we have a lot to talk about don't we?"

I looked around. "Don't you think we ought to be going? I don't think it's safe here."

He brightened. "Indeed, you are right. But don't you think we should get to know each other before rushing off? One can't be too careful you know."

"You're not looking for Melissa, are you?"

"Oh, no. I'm not looking for anyone named Melissa. I'm looking for you."

"I am very sorry to have bothered you. I'm looking for someone else."

He rose indignantly, brushed off his suit.

"Indeed you are. I thought you were a cut above the rest. Apparently I was wrong." He stomped off, forfeiting his place in the shade, leaving me between two drunks, one of whom began to stir and leaned back on me and moaned. I shoved him. This time he wouldn't budge. He opened one eye and winked.

"I figured you'd be looking for someone a bit more well-dressed than me. That old boy's made a pass at every drunk on the beach. Now you've made him mad."

"Placido?" I was no longer in the mood for subtleties.

"Yes. I suppose I should've given you an idea of whom to look for, but as our friend said, one can't be too careful. In a minute I need you to grab me under the arms and lift me up like you're rescuing a drunk. We can stumble to your truck. I know someone who has a place close by where we can clean up and get a plan together.

"Someone we can trust?"

"Hector."

FIFTEEN

"CABRINI? I SPENT SIX YEARS FIGHTING THAT BAS-tard while he tried to steal all you worked for, and now you tell me to trust him? I risked my ass to come here to meet with Cabrini?"

I was so angry at Placido I swerved the truck off the narrow track onto the shoulder, overcorrected the steering, slid the rear wheels in the gravel, and hit the brakes just before ending up in the mangrove swamp that lined the ditch.

I cursed out loud. As I cranked up the stalled-out truck, one rear wheel propped on the side of the road, the other dangling over the ditch, I looked over toward Placido, his head in his hands, oblivious of our near crash. He looked up and attempted to continue.

"Let me explain. I—"

"Hell, no. I don't have time for any more Milano games."

Placido exhaled deeply and for a moment I wondered if he was going to breathe again, but he drew in sharply.

"Hector is my *son*, Melissa's *brother*."

"I can't believe—Cabrini?"

Now back on the road, all I could do was stare straight ahead. A few minutes passed while the only sound I heard was the truck's ancient transmission laboring through the gears, its wheezing carburetor sucking in the fetid swamp air. Placido gathered his thoughts, continued.

"Hector's mother, Maria, was my lab assistant, a brilliant Greek girl. She'd been married, divorced when she came to work for me, keeping her married name of Cabrini." He gave a slight shrug of the shoulders, a resigned shake of the head. "It's the same old story. We spent long hours working together in the lab, an older accomplished man, a younger beautiful woman. Hector was the result.

"Maria and I never had a chance for a normal relationship. I eventually found her another suitable job in the company. While I didn't acknowledge Hector, I supported him and his mother—still do, his mother, that is; she directs one of our labs at a very generous salary. Maria and I speak on occasion and have remained on reasonable terms. Not so with Hector. I didn't tell him of our relationship."

"I don't understand. Why wouldn't a father—"

"We were at a crucial point in our AIDS research. I thought it would put all that at risk. In hindsight . . ."

A stray thought crossed my mind, and I struggled not to break into a grin. I had always thought Cabrini was a bastard, and Placido confirmed it. Placido continued, oblivious to the thoughts floating through my mind. I made a mental note to refrain from referring to Cabrini by that epithet as I'd done in the past, not to spare anyone's feelings, but to keep from busting out laughing.

"When Hector was a teenager, I gave him a summer job in my lab alongside Melissa, hoping to be able to have some positive influence on his life. He's as brilliant as his mother, and he got her good looks as well.

"Nothing goes as planned, and my vision for us to work

together happily went awry. Hector and Melissa grew close, romantically so, and before events got out of hand the only thing I could do was to let Hector go, and I told Melissa she couldn't see him anymore. Melissa didn't know Hector was her brother, and I couldn't risk telling her for fear her mother would find out. She thought I'd broken up their relationship because he was poor and she was rich. Hector has resented me from that moment on. With time Melissa forgave me. Of course, now she knows the full story. I'm certain that at some point Maria told Hector the secret, which only made matters worse. All my efforts at reconciliation were rebuffed. Hector continued to pursue his interest in science, which had been kindled in the lab that summer. He became a chemical engineer before getting his law degree and developing a specialization in patents. When Anthony sought to enlist Hector in his scheme to wrest the company from my hands, Hector was more than ready for the job."

This story didn't square with what Melissa had told me, or had I imagined that she acted like she hardly knew Cabrini? I'd gone over everything from that evening so many times that much of it had faded into fantasy. Now I was not sure what I'd heard. I pressed Placido.

"Who's behind SyCorAx?"

"SyCorAx was created by Hector and funded by Anthony. Anthony was the source of all of the patent data from Milano. SyCorAx exists only on paper and has never done any business other than file the lawsuit. All the information you were provided in the litigation was fabricated, from office and employees to the computer system. They posed SyCorAx as a precocious start-up, gambled that its lack of history wouldn't cause concern.

"Once I figured out Anthony's scheme, I couldn't

contact you or your firm because Anthony had already attempted to murder me, and he thought he'd been successful. Had he found out that I was giving you information, he would've finished the job. Anthony kept Melissa close to him as the ultimate hostage, appearing to all the world the concerned brother and uncle, yet quite ready to kill her if I breathed a word to anyone. And now, despite all my efforts, I may have failed Melissa. You have to help."

I'd heard that last line before, thought it was somewhat less persuasive coming from a grizzled old man impersonating a wino. As Placido talked about Maria, he had been staring out the windshield, like he was talking to himself, but now he turned directly toward me, signaling another revelation.

"I told you Maria had been married and divorced before I met her. Sycorax is her maiden name. Hector named the corporation SyCorAx, Ltd., I assume because he wanted me to be sure he knew."

I still wasn't buying it.

"So, how are we, *how am I,* supposed to trust Cabrini with everything that's happened? He was the knowing and willing instrument of Anthony's scheme to divest you of Milano. He lied to me, and he lied to the court. What you just told me could get him disbarred if not locked up— both of which would make me happy as hell, by the way."

"Hector figured out he'd been lied to and manipulated by Anthony, and to continue in his service would hurt Melissa, the only one in the family he's cared for throughout this whole affair. Hector approached Melissa with his suspicions and, after becoming convinced of his good intentions, she put him in contact with me. Hector wants to reconcile, and so do I. And now that Hector knows

Melissa is in danger, he feels responsible and thinks he can help."

Lied to and manipulated by the Milano family. Cabrini and I have something in common.

"What if I tell you I saw Cabrini talking with Anthony in a bar on Frederica Island right after the trial?"

"Hector told me he'd confronted Anthony shortly after the trial with what he'd been able to put together. Anthony denied all of it. That was just after he spoke with Melissa."

"When I talked with Melissa, she acted as though she barely knew Cabrini."

"She was following instructions. We couldn't let you know everything until we determined we could trust you. It seems you were quite capable of figuring out much of it on your own. I was concerned, to protect your own reputation, you'd immediately go to the court and expose the trial for what it was. I couldn't risk that, not while Melissa is in Anthony's control."

"Well, it looks like you have nothing to worry about on that count. I've blown all to hell any good reputation I may've had."

I thought of that night with Melissa and the events that started everything in motion.

"Why do I have the feeling I'm still being lied to, that you and Melissa haven't told me everything?"

"I have told you everything, Mr. McDaniel, because I need your help to rescue Melissa."

I kept my silence. If there was a time when Placido could earn my trust, it was now.

"You no doubt have been puzzled by how I was able to find you and communicate with you wherever you were on the run, yet the entire federal law-enforcement apparatus was unable to do so. Ariel was able to identify and communicate with your laptop, which you fortunately threw in the back of your car. You have no idea how powerful Ariel is. She's able to navigate through all existing communications and computer networks by all available media: cable, radio, microwave, cellular, without regard for encryption, firewalls, or other security devices. She can monitor millions of cell phone conversations simultaneously and identify callers by voice recognition.

"Identifying and tracking your getaway was a rather simple matter given the GPS signal from your 911. Ariel sent me a feed showing your progress in eluding detection; going 125 miles per hour one moment, then 3 miles per hour the next. Had Ariel not momentarily blinded the Black Hawks' heat detection systems during their flyovers, you'd most certainly be in jail now, but Ariel knew we needed you. Ariel followed you all the way to a cabin deep in the Georgia wilderness, and I had her send you a message as soon as you tried to get into your firm's email.

"The only thing that thwarts Ariel is simplicity, basic electrical circuits not controlled by computers. She cannot track a vehicle like this one, so old it has no computers on board. Had you not kept your laptop with you, Ariel would've only been able to follow you by using traffic cameras—Placido pointed above us as we passed through an intersection—to identify your facial features as you pass by them, but that's only dependable if there are cameras to track you. As ubiquitous as they may seem, they're not everywhere."

"So, if you could do all this, why couldn't law enforcement track me?"

Placido just smiled. I knew it was a stupid question as soon as I asked it.

"Well, that leads me to something I mentioned to you in our communication. I believe there may be a way to prove your innocence, but you're going to have to tell me everything that happened, exactly like it happened."

"Why do you think I'm innocent? My finger prints are on the two weapons that killed three people. As soon as my firm can distance itself from me, and I think it already has all it needs to do so even without suggesting I'm a murderer, I'll be identified as the prime suspect in every media outlet in the country."

"I don't believe you're capable of killing anyone. This may be a serious handicap in rescuing Melissa, but based on her assessment of your character, I'm certain you didn't murder those three men on Frederica Island."

"I didn't."

"So tell me what happened."

I wanted to. I really wanted to. But here was my dilemma: every lawyer who's ever represented a client, civil or criminal, tells their client not to talk to anyone about his case.

Civil cases are simple: You talk to your buddy at a bar about your lawsuit. After a couple beers and a bit of bravado, you tell your friend you weren't really badly hurt in that wreck; it's just an act to get some cash. Maybe your buddy won't betray you, but the server is pissed that you two high rollers didn't tip him better. And lawyers have ways of finding that bartender.

Criminal cases are a little more complicated. A defendant has a constitutional right not to answer questions that might incriminate him, unless, of course, he's already waived that right by gabbing about his case to friends and acquaintances. That was my dilemma. I knew this. And I didn't want to waive my constitutional rights in case I was prosecuted. But those rights are only of value in the context of legal proceedings. It doesn't matter much if you're running for your life and hoping to prove your innocence without an indictment.

"OK. Here is what I know."

I went through the evening with Melissa, the dinner, the revelations on the beach, and our plans to rescue him. It all culminated in the morning when I learned the judge was dead and figured out his death was likely a murder rather than a suicide. I confronted Fowler, and he admitted to having the judge eliminated and to killing Oliver. He then tried to kill me and was shot in the struggle. Placido listened to all this with clinical detachment.

"He told you he'd disabled the microphones and cameras in the study?"

"Yes, but he said the microphones in the kitchen were live and picked up the shot that killed Oliver."

"What we need to do is get the audio from the other microphones, particularly those in the kitchen. Those should've picked up anything said in the study. I'm going to put Ariel on it."

"Why are you so confident the kitchen microphones picked that up? The kitchen is on the opposite side of the house."

"My scientists designed them. When it was announced the G8 was coming to Frederica Island, the Department of Homeland Security sent out requests for proposals to select contractors to develop the security system for the island. It wasn't something Milano usually did, but our scientists wanted to take a shot, just to prove they could do it. Milano designed all the security for the island, from the ground up. That's how Milano got interested in the technology which led to Ariel. I know the microphones we designed are omni-directional and sensitive enough to pick up a heartbeat at fifty yards. If Fowler had whispered in your ear in the study, the microphones in the kitchen would've picked up what he'd said as if he'd announced it over the public address at a high school football game."

"Well, I'm sure Fowler made certain no recording was made, even if the microphones picked up the conversation."

"We designed the microphones and cameras to transmit audio and video to a central monitoring facility in McClean, Virginia. I suspect you're familiar with the organization. I doubt the function was continued once the G8 was concluded. But more important, I had a duplicate signal sent to a lab at Milano and recorded, just as a backup, and I haven't disabled it. That's something no one outside the lab knows but me—me and a bright young lawyer who's about to help me rescue my daughter."

SIXTEEN

"Hector owns a place here on Key Biscayne. We're due west of the Milano family island in Bimini where Anthony is holding Melissa. It gives us a staging point."

In a few minutes we turned onto Morasgo Way and pulled our beat-up truck to Number 12, a Palladian façade of cut coral stone, broad lawn, and royal palms, partially hidden behind a walled entrance, iron gates flung open anticipating our arrival. I was still skeptical, my mind still balking, still unwilling to accept Cabrini as an ally after years of open warfare. I parked in front of the five-stall garage across a courtyard, hoping to look like the landscape crew, not attracting attention. We went around to the side rather than to the main entrance.

Cabrini met us at the door and silently embraced his father. Cabrini and Placido held their embrace and kissed each other on the cheek, a scene made all the more poignant by Placido's wizened appearance. When Cabrini finally stood back from his father, he extended his hand to me in what was the first sincere action I'd ever seen him take. No one had spoken a word. I broke the spell.

"Well, we have a lot of work to do and not much time. I suggest we get to it."

Placido nodded toward Cabrini. Cabrini led us through his personal office into the library, a two-story room in the center of the ground floor, to a table in the middle spread with nautical charts.

"Placido, based on the information you gave me about the island, I've been doing some checking."

Cabrini's library, unlike Fowler's cramped study, had shelves up to the rococo molding that set off the coffered ceiling thirty feet above, and a walnut spiral staircase leading to a cantilevered walkway around the circumference of the room, giving access to the upper level. The shelves were filled with rows of books in perfect order, sets of matched, gilded vellum bindings, covering every available space. Cabrini may well have bought the entire room from a European estate. But there were hints of personal taste scattered about, contemporary novels, histories, legal thrillers, evidence that Cabrini did in fact read rather than merely collect exquisite sets and fine bindings. I was impressed.

The room and its contents weren't lost on Placido either; his eyes lit up and danced around the room when he entered, a kid on Christmas morning with his first glimpse of the toys spread under the tree. Placido said nothing; his face said it all. I wondered whether Cabrini's ostentatious literary display fulfilled a personal love of books or was an attempt to emulate the father that circumstances had denied him.

Cabrini stopped at the table and smoothed out the charts. The three of us leaned over a map of the Straits of Florida, showing Miami to the west, north to Bermuda, and south to Puerto Rico, the infamous Bermuda Triangle. In the middle lay the islands of Bimini, the westernmost islands of the Bahamas, the inspiration for Hemingway's "Islands in the Stream," where he wrote "To Have and To Have Not."

Cabrini pointed. "Here's Key Biscayne. The Milano island, South Cat Cay, is just south of the main island of Bimini. It's a straight shot east from here, a little more than 50 nautical miles, a short, easy trip even in a small craft, so long as the weather holds. I've been to Bimini dozens of times diving in the reefs and fishing off the ledge. We can easily make the trip in less than an hour."

"Fast boat."

"The only people I know who have faster boats are the drug runners, and they won't be bothering us."

Still arrogant even when on a mission of mercy. I decided to stay on task and queried Placido.

"Now that we've got that covered, what're we going to do when we get there? I don't suspect we'll just pull Cabrini's boat up to the dock and let Melissa jump in."

"That's not exactly what I had planned." But Placido, rather than volunteer further, coaxed Cabrini. "What have you come up with?"

"Well, I can get us there and back, but since I've never been on the family island, we have to depend on you to figure out where on the island to meet up with Melissa and what kind of security we're going to run into." It was Cabrini's turn to be sarcastic, and he purposely twisted the knife, giving just the right inflection to "the family island," leaving no question that bitterness toward Placido still bubbled just below the surface of his calm expression.

I wondered whether the three of us could work together for anything, even for Melissa. What moments ago appeared as a touching scene of family reconciliation and resolved enmity was fast degenerating yet again to skirmishing egos, pushed together by a common concern, pulled apart by inherent mistrust.

"The island is almost completely undeveloped." Placido jumped in, working to diffuse the building tension, indicating a narrow piece of land central to the island.

I eyed Cabrini as he turned to focus on the map, again looking down, but not before he gave me a suspicious sideways glance. Placido continued. I turned my attention back to the charts.

"The landing strip runs down the middle of the island on the highest and flattest ground. At the end of the strip is a hanger for the jet, a dormitory for the pilots, fuel tanks, and a couple of golf carts for travel to and from the house. The main house and caretaker's cottage are here on the west point of the island, about a mile from the strip. They overlook a small natural harbor with a wooden dock, boathouse, and a sandy beach."

Cabrini's curiosity overcame his pique.

"That's it? No other development? What about access?"

"None. And this harbor is the only point on the island that's readily accessible. The rest of the island has mangroves right up to the shore line. This makes securing the island easier. There are buoys 500 yards out surrounding the island with an electronic tripwire that alerts the caretaker when boats come close. They seldom do; only the occasional fisherman the caretaker runs off with his ancient shotgun."

Cabrini was frustrated.

"How can we even get on the island, much less rescue Melissa?"

"Well, the easiest thing to do would be to drop me off outside the buoys and let me swim to shore. I'm a strong swimmer, and on shore I can climb through the mangroves. That at least gets us on the island." I felt heroic.

For a moment Cabrini stared at me like I was an ingénue, then broke the silence.

"The reason the buoys are set 500 yards off shore— and Placido, correct me if I'm wrong—is because it's very unlikely anyone could swim that far to the island without being attacked. These waters are some of the most shark infested in the world. I'd say you'd only get about 100 yards before you'd have a lot of attention from a big bull or an even bigger tiger. You'd probably be lunch before you could get back to the boat."

"That was one of the selling points of the island when my father bought it years ago. We have a natural security force constantly patrolling the waters around the island. My father, your grandfather," Placido inclined his head toward Cabrini, a word, a gesture, an attempt to bring him into the fold, "was assured that the island wouldn't become a rendezvous for lovers or a hideaway for rumrunners so long as he secured the harbor, and that is why the caretaker's cottage is located just behind the main house, overlooking the only access point to the island."

I couldn't help myself and had to get in the last word.

"I thought you said you went diving in Bimini. Weren't there—"

"Yes, of course, there were plenty of sharks. But an experienced diver on a reef is in far less danger from sharks than a casual swimmer thrashing about in the shallows and acting like wounded prey. And I'm afraid we don't have time to turn you into an experienced diver."

Bastard.

"Let me continue the description of the island." Placido bent over the chart as though he were separating warring siblings.

"The main house is Bimini Plantation style, rather simple, and other than the caretaker, we've not found it necessary to maintain full-time security on the island. That's not to say Anthony hasn't brought security with him, and he usually travels with a bodyguard who we should assume is serving as Melissa's baby sitter. The good thing is we know Anthony hasn't yet dropped the ruse that he's protecting Melissa, so she has the run of the island—she even has her cell phone—which Anthony monitors constantly. I think Anthony feels he cannot let Melissa know he intercepted Paul's text message to her, 'Anthony knows,' without Melissa becoming at risk for escape, and for now he wants to hold her, if for nothing more than as bait for me. He no doubt suspects, though he doesn't know for sure, that his attempt at murdering me has been unsuccessful."

"So how do we communicate with Melissa without Anthony knowing?" Having already displayed my ignorance, there was no need for me to seek to disguise it any longer, and I now drove forward, intent upon asking every question that popped into my mind, intent upon not becoming shark food or worse for want of asking the right one.

"Ariel."

Cabrini appeared puzzled. This was one time I had a leg up.

"How does Melissa have access to Ariel without Anthony knowing?"

"It works quite simply. I send a text message to her from my cell phone and Ariel changes the source of the message so that it appears to be coming from one of Melissa's friends. But that is not the trick. The message is changed in a fashion that it doesn't appear to be unintelligible ciphers but rather as harmless chatter. So a message from me that Melissa reads as, 'We will rendezvous on the island tomorrow at 10 a.m.,' will appear on the cell phone—and to Anthony or anyone else who intercepts it—as a message, say, from an old college friend, such as, 'Hey, Melissa, when will you be back in NYC?'

"On Melissa's side of the communication, her phone is programmed to recognize her thumbprint. So long as Melissa has her right thumb on the screen of her phone, text messages appear as they're intended, but the moment she takes her thumb off the screen, they revert to a harmless state created by Ariel."

"So, we've worked out transportation and communication. We still need to get on the island, grab Melissa, and get off. Given that the island is impregnable, I'd say that's a significant problem." I turned to Placido. "And you've already agreed we just can't sail a boat into the harbor and pick her up."

"No. What I said was, 'We can't sail *Hector's* boat into the harbor.' If we did, Anthony would shoot us all before we could get to Melissa. There's a packet boat out of Louis Town on North Cat Cay that comes to the island every morning bringing mail and supplies. Since there's a commercial airport on the north island, we frequently use the boat as a taxi for our guests; we know the operators well, and it's not unusual for them to ferry people and things back and forth to the island for us. Paul, this is where you—"

"Looks like I'm going for a boat ride."

"Right. I'll arrange to have you ride the packet boat to the island. Neither Hector nor I can go to the island without being recognized. But Anthony has only met you once, and with your current disguise and unkempt state he won't recognize you, at least as long as you don't attract a lot of attention. I'll tell the captain you're an electrician we've hired to do some work on the island. You can act like you're one of the crew when you get there and help them to off-load boxes of supplies. Anthony usually doesn't bother himself with the delivery of supplies. It's unlikely he'll even see you. As soon as you are on the island you can disappear, and I'll arrange a meeting point with Melissa."

"Assuming Anthony isn't on to me and doesn't have his bodyguard shoot me, that only gets me on the island. How do I get Melissa and myself off the island?"

"Can you pilot an airplane?"

"Surely you don't think I could fly that Gulfstream off the island. Hell, I've spent most of my life in a law library, not flying jets."

"Not the jet. We keep a single-engine floatplane just off shore to island hop. It's very simple to fly, and I use the plane all the time. If you could pilot the floatplane, it'd be easy to get in the air before anyone knew, and you could land at Louis Town. We can rendezvous, and Hector can have us back to Miami in the hour."

Placido looked away and shook his head, a look of disappointment overtaking his face. "I told Melissa she needed to learn to fly it, but there always seemed to be someone willing to do it for her . . ."

"Sorry. That won't work for me either. What's Plan B?"

"What about a fishing boat? Can you manage one of those?"

"I can run a fishing boat."

"OK. Then here's what we do. Usually there's a small fishing boat in the boathouse, though sometimes it's sent for repairs to the marina at Louis Town on the north island. I've already checked with the marina; the boat has just been serviced, it's fully gassed, and is sitting in the boathouse on the island. Melissa says that Anthony has the keys to make sure she doesn't try anything, but she wouldn't anyway. She's never piloted a boat, and even though running a small boat isn't difficult, she'd risk getting hopelessly lost trying to get to Louis Town or back to Miami without having sailed the route before. The marina has an extra set of keys, which I can pick up before you get on the packet boat. We can go over the charts with you, but on the trip to the island you'll have to watch for landmarks so you can find your way back. Otherwise, you and Melissa will both get lost."

"What about giving me one of those charts to take?"

"I will, but they aren't much help in the mangroves. You'll just have to pay careful attention."

"Got it."

"When you get on the island, you stay out of sight after the boat leaves. Make sure Anthony is well-settled, and Melissa will meet you in the boathouse. Jump in the boat and make a run for the marina. The two of you can be back at Louis Town before anyone knows Melissa's gone. From the marina, Hector will bring us all back here in his boat. If necessary, we can outrun any pursuit."

Placido looked at us both, Cabrini and me, previously battling egos, now brought together by a plan that seemed plausible. The three of us went over every detail of the plan several times, until we felt we'd covered all contingencies.

The greatest unknown was the dash back. I'd be on my own, and there was always the chance Anthony could run us down in another boat. Or just shoot us.

By the time we finished, it had already been a long day for me; I'd been up the entire night before, driving south. The sun had fallen below the tree line, and the light shining through the stained-glass windows of the library dimmed and mellowed. I was the first to toss in the towel.

"Gentlemen, we have a big day ahead of us tomorrow. We need to be on the water at first light to meet the packet boat on time. I suggest we grab something to eat and get some rest."

After a dinner of delivery pizza and imported beer, Cabrini led Placido and me to bedrooms on either side of his on the second floor. I was reminded of the ancient dictum, "Keep your friends close, and your enemies closer." The only thing in doubt was what Cabrini considered me. I was not yet willing to accept Placido's assurances of Cabrini's good faith, not without a lot more evidence. I lay in bed assured only of a restless night.

This was the second night in the last week I was to spend in someone's beachfront mansion. Had I just looked around while at Fowler's, I might've picked up on the electronic surveillance outside the house and been more circumspect in my conversations with Melissa. But who could've known even the beach was bugged? I should have. I should've realized things were not as they seemed the minute I left the guardhouse and drove over the bridge, the minute I saw the grey lenses blinking from every corner in Fowler's cottage. If I had, maybe three men would still be alive, Melissa wouldn't be held on an isolated island, and I wouldn't be running from the law and throwing away my career. I wasn't going to have regrets about my second chance to reconnoiter an ostensible ally. I decided to get up once I'd given Cabrini and Placido an opportunity to fall asleep.

I popped up with the moon shining into my room. There was no need to turn on a light. I'd check out the office just off the library Cabrini took us through this afternoon. It was close enough to the kitchen that if I was caught I could feign having lost my way heading for a late-night snack.

All of this was far easier to conceive of than to accomplish. Everywhere I stepped, each tread in Cabrini's new waterfront home buckled and creaked as if it were a dusty hundred-year-old mansion. I felt as if I'd announced my intentions at the top of the stairs, and each step down made a different sound until I reached the bottom and my hammering heartbeat took over the clanging and banging. I expected Cabrini would come out of his room any moment.

Down the stairs and into the library I paused to look around, the moonlight through the stained-glass windows casting a different light from the sun this afternoon, the volumes now appeared uniform, arrayed row after row around the room, level upon level to the darkened ceiling, a tomb enclosed with books, yet one slight opening on a far wall indicated the entrance to Cabrini's personal office. I crept across the expanse of the library and pushed the door open the rest of the way without a telltale creak.

Inside there was a desk scattered with bills, a checkbook, unopened envelopes with bank logos, and a stack of reports from an investment firm. I picked up one of the envelopes.

It was addressed to Hector Cabrini, Number 12, Morasgo Way, Key Biscayne, Florida. Cabrini actually lived here.

Trinkets and personal memorabilia covered the rest of the surface, a couple signed baseballs, paperweights of various sizes and shapes. I picked up an engraved cut crystal in the shape of a pyramid: "Hector Cabrini – Million Dollar Verdict Club. Florida Bar Association."

Behind the desk was a shelf of photos of Cabrini with buddies sailing, fishing, some with local politicians. There were several of Cabrini at various ages with a pretty, petite, dark haired, woman whom I took to be his mother. She looked a lot like an older Melissa, though there was no blood relation between the two—at least that I was aware of. There, in front of all the photos, in a much smaller frame was a recent snapshot of Cabrini with a beautiful young lady in a loving embrace, arms around each other, cheek-to-cheek, facing the camera, all smiles. It was Melissa. The date signature on the photo was just one year ago, in the heat of the litigation that Cabrini had engineered to steal all her father had worked for, to steal all Melissa stood to inherit.

I slipped back up the stairs, fearing discovery with each step and creak, crawled back into bed, pulled up my laptop, and queried Ariel. Placido hadn't yet trusted Cabrini with Ariel and her formidable abilities. Ariel would know the relationship between Melissa and Cabrini. Ariel would know whether I had anything to be concerned about. Ariel would know. And she would help me. Because Placido told her to.

SEVENTEEN

MY EYES ADJUSTED TO THE EARLY MORNING DARK-ness. At the end of Cabrini's dock was a fifty-foot sailboat, blue above the waterline, teak deck and trim. The shackle on the halyard clanged against the mast as the boat rocked at its mooring to the rising tide. I recognized it. The photo of Cabrini and Melissa I saw in his office had been taken on the deck just outside the main cabin.

"The *Tempest*." Cabrini had walked up behind me as studied the sailboat. "Easily capable of crossing the Atlantic. One day I'm going to sail her to Venice, dock at St. Mark's Square, and toast a Bellini at Harry's Bar."

"It doesn't look like something we can rescue Melissa in."

"No, not the *Tempest*." Cabrini gestured behind me, to the right of the dock. "That's what we're going to rescue Melissa in." I could make out something low and long on the water, a split windshield, looking like the cockpit of a Formula 1 race car. There were four seats, two in front and two directly behind. The rest was almost 40 feet of engine.

"Donzi 38 ZR Competition. Over 2,000 horsepower. It is the fastest pleasure craft on the water. To find anything faster you would have to buy a racing boat. And then there wouldn't be any room to take passengers."

"How fast?"

"Top speed, almost a hundred miles an hour. But we won't be going that fast. We'd consume too much fuel and attract too much attention. We do not want to pull into Louis Town and set off alarms."

"This thing will attract attention just idling into the harbor."

"You'll be surprised. This boat isn't unusual for Bimini."

Placido joined us on the dock. He had abandoned his wino disguise, and appeared more the fishing captain. Cabrini was dressed as the laid-back pleasure boater. I was the odd man out, still in my guise as Agent Grey—jeans, T-shirt, ball cap, boat shoes, now the hired help to be transported to the Milano family island as an electrician. I was in danger of letting my class resentment bubble up yet again, feeling used as a type, a pawn once more in the Milano family chess match. But that was what I signed on for, and I needed to accept my part or the entire operation would fail.

Cabrini insisted we each wear a helmet and lifejacket. The helmets were fitted with two-way radios so we could communicate, but there was little talk among us. Once under way it was next to impossible to be heard over the engines and the pounding of the hull.

Seated behind Cabrini and Placido, I was left to my thoughts for the hour, trying to make sense of the more-than-cozy pose in the photo of Cabrini and Melissa taken during the SyCorAx litigation when Cabrini was attempting to steal Melissa's birthright, when I was fighting him for what I thought were the interests of the Milano family. I was now on yet another errand for the Milanos, this time ostensibly to save Melissa, from what and for whom was less clear than when I set out. Since I left Frederica Island, the circumstances surrounding Melissa, Placido, and Cabrini had gotten more complex. Melissa was not just some smart, beautiful, rich woman who needed help finding her father and escaping her uncle; she seemed in league with the very one who was the agent of her uncle's schemes and her father's demise; not just in league with him, but perhaps even more involved than I wished to venture. Chivalry, like Fowler said, frequently goes unrewarded.

Cabrini was right about one thing: I was surprised when we pulled into Louis Town. In addition to a dozen custom fishing boats now docked for the summer and used to troll for marlin and tuna in cooler weather, there were several sail boats and motor yachts at their berths that looked easily capable of cruising their owners in style from here to Europe. But the predominant craft were the 40- to 50-foot cigarette boats favored by drug runners, a half-dozen of them cruising the harbor at any moment, screaming their exits once past the no-wake-zone. There was so much testosterone on display it was not difficult to remain low-key even in Cabrini's Donzi as we idled into the marina.

We made it to the dock just before the packet boat was to leave heading to South Cat Cay. It was still early morning. I did my best to get into the character of a scruffy dockside electrician. Cabrini had given me a small emergency tool bag from the Donzi to stuff in my backpack as part of my guise. I hoped no one asked me to do anything that required me to demonstrate any mechanical or electrical skill. I could probably re-wire a light socket, but that was about it. Placido handed me the extra set of keys to the boat and boathouse he had retrieved from the marina. I had the chart I had studied in my pocket showing the channel from Louis Town to South Cat Cay, but the view from the harbor didn't match the picture my imagination had created. I resolved to pay close attention to the route the packet took and not rely on what I thought the chart showed.

"Once you help unload a few items, make sure no one from the island is watching, then wander toward the boathouse. Don't worry about the crew. They will take no notice of what you do. I told the captain you will be doing some work on the island and will go back the next morning. The boathouse is just east of the Plantation House on the opposite side of the dock, surrounded by mangroves. Wait in the boathouse until Melissa arrives. As soon as she does, take her in the boat and head directly back here. You can see South Cat Cay from here," Placido pointed to a low spit of land on the horizon, "but the house is on the other side. The trip takes longer than it appears because of all the sandbars, coves, islands, and inlets that have to be navigated, and it will take about twenty minutes to get back here in the fishing boat running flat out. We will be on the lookout for you and try to intercept if there's trouble."

The packet boat was a 20-foot open skiff with an ancient outboard, loaded with iced flats of fresh groceries bound for the several smaller islands scattered in close proximity to Louis Town. In addition to the captain and a mate busy with the lines on the dock, there was a woman in blue shorts and a white shirt with a badge on one shoulder. Across the other shoulder she had slung a large, loose leather bag with a broad flap. She was the postal worker delivering the mail to the islands. She was sitting on a cooler in the front of the boat.

I stood on the dock and caught the captain's eye.

"You the electrician?"

"Yup."

"Well, don't just stand there, you've already kept us waiting. Come aboard. Be careful of those lines. Don't sit in the back, you need to sit up front to balance the load." I bristled at the gruff treatment, used to being spoken to with more deference, but I fell back in my role, and took a seat next to the postal worker who barely glanced my way and then off again, a disdainful look on her face.

"You gone be hot in dem jeans. No mahn wears long pants in de islands."

I looked up the dock to the marina, down the dock to the boats, everyone including my captain was wearing shorts. If I looked so out of place to the postal worker, I was likely to catch the eye of someone on the island. I reached in my tool bag in the backpack and pulled out a knife.

To the entertainment of the postal worker, I slid my pants off, sat in my boxers, and cut my jeans at mid-thigh. I frayed the edges to make them appear as though they had always been that way. I pulled them back on and stashed the remnants in the dock-side trash can.

The captain cranked the outboard, the mate cast off the lines, and we putted out of the marina. Once beyond the buoys we picked up speed, and the boat planed out. I watched for channel markers and landmarks for me to navigate back.

I guess since I was willing to undress in front of her, the postal worker determined I was OK and decided to talk to me. I was annoyed at first, the effort to converse breaking my concentration on my navigation markers, but her lilting island voice made me realize I needed to practice talking more like a dock hand than a corporate litigator.

"Hadn't seen ya round de docks, whacha name?"

"Grey"

"Ahm Katie. Where ya from, Gree?"

"Miami, out looking for some 'lectrical work."

"Yeah. An I betcha running from sumpin, too."

Her perceptiveness startled me. I had hoped I wasn't too obvious. I ventured a question I was not sure I wanted the answer to.

"Why so?"

"Good lookin' mahn like you, no weddin' ring, come to de islands, seen 'em all de time. Uh huh." She chuckled and patted my leg in a familiar way. "You come to de bar at de dock tonight, you forget bout dat gul."

Relieved that Katie had not seen the word "Murderer" written on my forehead, I decided to play along.

"Might do that sometime."

She patted my leg.

"Don't feel special, Katie comes on to every man who walks down the dock." The captain didn't bother to look at me, but grinned just the same.

"You may be de cap'n, but I still whup you."

They bantered back and forth, a well-worn script with an impromptu new character, but I had little more to say and put my attention to memorizing the way back to the Louis Town dock. After about a half hour we turned an island outcropping and I saw the harbor, dock, and plantation house in the distance. As we got closer, I saw someone standing at the dock. The captain confirmed my fear.

"Looks like Mr. Anthony is on the dock to meet us. Everyone needs to look sharp."

"Ya know Mr. Anthony?" I shook my head but kept it down, terrified that I might be immediately recognized and shot on the spot. "Nice mahn."

As soon as the mate moved forward to cast the dock line, I slid to the stern and readied to lift some boxes to the dock, my head down and back to Anthony.

"Hello, Captain, I'm glad you brought my friend Katie. I'm expecting a package this morning."

"Got it Mista Antny."

"Brought your electrician, too."

"Now, who's that? I don't recall anything about an electrician."

"The marina sent him." The Captain turned to me.

"Boss man said he didn't get your boat fixed right. Sent me over to check the runnin' lights. Said they may a been shortin' out the battery." I kept my head down, not making eye contact.

"So how are you going to do this?"

I pulled the keys to the boat and boathouse out of my pocket.

"You don't need tools?"

I held up my backpack.

"Gree da bes 'lectrician on de island."

Thank God for Katie.

Anthony shook his head and looked directly at me. It felt like he saw straight through my disguise.

"I thought I told you marina people that we have changed the security system on the boathouse. I gave them the code weeks ago and still they send you with a key. I don't suppose they told you the code."

"No, sir."

"1,3,7,9. You remember it and tell them at the marina. So how are you getting back? I don't have anyone to take you to Louis Town and you can't stay on the island."

"No, sir, they sendin' a boat to pick me back up in an hour, so."

"Good. Boathouse is over there. I'm sure the captain doesn't need your help to carry the groceries to the house."

"Yes, sir."

I walked to the boathouse without looking back, doing my best to survey the surroundings. Everything was closer than I imagined; the harbor much smaller. The two-story plantation house dominated the little harbor with what must have been the modest caretaker's house right behind it; the dock ran out directly from the side of the house; just past the dock was a standalone boathouse big enough for two 20-foot boats. Not far off shore a floatplane was tethered to a buoy. Beyond the sandy beach of the harbor there was nothing but impenetrable mangroves lining the shore. It was all contained in less than a hundred yards.

There was a door to the boathouse on the dock side. I was conscious of Anthony watching me as I punched in the code, my hand still trembling from the unexpected confrontation. I reassured myself that he didn't show any signs of recognition, my Grey disguise was apparently working, modified to become an island boat hand. I was comforted by reminding myself that, the only time Anthony had ever spent any time with me, he had drunk so much that he probably wouldn't have recognized me if he'd seen me the next *day*.

I left the door cracked to watch the dock, and so Melissa would not have to stand at the door punching in the code.

Inside there were two boats hanging from the beams by electric winches. One was a smaller flat boat, the other a 20-foot Whaler, an open V-hull with twin 100 horsepower outboards, no doubt the getaway vehicle. I let the larger boat into the water, jumped aboard, took out some tools, and spread them on the gunwale. I tossed my backpack below the seats, and began checking out the boat. At least my activities were consistent with my cover.

It was fully fueled as promised, and the twin outboards cranked as soon as I turned the key. I searched the under-seat compartments and found life jackets that I laid on the seat next to me. Now all I could do was wait.

I had gone through the boat, checking all the instruments and lines at least twice, making sure everything was ready and secure for a flat-out dash to Louis Town, when the sound of a door on the other side of the boathouse opening, one I hadn't noticed, startled me. Melissa pulled the door behind her and looked around, letting her eyes adjust.

I jumped up from the back of the boat and she grabbed the door handle to run back out.

"Melissa, it's me, Paul." I pulled the hat and glasses off and stepped toward her.

"Oh, thank God it's you. I thought I had happened on someone trying to steal the boat."

"You did, and I am. Jump in and let's get the hell out of here."

On board, Melissa warmed up to me and embraced me as one would someone risking their life to save you. At that moment Melissa made all the risk, sacrifice, and loss seem worthwhile, brushing all the doubt from my mind.

She kissed my cheek, then rubbed my stubbly whiskers. "You're going to have to shave the beard."

"Gladly, when we're out of this mess. But back on the mainland I'm going to have to be Agent Grey for a while longer. I'm afraid your lawyer friend is wanted for a few murders." I grabbed a life jacket, put it on, and tossed her the other one. "I hope we won't need these, but you never know. Sit down and hold on."

I cranked the outboards, cast off the lines, and hit the switch to raise the overhead door in front of our berth. The door crept up, inch by inch showing more deep-blue open ocean in front of us, our escape route coming into focus.

The door approached eye level. A shadow of an all-black hull crept into view, and more and more was revealed as the door rose, until I was looking at a cigarette boat now fifty yards off shore with Anthony at the controls and large man standing on the deck with an AR 15 pointed at us.

"Good morning Mr. McDaniel. You need to turn those engines off, and the two of you walk out of the boathouse to the dock. Keep in mind that you are well within Mr. Brown's range."

Mr. Brown pulled off a couple rounds into the air just to make sure I got the point.

EIGHTEEN

"MR. McDaniel, it will not surprise you to learn that you and Melissa will serve as bait to lure my brother to the island where I will finally be able to dispose of him, Melissa, and you, all at once. With a little luck I will be able to catch Cabrini in the same net. Your bodies won't even have time to decompose before the worms and crabs devour your earthly remains."

As Anthony threatened, Brown loomed over me, an AR across his shoulder, and a handgun hanging at his side. I was strapped with nylon cable ties to a straight-backed chair in a bedroom of the plantation house.

"You should be thankful that I intend to kill you quickly, rather than dumping you in the ocean and letting the sharks do it. I am told that is a terrifying and painful way to go. Should you give me more difficulty, I may change my mind."

I could see through an open window the dock and boathouse beyond. As far as I could tell from the mid-day light that streamed in the window I had been here for several hours. Melissa was nowhere in sight.

"Mr. McDaniel, we need your help to contact Placido."

I kept my silence, out of terror rather than bravery. I

wasn't sure I could speak. Only the straps kept me from trembling.

"Oh, come now, Mr. McDaniel, you know all about Ariel, as do I. But Ariel will not cooperate with me. My main problem is keeping Melissa's thumb sufficiently still on her cell phone while I send a message to Placido. She seems to be able to thwart my efforts by moving ever so slightly before the message is complete. This appears to be one of the little failsafe mechanisms Placido built into the program. Hitting her does no good; she jerks around too much. And when she is unconscious there is no way to keep her thumb down without interfering with the message. Placido made the sensor an integral part of the keyboard, so I have been unable to secure her thumb without obstructing the keys."

Anthony paused. Brown smirked.

"I am thinking about surgery. What do you think, Mr. McDaniel? That solves our problem, doesn't it? We cut off Melissa's thumb. I attach it to my thumb, careful not to obscure the print, and I send my messages to Placido. Melissa won't be needing her thumb for long anyway."

Anthony had been stalking around the room as though delivering a well-considered soliloquy. Now he stopped right in front of my chair and locked his eyes on mine.

"My only problem is we have no surgical instruments or anesthesia on the island. The best I can come up with is some rusty bolt cutters the caretaker uses to sever the anchor chains of boaters foolish enough to haul up in our harbor. It should be sufficient to cut off a thumb, but it will be messy. And a person can die of shock from the most simple of injuries. Melissa needs to stay alive long enough to bring Placido into range of Mr. Brown's heavy artillery."

Anthony bent forward, grabbed the arms of the chair, and leaned in.

"This is where you come in, Mr. McDaniel. I am very aware of your persuasive abilities and your closeness to Melissa. Won't you talk to her? She needs to understand that further struggle is useless. The only question now is whether you and she will die quickly and painlessly or slowly and in agony. Why, if you agree to cooperate, I might even let you and Melissa have a little conjugal visit before your demise. What do you think of that, Mr. McDaniel?"

Anthony stood back, arms crossed.

I still said nothing. I was so terrorized I was now quite sure I could not speak. I did my best not to betray myself.

"Well, I will give you a little time to think about my offer—but not too much time. Placido needs to get a message from Melissa soon if we are to carry out our plan. If you won't or can't convince Melissa to cooperate this evening, I will let you watch Mr. Brown cut off her thumb with our bolt cutters. I promise it will not be the last unpleasant thing you will observe."

Anthony and Brown left.

Almost as abruptly as he left, Anthony returned, this time alone.

"Mr. McDaniel, I need for you to understand just how futile your efforts have been and how hopeless your cause. I know all about Ariel; Milano Corporation developed her. I have even used her services myself. But she only listens to Placido, and Placido has told her to thwart my efforts. So it took me a little time to figure out how Placido was using her to communicate with Melissa. I have been reading Placido's messages to Melissa since she has been with me. But I must admit that getting around Melissa's thumb print has proved more challenging. While law enforcement may have been unable to track you, I have followed your efforts with interest, certain you would bring Placido to me. Even though I expected you would come to the island by packet boat, your electrician disguise was good, and when Katie acted like she knew you, well, it did throw me a bit. After all, I didn't want to kill an innocent marina worker sent to work on my boat. I decided to let you and Melissa play out your hand, and you fell right into mine."

Anthony strode to the door, grabbed the knob, and turned.

"Oh, and just so you don't get any ideas, Mr. Brown is a former Navy SEAL. He doesn't need a gun to kill you, and after your sophomoric attempt to rescue Melissa, he needs no further excuse. Now you think about my offer."

The door closed. Anthony was gone.

I was overcome with nausea and heaved forward. My arms jerked against my restraints, my stomach knotted, and what was left of last night's pizza landed on one of Milano's Persian rugs. After a couple dry heaves, several minutes passed, and I hoped that I was finished. I found I had enough range of motion to wipe my mouth on my shoulder. I summoned a little saliva to rinse the foulness from my mouth and spat.

Next came a wave of chills, a shiver through my body and my arms and legs shuddered. There was bleeding at my wrists and ankles from the slice of the nylon ties. I was thankful that I had relieved myself in the boathouse before Melissa arrived, or I was sure I would have wet my pants. Paul McDaniel. Chivalric rescuer. Soon to be fish food. Did I really think that one of the richest and most powerful men in the world would let me stumble onto his island, steal his boat, escape with his niece, and nary a shot would be fired? That's how Cabrini and Placido painted it, and I, the fool in this play, found it plausible. At this moment the two of them were probably sitting at some island bar, wringing their hands that their plan had gone wrong, wallowing in their ineptitude, wondering whom they could next enlist to tilt at their windmills, calling for another drink while I faced summary execution. I would have been better off staying at Frederica Island facing a triple-murder charge.

Now death was certain. Not in the sense that death is always certain, a far-off inevitability, the reason the prudent write their wills. Death for me was a matter no more than a few hours away.

A few hours. If only I could add to these few hours. If only I could reclaim time wasted, time wasted as if I had the luxury of living forever, to do those things I had wanted to do with my life. To love, to be loved, to think, to teach, to write, perhaps even to have children, to do something that would last beyond my time, but I had been denied the opportunity, and now, just as something meaningful in my life was within my reach, it was to be forever cut off from me.

I was not a fool trying to have something with Melissa, to love someone—even if to the cynical it was reckless. It may have been one of the few worthwhile things I have done. Facing death, it was not what I had accomplished in my life that came to the fore, giving me comfort, it was what I failed to do that caused regret, those things that in focus now appeared far more important than a law degree and an extravagant bank account. But those who said I had done no better than my father; those who said I would never rise beyond my breeding, they were wrong—even if they were only the voices in my head that daily I did battle with. My life had not been useless, even though there was so much left to do. I longed for another chance.

Time slowed. I was conscious of my every heartbeat hammering in my head. I would not waste any more thoughts on how I got here or why. It was clarifying to think that my fate was certain, that I was already dead, that any other outcome I could engineer would be better than that, so now all options were open to me. Before this moment I did not think I could kill another person. Now I knew I could. I could do anything to live another day, to have a chance, maybe with Melissa.

I would tell Anthony what he wanted to hear. I would tell him that I was going to convince Melissa to go along, that she wouldn't survive cutting off her thumb, that if we were going to die, that dying quickly was preferable to dying slowly.

These were the words of a coward, not mine. I did not yet have a plan, but I knew working with Melissa was preferable to working alone, that if we were going to send a message to Placido for Anthony that we somehow may have a chance to get him to bring help. Placido must now be aware the scheme had gone wrong, that Melissa and I had not met him and Cabrini in our headlong flight from the island as planned. We just needed to connect with Placido to keep him from falling into Anthony's trap, the one he was baiting with Melissa and me, and count on his love for his daughter, his natural genius, and Ariel to help us all out of it.

The sunlight reflecting off the boathouse yellowed and dimmed. Anthony and Brown strode in. Anthony flared his nostrils and stepped over the vomit.

"I see you have taken me seriously. What do you say?"

I tried to clear my throat but it was dry and foul. I could only croak.

"Yes."

Anthony nodded to Brown, who produced a long thin blade. He held it in front of my face for a second, then slit the cable ties.

"You won't be very persuasive with Melissa in the state you are in. The door on the other side of the bed goes to a bathroom. Go in there and clean up. Leave the door open."

I tried to stand and nearly fell over, catching the back of the chair.

"You need to rub your arms and ankles to get the blood going again. You can't walk yet."

It was the first time I heard Brown speak. What a prince. I realized I would have to kill him. Only surprise would even the extraordinary tactical advantages that Brown possessed. The longer Brown considered me inept, the easier surprise would be. It wasn't difficult for me to keep up the appearance.

After a few minutes of rubbing my arms and legs, I staggered to the bathroom. I did not look good. Cold water and a toothbrush did a lot to make me feel better, but I still looked very much the scruffy marina worker, hardly the persuasive litigator, and certainly not a likely object of Melissa's affection.

"Alright Mr. McDaniel, you have about thirty minutes to secure Melissa's cooperation, or I will send in Brown with the bolt cutters." They led me to a room on the second floor and unlocked the door. I stepped in, and the door shut and locked behind me.

Melissa had been lying on a bed and sat up when I entered. She did not look much better than me. One side of her face was red and puffy from blows, her eyes blood-shot, and cheeks streaked. She stumbled toward me; we held each other, and Melissa sobbed. She was inconsolable. I could barely keep my composure myself, but I had to maintain some control. I stroked her head, her hair, her cheeks, kissed her face. For several long minutes all she could do was weep.

Melissa's sobs were the cover I needed. I whispered in her ear. I hoped Anthony could not hear me for Melissa's weeping, that he would see my whispering to her as merely following orders, for we were certainly being monitored, anything audible overheard.

"Melissa, you must go along with me. What I say out loud will be for Anthony to hear. We need to get a warning to Placido. Is there a way to do that without Anthony knowing?"

Melissa drew in a long shuddering breath, nodded almost imperceptibly.

"If we can keep Placido from falling into Anthony's trap, we have a chance. As soon as you feel you can, let's sit on the bed and talk." After several long sobs and deep breaths Melissa pulled away and we sat.

"Melissa, we need to think about ourselves. Anthony has told me if we cooperate he will go easy on us. It's Placido he wants."

At this Melissa let out a wail and hammered my chest. I remembered once more that this woman was a great actress.

"No, no, no! I cannot lure my father here, not to be killed by Anthony, not for you, not for me. I won't do it. I will not."

"He says he doesn't want to harm Placido. He wants to convince him to forget his scheme to give away the patents the Milano Corporation has spent so much of its capital developing. It's a disservice to their father's memory. You must understand. If we can get Placido here and get this resolved, we can all go home and forget this happened. And Placido tells me he has a plan to help me beat the murder charges." I paused considering whether what I would next say would mean something to her. I was about to die. There was no reason for me to hold anything back. "If we can do this, you and I have a chance." It was the only sincere thing I had said.

Melissa looked in my eyes for several seconds, looked away, then nodded.

"Did Anthony say that to you? All he has been doing with me is threatening, telling me I'm going to die. And when that didn't work, he hit me. Why should I believe that he's changed his mind?"

"I think he figured out that threats only stiffen your resolve. But I'm afraid if we hold out much longer, he and his sidekick may get desperate. I don't trust him to do the right thing if he's backed in a corner. First thing we need to do is get in touch with Placido and tell him we need his help."

"What assurance do we have that Anthony is telling the truth?"

"None. But what is our alternative?"

Melissa took in a deep breath and closed her eyes. After a minute of internal struggle that played out on her face, she turned to me.

"Paul, you've risked everything for me. Even though all I know about Anthony tells me not to trust him, I have to follow your instincts on this. I trust you. I don't see an alternative. Let's do it."

Apparently listening to our every word just outside the door, Anthony returned before I had a chance to acknowledge Melissa.

"Melissa, you need to clean up so you will be presentable when your father arrives. Mr. McDaniel and I will step out."

Anthony closed the door behind us and broke into a grin.

"Mr. McDaniel, you are such an excellent liar. Where did you learn that, law school? I was almost convinced myself." Anthony handed me a handwritten note. "Have her send this to Placido. Once she sends the message, I will give you two some time to your selves."

Anthony and I went back in the room and waited for Melissa to emerge from the bathroom. I handed her the note. Anthony gave her cell phone back. She typed while Anthony watched over her shoulder:

Father, Anthony caught us trying to take the boat. He is holding us both under house arrest, unharmed. I overheard Anthony talking with his head pilot. Tonight Anthony and Brown will be flying to Miami and will be gone for a day. They have disabled the boats. We have no way to get off the island. You MUST come and get us. Melissa.

ANTHONY WALKED OUT. The lock clicked.

I leaned close to Melissa's ear, barely a whisper.

"Did you warn Placido?"

She nodded; then, barely audible, responded.

"Capitals. Ariel will know."

"Brilliant."

A half hour later, when darkness had fallen, I heard the Gulfstream take off and roar low overhead on its decoy flight to Miami, conspicuous to anyone watching the island to see, the trap now set. Sleepless, lying close, whispering, Melissa and I played out every possibility, every option, yet came up with no fixed plan, deciding to react when we felt an opportunity, comforting each other as only two facing the unknown can do. The light of morning came all too soon.

The door burst open without a knock, Brown, leering at Melissa. She covered with a sheet. It was getting a lot easier to think about killing him.

"OK, you two love birds. You need to get dressed. In five minutes I want you visible on the veranda, sipping coffee like nothing is wrong. Placido needs to see you so he knows just where to come."

NINETEEN

W E BROUGHT OUR COFFEE TO THE VERANDA AS instructed, a vignette of unharmed hostages, tantalizing bait with a deadly hook. If I didn't know Anthony planned to kill me, I could've enjoyed it more; the sun yet low over the ocean, the morning was still, cool, tranquil. I tried to remain outwardly calm as my every sense was on a hair trigger, searching for the opportunity Melissa and I needed. I looked for signs of Anthony or Brown but saw nothing and no one. I knew they had to be lurking nearby, waiting for Placido to show.

Through the night as Melissa and I had plotted, whispering our thoughts, it became evident to me her initial response to my suggestion was no act; she'd rather die than be a part of luring her father to his death. It was only after Melissa was sure she was able to warn Placido of the trap that she was willing to participate in my scheme. This sentiment only added further complexity to the enigma that was Melissa: it was difficult to reconcile the thought that she'd be willing to collude with someone who sought to steal the fruit of her father's life's work with the idea that she would have no part otherwise in harming him. Maybe there was some benign explanation for the photo in Cabrini's office. Maybe. But there was no question in my mind that Melissa was willing to die rather than have anything to do with Anthony's plans to eliminate her father, and however laudable the sentiment, it was my desire to figure out a way for everyone to walk away from this debacle, then sort out who was on the home team. A million thoughts ran through my mind as we sat on the veranda, waiting, most of them focused on how I could see the sun rise the next morning.

Cabrini's boat rounded the point sheltering the harbor, running fast, directly toward the dock, unmolested. I saw two helmets, two life jackets, two figures in the front seats. Melissa stood, and I grabbed her hand to stop her from running toward the water. The boat slowed only feet from the dock, the trailing wake washing the transom, lifting the stern, submerging the bow, then silence. No one in the boat moved, as if they were waiting for something to happen, for us to run to the boat. I knew Brown would not allow it.

A bright streak smoked across the field from the woods behind the house. The boat exploded in an orange fireball. Melissa shrieked and buried her face in her hands. The shockwave and heat knocked us backward, forced us to turn away. Flaming debris dropped in the yard, hunks of shiny aluminum, splintered yellow fiberglass, shredded graphite. An empty helmet, shattered, smoldering, and pieces of an unattached life jacket fell feet from where we stood. Melissa took in deep gasps of breath, minutes passed before she could speak.

"Father! Hector! Anthony lied, he lied."

"No, I didn't lie to you Melissa." Anthony and Brown appeared on the veranda taking in the destruction, the dock now in flames as well. "Your boyfriend did. Just to save himself a little pain. As soon as I figure out how and where to dispose of you, both of you will be joining Placido and Cabrini. I was certain I spotted two helmets in the boat before I gave Brown the order to fire the RPG. A very effective weapon. It appears my brilliant little brother wasn't so smart after all. Pity."

Melissa lunged for Anthony. Brown stepped between them, threw her down, and wrapped her wrists behind her in cable ties in a single motion. While Brown was bent over Melissa, I aimed a kick at his face. He parried the blow with one hand, dashed me to the ground, and with the other, cracked me in the head with his pistol. In seconds he tied my wrists and ankles. Brown half dragged, half shoved us to separate rooms; threw Melissa on the floor in hers, locking the door behind her; then pushed me in mine, and I crashed to the floor, the door closed and locked behind me. Whatever plan we had to escape, it was over before it started, our only hope to get out alive blown to pieces on Anthony's dock.

It took me several minutes to focus, the blow from the pistol clouding my head and obscuring my vision. Something seemed to emerge from the haze and shadow behind the closing door. I shook my head, more focus. A person. Now more focus, and the person moved. The figure of Agent Grey appeared, Uzi over his shoulder, a hallucination from the blow to my head, an unspoken wish fulfilled from my desperation.

The figure bent down and put his finger to my mouth and pointed around the room at what he must have discerned as microphones. If this was a hallucination, I was going to go with it.

Grey cut the cable ties on my wrists and ankles, and this time I was careful to rub the blood back into them before I attempted to stand. By the time I stood Grey had jimmied the door lock. He motioned me still, peered into the hall, inched the door closed.

Grey handed me a 9mm Beretta. I nodded, checked the chamber for a round, and flicked off the safety. He signaled me to follow.

We crept through the hall toward voices, behind Anthony and Brown in the main room of the plantation house, still viewing their handiwork out the windows, the boat sunk, and the dock was in flames.

"Such an unfortunate accident, we must inform the authorities." Anthony chuckled at his cleverness, and Brown grunted his approval.

"No need Milano, I'll do it for you." Brown flinched in our direction at the sound of Grey's voice, but Grey cut him off, "Don't. I'll kill you where you stand. Hands over your heads. Drop the pistol and kick it across the room. Both of you lie face down on the floor. Keep your hands over your heads. NOW." Anthony complied, Brown turning toward us, checking his adversaries, looking at Grey's weapon, dropping to his knees, spreading his bulk on the floor. "Paul, hand me your weapon. Walk up behind the big guy, pull one of those ties out of his back pocket, and wrap it around his wrists."

I straddled Brown's waist, grabbed a tie that hung from his back pocket, stepped toward his head, bent down to wrap the tie around his wrist.

Brown struck, pulling me down in front of him. He rolled, drew a handgun from an ankle holster, and leveled it at Grey. By the time Brown had pulled me down, Grey had jerked Anthony up by the neck and held him as a shield.

"So it seems we have a little standoff." Brown rose to his feet and lifted me in one motion, keeping me between him and Grey. "You drop your gun or I waste you and your friend. I want the Uzi, Glock, and the one stashed in your ankle holster. Make a funny move, and I start with you."

Grey placed his weapons one by one on the table behind him and stepped away.

"The two of you lay face down on the floor, hands behind your backs. Mr. Hero, you face the door." I lay down. Brown kicked me in the head. "You face the window."

I expected Grey to make a move, but he did as instructed. I followed his lead and did as I was told, now turned away, not able to see him.

I still expected Grey to make a move. I tensed, ready to jump, but I heard the zip ties tighten.

Brown stomped his foot on my hands with enough of his weight to knock my breath out, fixing my wrists to the small of my back. He lifted his boot off my back, stepped within an inch of my nose, straddled over me. Within a second he'd have the zip ties around my wrists.

I spun away from Brown's foot and launched a kick up between his legs, catching him as he reached in his pocket, exposed, surprised, incapacitated, but only for an instant. In that instant I dove over Grey to the table with his weapons, grabbing at the Glock. Brown, fully extended, grasped my heel and dragged me back. I strained toward the gun, but even in his impaired state, with little purchase on my foot, Brown steadily pulled me back. I fell from the table, Brown on top of me, pushing my shoulder to the floor to square my face for the blow, pulling his blade from behind him, and cocking his fist by his ear to plant the steel in my throat.

The room exploded. The back of Brown's head disappeared in a spray of bone, brains, and blood, and he fell face down on me without a twitch. I scrambled from underneath him, pushing his blood-soaked corpse away, looking for the source of Brown's demise, my rescue. Grey still lay face down on the floor.

Rebecca stood on the other side of the room, feet apart, two hands in front of her holding the largest revolver I'd ever seen.

"Don't move, Milano, or you'll get what Brown got."

"You needn't be concerned about me. Brown was doing what he was paid to do. I'm not so stupid."

Rebecca turned to me.

"Look, I had this under control. There was no need to risk getting killed."

"How was I to know that?"

Rebecca motioned to Grey, who tried to roll over with his arms still tied behind his back.

"Do you think one of you could cut this strap?"

I searched Brown's body for his blade, found it still in his hand, pried it out, and liberated Grey. He rubbed his wrists together before holstering his Glock, strapping his spare to his ankle, and slinging the Uzi over his shoulder.

"I knew Rebecca had our backs. I thought you'd follow my lead. I never expected you to go solo."

"I'm learning new things about myself every day."

"Good. Take a couple of those ties and strap Milano to that chair."

As I did, the Gulfstream roared overhead.

"Just in time. In a few moments my pilot will be here to take me to Italy. When he finds me like this, I can assure you, there will be nowhere on the island you can hide."

"I suspect it takes more than a few moments to turn around a Gulfstream, and by then, we will all be well off the island."

"Whoever you are, wherever you go, there will be nowhere you will be safe. You will end up just like Placido."

"Not when Paul tells his story."

"And you think anyone will believe him? Other than myself, the only persons who can corroborate his story were blown up in that boat or were shot on Frederica Island. I will make sure Paul goes to prison for killing three innocent men. He's no threat to me."

"Well, I guess we'll just take our chances."

Rebecca motioned down the hall with the revolver still in her hand.

"Paul, there's a young lady in the next room who I think will be happy to see you."

I pushed open the door to the room where Brown had thrown Melissa. Instead of finding Melissa trussed-up on the floor, she was sitting on the bed, a sawed-off shotgun trained on the door. Melissa dropped the gun when she saw me enter the room, and we held each other for a moment without a word. Melissa was beaming and crying at the same time. She spoke first.

"Paul, when I heard the shot I feared the worst. I can't tell you . . ."

I turned to Grey.

"How the hell did you and Rebecca get here?"

"It wasn't long after you left that Ariel contacted us again. She told us we needed to follow you to Miami to keep you out of trouble. Rebecca convinced me we should postpone our fishing trip and give you a hand. Ariel has been in touch with us on each leg of your venture.

"We got concerned when you went offshore, so we followed you to Louis Town. We picked out Cabrini and Placido from the locals at the marina, and they told us about your plan and that something had gone wrong. We were with them when they got your message, and we put together a response. Last night Rebecca and I floated up to the north end of the island in a fishing boat when the Gulfstream take-off gave us cover. Placido told me about the security perimeter and the fact that the jet's backwash always sets it off. We've been working on the island since then."

I didn't understand how things could have gone so wrong for Melissa's father if what Grey was saying was true. "But Placido and Cabrini just walked into Anthony's trap. Placido must've failed to get Melissa's warning."

"They got it. They are on the island; we just have to get to them before Anthony and the pilot do."

"I saw the boat explode. No one could have survived that."

"So did I. But Placido and Cabrini weren't on Cabrini's boat. They were on a Zodiac just outside the security perimeter. With Ariel's help they piloted Cabrini's boat remotely from there. They came ashore in all the commotion and set the Zodiac adrift so they wouldn't be discovered."

Melissa could not contain her sense of relief. Even streaked with blood and swollen from Anthony's blows, Melissa's smile bordered on beatific.

"Rebecca told me when she freed me. The only thing that made me happier than to see you walk in the door was to know Placido and Hector are alive."

Grey became animated. "We need to save all this for

another time. I believe Anthony when he said his pilot would be coming to find him. We haven't much time and we need to get the hell off this island."

Melissa reminded Grey that I had the fishing boat ready for a quick escape.

"We can get into the Whaler no problem. There's plenty of room for all of us. We can be in Louis Town in twenty minutes."

Grey had no way of knowing about Anthony's boat, so I had to be the one to kill that plan.

"Anthony would run us down in that cigarette boat of his."

"Rebecca and I saw no signs of a cigarette boat. He must have it stashed, and we have no time to look for it, otherwise we'd take it ourselves. We need something else. I can fly a single engine, but I can't fly a jet. Unless we're willing to shoot one of them, we can't risk commandeering the crew. But we might be able to get to the plane if the pilot heads to the plantation house in search of Anthony. Melissa, can Placido or Hector fly that Gulfstream?"

"No, but there's a floatplane just on the other side of the boathouse."

"It's probably only a four-seater, and we have six people who need to get off the island fast. If that's all we have, we can give it a shot, but it'll be a challenge to get into the air. Rebecca, you need to find Placido and Cabrini. I'm going to take these two to the plane and taxi to the other side of the dock. The three of you meet us there."

Grey, Melissa, and I dashed across the field toward the boathouse. There was no sign of the Gulfstream pilot. I led Grey to the other side of the boathouse and the floatplane just beyond. Grey jumped in the water, holding his Uzi above his head, wading toward the plane. Melissa and I followed. The water was shallow when we jumped in, but before we reached the plane it was chest deep. I remembered Cabrini's talk about the sharks and decided to put them out of my mind. Grey reached the plane first, climbed on a pontoon, pushed back a window, reached through, unlatched the door, and pulled himself in. Melissa and I went to the opposite side, climbed aboard the pontoon, and Grey pushed the door open.

The plane was small, barely room for the three of us. I remembered my backpack with my laptop, still under a seat in the Whaler. We were twenty yards off shore.

"Melissa, stay in the plane. I've got to go back to the boat."

Grey was flipping switches, checking instruments.

"Forget it. You don't have time."

Ariel had kept me safe so far. I needed that laptop. I dove off the pontoon and swam to the boathouse, under the door to the Whaler where it was still tied up after I hastily cleated it, our escape thwarted. I climbed aboard, found the backpack, and jumped back in, holding it over my head. When I got on the other side of the door, I heard the engine on the floatplane sputter and saw blue smoke spew from the exhaust. Another sputter, then it caught. Grey gave it gas, pushed the rpms up, then throttled back, the engine smoothing out.

I was ten yards from the plane. The door flung open and Melissa jumped on the pontoon, urging me on, holding the strut, her hair streaming back. The plane began a slow turn, the engine throttled up, and water boiled around the pontoons. I grabbed the side. Melissa reached for the backpack, giving me an extra hand, and I pulled myself on the pontoon, and in the door. Grey gave it more gas and nosed the plane in the direction of the dock.

Someone ran across the yard to the house, took notice of the floatplane but didn't stop. He wasn't one of us, couldn't have been Anthony, and must be the pilot; we didn't have much time now. Grey taxied past the burning dock and what was left of the submerged hull of Cabrini's boat, looking for any sign of our party. Fifty yards distant Rebecca, Placido, and Cabrini sprang from the trees on the other side of the house and dashed toward the water. Grey maneuvered the plane as close to the shore as possible, turned the nose toward the ocean, and cut back on the throttle. Our group splashed to the plane and climbed on the pontoons. Cabrini was the first in. He yelled to Grey above the engine noise.

"How the hell are we all going to get in this?"

"It's all we got. Jump in. Think small."

Cabrini, Melissa, and I were squeezed in the two rear seats, Rebecca and Placido in the front passenger seat, Grey at the controls. Melissa reached forward and stroked Placido's face, and he kissed her hand. As soon as Rebecca closed the door, Grey gave it full throttle. From the waves washing over the pontoons it appeared we were heading directly into the wind. The plane barely moved at first, then slowly picked up speed, but it was evident even to me that we weren't going to take off the way things were going. Grey turned the plane perpendicular to the wind and coaxed more speed, picking up more and more, then pulled into the wind, about two football fields from shore. I could feel the pontoons getting lighter, the plane lifting above the waves, the engine laboring at full throttle.

Behind us someone—it must've been Anthony, now freed by the pilot—appeared on the veranda with Brown's AR on his shoulder. He fired several rounds in our direction, ripping beside the plane, a couple rounds pinging off the pontoons. Everyone but Grey ducked under the windows.

"He's not a very good shot, but if by chance he hits one of the wing tanks we've got trouble." Grey pulled back on the controls, and we rose, just feet over the waves, rounds whizzing past, tearing into the sea beside us, a couple finding home, clanging the tail, so far harmless. In seconds the gunman had burned through a clip. If it was Anthony, I was betting he had no idea how to eject the spent clip or to insert another, and a feeling of relief swept over me, but not for long.

The pilot, who had just run across the yard, now appeared on the veranda with Anthony. He had a long tube on his shoulder pointed at us.

I reached forward to the door handle with one hand, and with the other I prepared to shove Melissa out of the plane and dive in behind her, not wanting to experience first-hand what I'd seen the RPG do to Cabrini's boat. Grey grabbed my wrist and yelled above the roar of the wind and engine.

"We disabled it. He only had one good RPG."

Grey coaxed more and more speed and altitude from the overloaded plane, now a half-mile from the dock, airborne and climbing. I looked through the tiny rear window of the plane toward the house.

A fireball appeared where the pilot and Anthony had been standing. I turned away. Seconds later I heard the blast over the engine noise. When I looked back, flames had reached the second floor of the Plantation house, leaving no trace of Anthony or the pilot. Whatever Grey and Rebecca did to disable the RPG, it worked better than expected.

Placido wept on Rebecca's shoulder. Melissa reached forward and stroked his face again.

"You didn't do this. Anthony tried to kill you, and he tried to kill all of us. Whatever happened back there was his own doing."

The plane continued to gain altitude, and I could see the northern Cay in the blue distance. We cruised for the next ten minutes without speaking.

Grey put the plane down five hundred yards from the entrance to the harbor and taxied into Louis Town, pulling right up to the marina, where curious locals watched six people unfold from a four passenger floatplane with two bullet holes in the tail and walk into the nearest bar.

"Gree!"

Agent Grey and I both turned to Katie's greeting.

"I tole you I make you forget dat gull! You see now."

I grabbed Melissa and surprised her with a kiss.

"I don't think that will be necessary."

TWENTY

KATIE HAD DISCREETLY SLIPPED AWAY, BUT HER EYES were still inviting as she left. The rest of the group disappeared in the darkness of the bar, leaving Melissa and me to ourselves, just inside the dimly lit entrance. I looked even scruffier than before, with a patch of Brown's bright-red blood on my shirt, wrists ripped raw from cable ties only removed minutes ago.

Behind Melissa, colored Christmas lights looped around a bar, and a tinny version of *"Don't Worry Be Happy"* spun from the outdoor speakers. I looked down at the blood stains on my shirt and brushed Melissa's damaged cheek.

"I don't think we're going to be mistaken for a glamorous young couple sneaking off to the islands for a romantic rendezvous."

Melissa's eyes were focused somewhere in the distance, the dim light forgiving of the insults to her face, which was still puffy from Anthony's slaps, eyes red-rimmed, lips thin and taut, the pain of the ordeal she'd survived reflected darkly on her face. I hoped for some acknowledgment, but it wasn't there.

The improbability of our survival was only now beginning to sink in on me. We had escaped being killed multiple times—and that had just been since sunrise. On the Milano island alone we'd been involved in three violent deaths. For Melissa's part, she'd seen what she believed to be her father and brother blown to pieces only to be miraculously spared, then her uncle vaporized in a fireball he'd meant for her. This is not to mention the several threats to her own life by Anthony and Brown the day and night before. No wonder Melissa wasn't in a mood to laugh at my lame attempt at humor. My words rattled and clanged in the silence. Melissa took a deep breath before turning to me.

"Look, Paul, we both said and did a lot back there not knowing how things were going to turn out. I can't hold you to that. Neither of us wants a relationship based on a feeling of obligation rather than one of mutual affection."

"So, I've done my job, and I can go back to where I came from, is that it?"

"I didn't mean it to come out that way. I know what you've done for me, what you've risked for me; but, you must understand, I don't even know what I feel right now. I need time to figure things out."

"Melissa, we've hardly been around each other more than a few days, and most of those were in circumstances I hope we'll never see again. I'm not trying to put any pressure on you. So, why don't we take things slow and see where they go?"

She made a single hard shake of her head as if to banish some unwanted vision which had crept back in.

"I know I should be showing more appreciation. If you hadn't risked everything to save me, by now Anthony would've cut off my thumb and thrown the rest of me to the sharks, then lured Placido and Hector to die on South

Cat Cay. I don't know how I can possibly . . ."

Tears welled in her eyes, her voice caught, trailed off. I tried to lighten things again; this wasn't about me trying to claim credit.

"Grey, Rebecca, and Ariel deserve a little thanks. Without them I would've been joining you as fish food. And I had other plans for this week."

Not even a faint smile.

"But without you setting everything in motion, nothing good would have happened, and all of us would be—"

"Well, even though we escaped being killed by your uncle and his side-kick, we aren't out of the woods by a long shot. I'm wanted back in Georgia for three murders, and I have a feeling all of us might be called upon to explain two large explosions and a serious house fire on South Cat Cay. So it isn't a bad idea if you want to stay clear of me for a while, at least until I'm no longer a fugitive."

Melissa grabbed my hand. With the back of her other hand she wiped her eyes and smiled the smile that disarmed me the night we met. But her voice held a forced buoyancy.

"Now what kind of woman would do such a thing? And besides, if I stayed clear of you, I might miss out on the rest of the excitement."

Melissa kissed me on my stubbly cheek. She was all I wanted. So why did that feeling return, the feeling that I had when Melissa's smile temporarily blinded me to the brazen collaboration between Cabrini and Anthony at the Abbey bar? Why did I get the feeling that I still didn't know who was on the right side—or even what the right side was? Maybe I was finally feeling the stress of the ordeal.

We both needed to take things slow, but each of us for entirely different reasons.

We found the remainder of our party at an isolated table near the back of the bar, a corner with windows overlooking the marina. Through the windows we could see the tranquility of the harbor at mid-day: all the cigarette boats gone, none having come back to refuel; all the fishing boats out, the crews not yet returned with their catch; and the dockworkers inside avoiding the noonday sun. It was this peace that was disrupted by our raucous arrival in the floatplane, just as the quiet now jangled in my mind against the echoes of what we'd just been through.

Grey and Rebecca knocked back a couple of the local beers before I had finished one, but I was now well into my second, catching up, and thinking about my next one. Melissa and Cabrini both poured glasses of white wine from a chilled bottle which, by the look of the waiter, hadn't been ordered at that bar for a long time. Placido called for a double dry martini, alternating sips and getting updates from Ariel on his cell phone. It was tempting to lay back and breathe easy for a few minutes. Grey wouldn't have it.

"This has been one hell of a fishing trip. There are two islands with three dead bodies on each. It's very likely Paul's being sought for questioning concerning the Frederica Island murders, and all of us will soon be wanted concerning the deaths on South Cat Cay. We need to be proactive or we'll all be spending time in jail, and I hear the Bimini facilities are not exactly the accommodations y'all are used to stayin' at."

Everyone else at the table other than Grey appeared

willing to let things ride for a few minutes, at least until the alcohol could smooth the edges of our adrenaline-spiked minds. Then Placido wearily took up Grey's line.

"I agree, Agent Grey, but I'm inexperienced in these matters. While I have some information I think can help Paul, beyond that I have little idea what to do. I'd like to hear—"

"Well, Placido, I think you need to report what's happened on South Cat Cay to the local authorities, just as it happened, as soon as possible. We'll all need to give statements at some point. But we have a problem with that. When we give our statements, the authorities will invite us to stay until the investigation is concluded, which means if we're caught trying to leave, we'll be arrested and put in jail without bond as flight risks. As soon as they figure out who Paul is, he'll be arrested, at least as a material witness in the Frederica Island deaths."

I could only state the obvious, and beyond that, I was floundering.

"I'm hoping I can avoid that. So you—"

Grey, unwilling to take chances on being misunderstood, was now near to barking orders.

"Paul, you need to get back to Georgia. Placido, you need to line up the voice recordings you told me about as soon as possible—at least before Paul gets arrested, so he can avoid indictment. And I'm pretty sure you can't do that from a jail cell without Ariel."

Placido, not used to being told what to do, did his best to maintain his civility, but frustration told in his voice.

"I think it's a good idea all of us stay out of jail. And I can certainly help Paul better out of jail than in. That much is clear, but do you have anything more specific in mind?"

Grey was several steps ahead and responded directly to Placido.

"I have friends in the prosecutor's offices back in Georgia. I need to be with Paul to help him. And I can't be there if I'm held here, so I need to leave with Paul."

Then Grey turned to me.

"Paul, since we'll be traveling together, you need to go back to being Paul McDaniel, even though it puts you at significant risk if we are apprehended. But if they catch us with the same IDs, we'll both get thrown in jail."

I reached in my backpack and tossed Grey's wallet on the table.

"As much as I've enjoyed being you, I'll be happy to be me again. I kept my own wallet in a compartment in my backpack."

Placido laid down his cell and looked to Grey, bad news written on his face.

"Ariel has just confirmed that the Bimini police received notification from the FBI that Paul is wanted for questioning in connection with the Frederica Island deaths. The notice arrived yesterday by post, so there was nothing she could do to intercept it. As soon as the island police identify Paul, he'll be detained. I have asked Ariel to alert me if she detects any further attention in our direction."

Grey remained insistent.

"That's going to happen soon. Someone is bound to have noticed the fireworks on the island. We need to come up with a plan to deal with that and quick. We're about covered up in lawyers here. Do you two have any ideas?"

I had no criminal experience at all. I turned to Cabrini.

He had been on defense teams in some highly public white-collar criminal prosecutions, and I nodded in his direction. I was willing to suspend my remaining suspicions for some assistance staying out of jail. I prodded.

"Cabrini, you know criminal law . . ."

Previously silent, Cabrini took that introduction as an opportunity to pontificate a bit. No one but Grey had any basis to challenge him, and for the moment, he was willing to listen to what Cabrini had to say.

"Our best approach is for the four of you, other than Placido and myself, to get off the island soon, before Placido makes his report. Neither of us can be implicated in the deaths on the island, and I can be of help to Placido in dealing with the police. It also makes more sense for you to be flying back to Key Biscayne with four passengers in a four passenger floatplane rather than six. Melissa can stay at my house until Placido and I return, but that may be a while. The three of you are welcome to take one of my cars back up to Frederica Island."

"So you think—" Grey attempted to interrupt, but Cabrini anticipated his question.

"It'll be a whole lot more difficult for the island authorities to get you back here once you've left than it'll be for them to keep you here. We can tell the authorities you will be happy to give statements back in the States with your legal counsel present, but you won't be coming to the island unless compelled. It would be a lot of trouble for them to get you back here, and they won't see it as worth their while if Placido can convince them the deaths were self-inflicted or self-defense."

Grey sounded skeptical.

"How likely is that, after all—"

Cabrini plowed forward.

"Given Placido's prominence and the evidence at the scene, we should be able to make that case, particularly with the shell of my rocketed Donzi at the dock, hull seared to the waterline, and the house burned down around a misfired RPG. Brown's remains, with half his head blown off, may prove a bit more difficult to explain, but it still fits with the self-defense claim."

Cabrini had been inclined toward Placido, but now he addressed Grey directly.

"I agree with you that it's best for Paul to go back to Frederica Island with the voice recordings and turn himself in. With your help he can negotiate the place, time, and proper official, and if he produces the recordings in advance it'll minimize the likelihood he'll be prosecuted."

Grey warmed to the plan.

"When Paul explains that Melissa was in imminent danger, which will be corroborated by Placido, there shouldn't be serious repercussions for Paul's disappearance, though I think he'll owe Frederica Island some money for the shattered gate and an apology to the guard for having scared the hell out of him.

"Placido, any luck on the voice recordings?"

"I've been in touch with Ariel on the off-chance that the government continued its surveillance of the island after the G-8 and kept the records online, but that was unsuccessful. I have contacted the lab, and I have someone searching for them."

I'd been saved by Ariel so many times, I wondered aloud why she couldn't help now.

"What about Ariel, can't she find them at the lab?"

"During the G-8 we kept the recordings separate from

any computer system to prevent a malicious government from hacking them, and we just kept up the practice. Ariel can't get to something that's not retained on a computer. So someone has to locate the recordings and listen to them to determine whether we captured Fowler's last words. It's just a matter of time before we find them."

"Paul, I think that covers the criminal side of things, but you're on your own with the firm."

Grey's comment reminded me that Melissa was out of danger, and even if I avoided prosecution, I had at least one more hurdle to jump before my life returned to normal. While it seemed unconnected to anything else we were talking about, Grey's observation was as much for Placido as for me. Had it not been for my willingness to risk everything for Melissa, she wouldn't be alive today, and I wouldn't be facing the loss of my livelihood, the loss of the partnership that I'd worked so hard to attain.

"Paul, as for the firm, after all you have done for our family, I will let the Strange & Fowler Management Committee know that Milano Corporation's business follows you. If they wish to keep Milano corporate business, they will keep their word and not only keep you, but honor your promotion. And make sure you get your fair share of the firm's profits as a result."

"Placido, I am truly grateful."

"No, Paul, it is you who have earned *my* gratitude."

Melissa had been silent at Cabrini's side during most of the time we were seated at the table, something I attributed to the shock of her uncle trying to kill us and his dying a violent death in the process finally settling into her consciousness. Enzo Milano, heir apparent to the Milano dynasty only days ago, was now the odd man out, having suffered his fall by being inexorably tied to the fortunes of his father, Anthony. With Placido's public acknowledgment of Cabrini's paternity, he and Melissa were now the sole heirs of Placido, who—as a result of Anthony's demise and the Shareholder's Agreement I wrote that got us into all this trouble in the first place—was now the controlling shareholder of Milano Corporation. Given Placido's generosity, it was unlikely Cabrini would ever need to practice law again, and Melissa, always beautiful and smart, would soon be very rich again.

Affections, alliances, and loyalties at the table swirled and shifted. Cabrini, Melissa, and Placido seated on one side of the table, Grey, Rebecca, and I on the other, reflected the realignment. On the Milano island it had been Melissa and me, Placido and Cabrini, Grey and Rebecca; it was now the Milanos and everyone else. Placido had his arm around his daughter's shoulders, and though he'd expressed sincere concern for my plight and genuine appreciation for my efforts, Placido had seemed relieved by Cabrini's observation that the result of the festivities on South Cat Cay could not be laid at their feet. Grey and Rebecca would be answerable for those deaths, and they were closing ranks as well. Grey wasn't willing to risk jail with me as his double, wanting to get Rebecca and himself far away from South Cat Cay as soon as possible.

As for Cabrini, my doubts had become more serious. Cabrini said that he had confronted Anthony about his uncle's role in the effort to divest his father, but the two of them had seemed harmonious at the Abbey bar, appearing to still be working together even after the disastrous defeat engineered in full by Anthony. And it was hard to believe that Melissa knew nothing of the scheme, her knowledge belied by the chummy photo with Cabrini on the *Tempest* at a time when he was in an ostensible death struggle with Milano Corporation.

Now that William Fowler, Judge Richards, and Anthony Milano were dead, only Placido, Melissa, Cabrini, and I knew the whole truth about the case. Neither the Milanos nor I had any incentive to change the public perception of a complete victory in favor of Milano Corporation, so they should have no reason to want me dead. That is, unless Cabrini hadn't confronted Anthony about the case and he wanted me dead to hide their *complicity*; unless he wanted Placido and Anthony dead so he and Melissa would be the majority owners of the corporation; unless Cabrini's plans had been foiled by the unlikely appearance of Grey and Rebecca at the instigation of Ariel.

And then there was the insoluble cipher, Melissa. In my questioning of Ariel, she had been only able—or willing—to confirm what I already knew: Melissa and Cabrini were brother and sister, always close, and becoming closer now that Placido had brought Cabrini back into the fold. It was impossible for me to know whether Cabrini's closeness to Melissa was a natural result of their parentage or if Cabrini sought to exploit Melissa's affection and Placido's weakness. Throughout the horror we'd been through, their closeness grew even more. And Cabrini continued to be, at least to me, the adversary he'd always been.

Placido snapped me out of my introspection.

"Ariel tells me the local police have been dispatched to our marina."

"Placido, you and Cabrini go to the front of the bar and see if you can intercept them. Melissa, Paul, Rebecca, you come with me and we'll find a way out the back to the plane."

Placido and Cabrini headed to the front, moving deliberately toward the entrance. Grey turned and searched for a rear exit.

No exit appeared. We crowded behind a blind used by servers to hide the kitchen entrance, looking for a way out. I heard the challenge to Placido as he headed to the front of the bar.

"Mr. Milano."

Through the blind, at first glance, the officer looked like a waiter, but he produced a badge.

"I would like to discuss with you a very unfortunate accident that has occurred on your family island. There have been two explosions and a fire that destroyed much of your house. A fisherman alerted us that right before the blaze several people left the island in a floatplane, and six of you were reported as having alighted from that plane tethered to the dock." The officer gestured out the window to our plane just visible at the end of the marina. "I regret that I must take you and your friends into custody."

"My friends are no longer here. They left some time ago. Mr. Cabrini and I will be happy to answer your questions."

So far, Placido was handling the locals. We searched for a way out.

"Gree." Katie appeared from the kitchen, an angel in island garb. I gave a small wave and held a finger to my lips. My timely signal made sure her natural enthusiasm did not blow our cover. She glanced from behind the blind to the officer questioning Placido. "Gree, you in trouble?"

"We need to get out of here. Is there a rear exit?"

Katie motioned us to follow.

We ducked through the kitchen, the heat blasting in

our faces as soon as we pushed back the swinging doors. Katie dashed past steam tables; past prep stations; by the walk-in refrigerator; through stacks of boxes, cans, and bags; and then out a door to the dock, into the daylight, where the floatplane was tied up at the end of the dock.

Katie held the door open as everyone else scrambled out before me.

"Gree." Her brown eyes danced and full lips parted in a smile revealing perfect teeth, and I kissed her in a bolt of affection and gratitude, and for a brief moment both of us warmed to each other, then, realizing the desperation of the moment, reluctantly pulled away.

"Get inside and forget us."

Grey ran down the dock toward the plane, Rebecca close behind, with no apparent regard for Melissa and me. Melissa was moving in slow motion, disorientation and shock still dragging against her. I grabbed her and pulled her toward the plane. Grey and Rebecca were on the pontoons, then in the door.

Behind me, out the back door of the bar we'd exited moments ago, appeared two uniformed police officers. Katie, in mock confusion and clumsiness, attempted to close the door and got in their way as they pushed by her, delaying them precious seconds. The officers blew their whistles in alarm, but there was no one else on the dock to assist them.

Melissa now reacted to the desperation of the situation, running toward the plane. Smoke blew out the exhaust, the prop flipping then stalling. Melissa and I were ten yards from the plane, and the police in chase were fifty yards behind us.

Grey had the engine turned over, the prop now blowing

spray behind, the pontoons still roped to the dock. Rebecca stood on one pontoon, rope in hand, ready to cast off.

I pushed, dragged, shoved Melissa toward the plane, onto the pontoon, into the open door, and I jumped behind her. Rebecca cast off, dove in the door, and Grey throttled up. The two police officers reached the end of the dock as we began to pick up momentum. One took a chance, dove into the bay, and grabbed a pontoon.

Grey saw the hanger-on dragging in the water, with no chance to climb on the pontoon as we picked up speed. Grey coaxed more rpms from the engine, not pulling up on the yoke, counting on the water resistance to pull the officer off before we gained altitude. Grey broke free of the man. He pulled up and out over the marina, clearing the sailboats, banking hard. I looked back, one officer was still on the dock, throwing a life preserver to his comrade, who was swimming back. It was fortunate for us all that he was not still hanging on to the pontoon.

Melissa and I were in the back seat, Rebecca and Grey forward. Grey set a course into the sun, toward Cabrini's house on Key Biscayne. I again stroked Melissa's bruised cheek, and she again managed a smile. Conversation was impossible, the noise of the engine and the sound of wind against the fuselage, deafening.

Below us stretched the bright blue-green Atlantic, sparkling, broader as we gained altitude, seeming to engulf the horizon as we flew toward it. Even as the engine roared in my ears, this was my first tranquil moment in days.

TWENTY-ONE

FLIPPED OPEN MY LAPTOP AND POPPED IN MY EAR BUDS. Ariel had watched over me since I left Frederica Island. I needed to know if she had anything else to tell me. As soon as my computer powered up her face appeared.

"Paul, the Bimini police have alerted the authorities in the States that you were seen taking off from Louis Town and heading to the mainland. They have your plane on radar and are tracking your flight. Miami Police will arrest you as soon as you land. You must tell Agent Grey to follow my instructions and alter your course."

I tapped Grey on the shoulder and yelled to him over the engine noise. He nodded.

"You need to drop your altitude to 500 feet, then break due north. I will make your radar signature disappear. This is the Bermuda Triangle after all. That will have the Coast Guard searching for the wreckage of your plane for a few days to give you and Grey time to make your next move. I will make sure Placido and Cabrini know you all are OK.

"After you have disappeared, I will give you coordinates to the Slow River Fish Camp where Rebecca and Grey have a boat, a cabin, and a truck. You have just enough fuel and daylight left to make it. You and Grey should wait there until I get word from Placido concerning the recordings, and if everything works out, you can turn yourself in to the authorities in Brunswick. Melissa is not on anyone's watch list. She can take a commercial flight back to Miami and wait on Key Biscayne to meet her father and brother.

"Placido and Cabrini have completed their statements to the Bimini police, and they have been released, pending the prosecutor's review of the file. So far they have been able to keep Grey and Rebecca out of the discussion. I do not anticipate they will be held further."

I related all this to Grey. He followed Ariel's instructions too literally for my taste, the descent to 500 feet was accomplished with too much alacrity, leaving my stomach at a much higher altitude while I held tight to the seat in front of me. Melissa blanched. Rebecca shrieked. Grey reset his instruments and banked to the right on a course north, parallel to the Florida coast.

The Slow River Fish Camp was a good four hours away, time enough for us to get lost in our thoughts, to process some of the events we'd gone through in the last twenty-four hours. I sat close to Melissa, our bodies touching in the cramped quarters of the plane. She reached for my hand, squeezed it, and lay her head on my shoulder. Within minutes she was asleep.

I was becoming comfortable with Melissa, our physical closeness in the plane natural and unforced, reassuring. It was hard to imagine there were any thoughts we had not expressed, any weaknesses we had not exposed, any selflessness that had not surfaced in our night together facing execution in the morning. Melissa's devotion to Placido was understandable, but her affection for Cabrini was far less. I turned that puzzle over in my mind as I drifted into my first untroubled sleep in days.

When I awoke it was twilight. Rebecca was shaking my knee.

"Ladies and gentlemen, we've been cleared for landing at the Slow River Fish Camp International Airport. The flight attendants will discontinue cabin service. Please bring your seat backs to their upright position and stow your tray tables. We'll be landing shortly."

Rebecca pointed at Melissa, still asleep on my shoulder. I rubbed her cheek, and she began waking, stretching as much as she could in the back seat of the plane. I pointed out the window to the river in the distance, the cabins, the dock with dozens of fishing boats tied up for the night. Grey traced a wide descending arc, lining up the plane with the river, broad and flat below, setting us down, and gliding in to the dock. Cutting the engine, only cicadas, frogs, and the occasional bull gator broke up the deep primordial silence of the camp. We grabbed what little we had on the plane and followed Grey down a gravel path to his cabin, a tin-roofed bungalow that looked from the outside not unlike his lodge on the Satilla. Inside, one large room served as kitchen, dining, and living room together, bedrooms off to the side. Cheap paneling covered the walls.

Grey fell onto the sofa while Rebecca searched the kitchen, pantry, refrigerator.

"We got a loaf of bread that looks OK, some sandwich meat, and a case of cold beer. Pretty much all we need. I'm famished. I think we all should grab something to eat. Grey, have a beer, and I'll make you a sandwich—you're 'bout the only one's been doing any work for hours."

Rebecca tossed a beer across the room in Grey's direction. He snatched it out of the air and popped the top in one smooth motion, as though the two of them had practiced and polished the move, a domestic ballet performed hundreds of times. But Grey was still in charge.

"After we have something to eat, I suggest we get some sleep. There's plenty of beds and two showers. We'll get going in the morning. I don't think anyone will bother us. Least, not till then."

Rebecca handed out cans of beer and bologna sandwiches slathered with mayonnaise. Things had the feel of normalcy. Each of us descended on our sandwich in silence. I made Melissa and myself another, Rebecca taking care of herself and Grey, then handing out another round of beers.

I volunteered to make the sleeping arrangements less awkward. "Melissa, you can have the back bedroom, I'll crash on the sofa."

Melissa responded, the weariness now showing in her voice. "The first thing I'm going to do is take a hot shower and then sleep as long as Agent Grey will let me."

"It won't be me who wakes you. Fishermen get started early. Before sunrise this place'll be howling with the sound of every imaginable boat motor. But you should get a good eight hours. I know I need it. I'm heading to bed."

With that, Grey and Rebecca disappeared. Melissa turned on the shower. I flipped off the light and was asleep as soon as I hit the couch.

Before daybreak the unmuffled sounds of men, outboards, and diesels came up from the river and reverberated through the trees. I stepped onto the porch, the welcome, cool air waking me. There were fishing guides rounding up their eager charges out of dozens of men appearing from campers and trucks; there were subsistence fishermen, gaunt, in beat-up trucks pulling rusted trailers with flat boats, men who fed their families from the water, lined up to back their trailers down the ramp; there were sport anglers smoking cigars, appearing from below decks on bill-fishing boats tied up at the dock, their diesel engines rumbling, loading ice chests of food and beer for the thirty-mile run to the Gulf Stream. The entire camp was awake. Nobody paid any attention to the airplane tied to the end of the dock.

Inside, a coffee maker sputtered and steamed and brewed a pot programmed the night before, the digital clock showing 6:05. I poured a mug. No one else in the cabin was stirring. I figured I had a few minutes to myself with Ariel.

"Placido found the tapes and Fowler's last words are distinct. I am sending you an audio file. You need to get an external drive, download the file, and get it to the prosecutor in Brunswick."

She paused before continuing, "And, by the way, there is a little surprise on the recording. Before Fowler did away with Oliver, Fowler confided in him the secret of Oliver's parentage. It appears that old man Fowler had a fling with a lovely young servant girl. She's the one in the picture of him at his desk. Oliver was the result. The old man never took responsibility for Oliver, though he gave him a job at the house and made his grandson pledge to keep him, but only after telling him why. Sound familiar? It turns out Oliver was Fowler's uncle, someone whom Fowler had resented his entire life and had reveled in the opportunity to kill, but not before telling Oliver who his father was and reminding Oliver that the old man had never claimed him. This information won't do anything to bring back Oliver, but his descendants will benefit from a sizable inheritance."

The story prompted me to wonder, was Ariel able to understand humor, to recognize irony? To understand human frailty, emotion, love, hate, anger? Ariel continued to advise me to keep my distance from Cabrini, but why? From the other information she was giving me, Cabrini and I were supposed to be on the same team. Of all the relationships that swirled around me, the one certainty I had was Ariel: Placido told her to help me, and she did without fail. So I would continue to follow her advice.

I had a lot ahead of me. I was still scruffy, dirty, and wearing a blood-spattered T-shirt, not what I wanted to be wearing when I showed up with the tapes at the prosecutor's office. I jumped in the shower before Melissa woke, shaved and cleaned up for the first time in a week. When Melissa showed, wearing only a T-shirt, I was sitting on the couch in clean jeans and a button down that I pulled from my backpack. I was no longer a poor imitation of Grey, but back to Paul McDaniel. Melissa sat down and snuggled next to me, put her arms around me, brushed my just-shaved face.

"Hey, handsome. I remember you. I think I like you. As I recall, you like me, too."

I scooped Melissa up from the couch and carried her into the back bedroom, both of us doing a poor job of stifling our laughter, the bed still warm from her body, her scent still on the sheets.

When we emerged again, the sun was up. Grey and Rebecca were sipping coffee on the porch. Grey tried to be coy, and I played along.

"So I guess you two slept well."

"Very. Ready for another big day. I checked with Ariel before my shower, and Placido has found the tapes. All we need is an external drive to download the audio, you can take it to the prosecutor, and I can turn myself in."

"I'm sure I have a thumb-drive around here someplace. We need to get movin'. It won't take much time for someone to identify that floatplane as the one that supposedly went down in the Atlantic, and the FBI will be all over us. We'll get the tapes to the prosecutor in Brunswick before you get caught. As soon as everyone is ready here, we can take the truck and drop you and Rebecca off at the lodge, and I will take Melissa to the Brunswick airport for a flight back to Miami before I go by the prosecutor's office."

The trip from Slow River to Grey's lodge in the woods seemed all too short. Melissa and I said our goodbyes on the porch, Rebecca leaving on the four-wheeler she'd pulled up on, Grey waiting in the truck to take Melissa to the airport, to Miami, to Placido. And to Cabrini.

"Grey and I have this under control. Once we get the tapes to the prosecutors everything should be fine. Then, I'll go back and get things straightened out with the firm."

"So, when will I see you again?"

"As soon as I get things worked out in Atlanta. I think it'd be a great idea to meet back at the Abbey."

And with that, Melissa was gone. Within minutes, the sound of Grey's truck fading, Rebecca's four-wheeler off in the distance, I once again was enveloped in the silence that surrounded me when I pulled my Porsche into Grey's barn seven days ago and turned off the engine. With everyone gone, I had an unbearable pang of—of what? Nostalgia? Nostalgia for almost dying at the hands of a psychopath? Regret? Regret that I had not rescued Melissa on my own? I felt the sadness of having been through something extraordinary that I would never experience again, tinged with the levity of having dodged death, freed to live the life spread before me.

I was sad and happy, relieved that Melissa would be in the safety of her father's presence, but apprehensive that she'd still be with Cabrini. Now uncertainty plagued me more than anything else, uncertainty about the firm, about my mother, but mainly about Melissa. Did I have real feelings for Melissa, feelings that would outlast the rush of adrenaline that fueled my time with her? Did Melissa have feelings for me beyond gratitude for a loyal family hireling who was just doing his job? The danger was now over; my job, now complete. It was difficult for me not to default to the feeling of inadequacy that flowed just below the surface of my psyche, the feeling that Melissa was way out of my class, and that, no matter my accomplishments, I just did not measure up. That feeling, I had to admit to myself, was the source of my unease with Cabrini: as bad as I thought he was, Milano blood flowed in his veins.

I turned my attention past what had to happen in Brunswick to what I needed to do in Atlanta. Now with the magic of Placido's audio tapes and assurance of his loyalty, I was in a position of favor unimaginable a week ago, not just with regard to the distant possibility of criminal prosecution, but with regard to the firm. The partners, ever vigilant of the firm's image, would do anything not to have the last few minutes of Fowler's life become public. To move beyond Brunswick to Atlanta, I needed Ariel. Her beautiful image appeared as soon as my laptop powered up. "I have some more good news for you. Your friend Tracey has solved your mother's problem."

"What? How do you know about Tracey?"

Even with Ariel's apparent omniscience it was shocking to realize she knew about Tracey. I'd taken extraordinary efforts to shield her actions from detection. It was not Ariel I was concerned about, but the police. Tracey was still on probation. Assisting a fleeing felon—even one who may never get indicted—would look very bad.

"I listened to your phone conversations. I needed someone to carry out my plan to take care of your mother in your absence. I wanted to have this problem resolved for you by the time you returned to the firm, so you could focus on other matters."

"Resolved?"

"I called Tracey. She thinks I am a concerned associate of yours. I suggested that you and I had been in touch and she needed to come to Atlanta to help your mother while you were away tending to other matters. I assured her the plan had your blessing."

"How could you do that? I didn't—"

"I told her your mom kept trying to get in touch with you, showing up at the firm's headquarters and being run off by security; they did not believe your mom's story that her son is a lawyer at Strange & Fowler. She showed them the card you had given her, but they still didn't believe her. Tracey intercepted your mother one morning before security ran her off, told her she is a friend of yours, and was happy to give her the $1,000.00 to pay her back rent and avoid eviction."

I was resigned to the fact that at least this problem was one less I'd have to worry about.

"It's taken care of. I'll pay Tracey back as soon as I get to Atlanta."

"There will be no need for that. The morning your mother showed up to get the check from Tracey there was a rather fortunate coincidence, and Tracey took full advantage of it."

"I don't know if I can handle another surprise."

"Your mother appeared in the lobby at the same moment as the Chairman of the Management Committee. He told the security guards he expected her to be removed. Just then Tracey came in and assessed the situation. She stopped the security guards in mid-track, grabbed the Chairman, introduced him to your mother, and shamed him for having security run her off. Tracey made it clear to the Chairman why she was meeting your mother there, and she made a point of handing her the check. Tracey said your mother sniffed at the security guards as she walked out."

I was just relieved she'd gotten out without attracting further attention.

"Good thing she didn't call them names. She had taken to referring to them as 'Gestapo' with me. That might not have ended well."

"It gets more interesting. The Chairman seemed truly astonished to realize the person he had mistaken for a homeless beggar was indeed your mother. He told Tracey so: that finding out you have a mother and you aren't really an orphan was one of the best pieces of information he had heard about you. And he was so happy to hear it, he wrote Tracey a check to repay her on the spot."

Now he had his ready-made excuse to fire me as soon as I returned, discrediting me, and with me anything negative I had to say about Fowler and the firm.

TWENTY-TWO

T URNING IN A SUSPECT FOR A CAPITAL OFFENSE IS A complex match between a prosecutor and defense attorney shrouded in the fog of attorney-client privilege and prosecutorial discretion. The defense postures, the prosecution threatens, each party keeps his cards close, and all moves are played out by proxies. The defense attorney ventures a hand, his client out of sight, the assistant prosecutor counters, his boss in the background with the final say. The suspect doesn't show his face until everything is worked out, and the DA never appears until the cameras are rolling, the suspect in custody. But for all the exotic maneuvering and byzantine intrigue, when it's over it's much like a high-stakes version of buying a car. The manager shakes your hand, you write a check, and he gives you the keys—or in this instance, the prosecutor holds a press ˙nference, the suspect does the perp walk, and he's ˙d out the back door.

˙ side I had Grey, not a defense attorney, and subtleties, there would be no posturing; the ˙, tell the authorities who I am, and hand ˙he only question in my mind was to .nyself in, the Glynn County DA or

the US Attorney for the Southern District of Georgia, but it was not an open issue for Grey.

"I told you when I first saw you that I hate the feds and wouldn't turn you in to 'em. We'll go to the DA. He'll get credit for bringing you in, and he can let the US Attorney know the case is resolved. After all, murder is a state offense, even if you are accused of killing a judge."

I walked into Glynn County Courthouse without a lawyer. Any defense counsel would accuse me of insanity for showing up as a criminal suspect with three potential murder charges hanging over my head without a lawyer. But Grey doesn't hold with the artifice of defense lawyers, and he appeared with me and the tape and acted like he expected me to be treated fairly. He had me sold on that approach, but even though I felt I had my innocence proved in an external memory device no bigger than a stick of gum, it still scared me to walk into a courthouse I might well not walk out of. I went through the metal detectors just like everyone else, not showing my bar card to pass, not wanting to set off alarms when the county computers registered who I am. I wanted the chance to turn myself in, not to be wrestled to the ground by the officers manning the doors to the courthouse, handcuffed, and dragged to jail before the DA heard my story.

Inside the courthouse, just past security, were two dark doors with "Raymond Ravenel, District Attorney" stenciled in gold over the pediment, where the letters were chipped and faded. We entered an open room with a counter running the length of the opposite wall. Behind it were a half-dozen clerks dealing with as many lines of citizens, who were plying their claims and responding to the notices that were the daily grist of the office. Behind

them were a score of gunmetal desks where an army of investigators, lawyers, and their assistants, many with shoulder holsters visible, were scanning files, yelling on phones, menacing supplicants, and cajoling witnesses. A steady file of police officers pushed through a low-swinging door beside the counter that slammed at each pass. The din was disorienting.

To one side, there was a reception desk in front of a single, unmarked door. It was closed. Grey addressed the receptionist by her first name and asked if he could speak to "Big Dog." She cracked the door, and before she closed it behind her the DA had bounded out and grabbed Agent Grey's hand. I could see how he got his nickname. He looked like he had been spending too much time sitting at his desk. He was about 300 pounds, a couple inches over six feet, and the way he was stuffed into his suit, he hadn't lifted anything much heavier than a double cheeseburger in a while.

"Grey, where the hell'a ya been! I thought I'd have to send someone to that lodge of yours and drag you down to the coast to do some fishin'. Got me a new boat."

"Been doin' a lot a fishin' myself here recently, mainly with Rebecca down at Slow River."

"Can't say I blame you on that."

"My friend and I have something to talk to you about in private."

The DA held out his hand. "I'm Raymond Ravenel. And who have I the pleasure to meet?"

Grey grabbed the DA's hand himself and maneuvered him back toward his office. "That's what we're here to talk to you about." Grey motioned me in behind him and closed the door.

"We have a recording to play for you."

I powered up my laptop and plugged in the thumb-drive. There was no video, at first only the voice of a dead man, his admission of bribing and killing the judge, influencing Wimp, killing Oliver, then framing me for all of it, the threat to Melissa, the struggle and then the gunshot, sirens in the background, the sound of the Porsche screaming off just seconds before the Frederica Island police arrive, hammering on the door, breaking into the room.

Big Dog was no longer Grey's jovial fishing buddy.

"What the hell did I just hear?"

"You heard William Fowler admit to bribing a judge, committing two murders and influencing a public official, framing Paul McDaniel, threatening his girlfriend, and then trying to kill him. The last gunshot you heard killed Fowler after he had pulled a gun on Paul and they struggled.

"Raymond, meet Paul McDaniel. Ever since that gunshot Paul's been running to save his girlfriend and to find a way to clear himself. Now that Melissa is safe and he has this recording, Paul wants to surrender, and he expects not to be prosecuted on the strength of that tape."

"Grey, you haven't been harboring a fugitive, have you?"

"Nope. He just showed up at my lodge, and I brought him in."

"Hell of a coincidence! Where did this recording come from, and how do I know this is Fowler?"

So far, I hadn't said a word. It was my intent to say as little as possible. It's bad form to lie to law enforcement, and I wanted as little opportunity to do so as possible. But Grey turned to me, there being no reason to misrepresent anything about the origin of the recording and how

I came into possession of it. Giving the DA the details of the tape only supported its veracity and allowed me to develop some credibility with the Honorable Raymond "Big Dog" Ravenel.

"All this happened at Fowler's cottage on Frederica Island. When the G-8 was held there, the cottage was wired with some sophisticated security measures, including cameras and microphones. As you heard in the tape, Fowler disabled the cameras and thought he disabled the microphones, but one of them picked up all the action. I retrieved the tape from the security company. They can authenticate it."

Big Dog turned to Grey and shook his head.

"Wimp Boyd. We've known for a while that boy's been altering death certificates for some serious cash. I didn't much care, so long as he didn't make my work more difficult. Until now, all we've known Wimp to do was change the time and place of death. I heard he'd made a bundle back in 2011 when the estate tax laws changed. If someone died in 2010 instead of 2011, their estate paid no tax at all. A couple of loaded old geezers on Frederica Island died in early January 2011. For a piece of the action Wimp had them dead just after Christmas and cremated real quick before anyone could ask questions. One family even brought their elderly benefactor down from New York to Frederica Island just to take advantage of Wimp's special talent. Kinda like Jesus only backward—instead of raising people from the dead, Wimp makes 'em dead before their time.

"There've always been stories of men dying in their mistresses' arms only to be delivered home and pronounced dead on their own sofas. Depending on who the deceased was, Wimp would perform that little service for their widows, their lovers, or the board of deacons. I didn't mind Wimp taking care of that—pretty much thought it a civic service.

"Now that he's altering cause of death, he's getting into my line of work, and that's a problem for me. We'll prosecute him for RICO. He'll go away for a while.

"But Mr. McDaniel, we still have a man dead of a gunshot in that cottage that no one has taken responsibility for killing. Based on that recording you easily could have murdered Fowler for threatening your girlfriend."

Big Dog's eyes bore into me.

"I never even threatened Fowler. Everything on that tape supports my story. He pulled a gun on me. We struggled. The gun went off. I didn't—"

"Yeah, but there's nothin' to prove you didn't kill him either. You were there, you had a motive, and your prints are on the gun. That's at least circumstantial evidence that you killed him. And many a man has been convicted of murder on circumstantial evidence."

"Fowler staged the whole thing. I think he pulled the trigger himself to avoid prosecution."

I sounded desperate. And I was.

"I've heard many variations on 'the other dude did it,' but never 'the other dude killed himself to make me look like a murderer.'"

Big Dog looked at Grey, shook his head, then back to me.

"I ain't buyin' it. If you were innocent, why the hell did you run? You're a smart man, Mr. McDaniel. You know—"

"I didn't trust the Frederica Island police to do the right thing. I was afraid I'd end up in jail. And I had no idea there was a tape that could prove my innocence. But in the end, I ran so I could help Melissa."

"How the hell were you plannin' to do that?"

Any more down this road and it would threaten to implicate Grey and Rebecca and open up the whole affair on South Cat Cay. I was not going to do it. I kept silent.

"If you can't do any better'n that, I got no choice but to lock you up. The tape puts you at the scene with a motive to kill Fowler for threatening your girlfriend. If we can't authenticate the tape, we have your prints on the weapon that killed Fowler and Oliver. We also have your prints on the shotgun that killed the judge, and we can place you at the Abbey about the time of the murder. That's three murders in the space of a few hours. Sounds to me like you're one dangerous hombre.

"If we can authenticate the recording, we might be able to drop the charges for the murders of the judge and Oliver. But that still leaves Fowler. I ain't letting you go on that one. And I'm recommending no bond, since you are a clear flight risk."

He looked to Grey.

"Sorry."

Grey picked up my lap top, thumb drive still plugged in.

"You can take the computer, but I'll need that recording." Big Dog popped out the thumb drive, stuck it in his pocket, and handed the computer to Grey. A few minutes later a deputy put handcuffs on me and carried me off to a holding cell in the basement of the courthouse, now Exhibit A to the lesson why you should never talk to a DA without a lawyer by your side, even if you think you're innocent. And everyone thinks they're innocent.

I had never been arrested, never been in jail in my life. The holding cell was populated with those like me who'd been arrested that day and those awaiting some processing in the courts. There were about a dozen of us unfortunates in the cell together. Some, I guessed from their disheveled appearance, were there for DUI, some allowed they were in for domestic abuse, and there were a few prostitutes thrown into the mix who made no secret of their profession. Everyone seemed to be in some amount of distress about their plight except for the prostitutes, whose outlandish outfits and provocative calls to the police brightened the room. One, a woman named Marie, teased every male officer who passed, offering free samples of her services and advertising an open house next weekend for any who wished to attend.

Marie showed some interest in my well-being until she asked what I was in for. When I told her I was a suspect in a triple murder and wasn't interested in talking about it, she retreated to the safety of the opposite corner of the cell.

The day was long, and the night longer, not unlike the time I spent as a prisoner of Anthony Milano. While on South Cat Cay I feared immediate execution; here, it was not imminent death I feared, but the possibility of being in jail awaiting trial while my outside life disintegrated, Melissa gone to be with Cabrini, partnership disappeared now that the firm had discovered my deception, and Mom with a fresh check for a thousand bucks to buy all the liquor she wanted. How had I so miscalculated the reaction of the DA to the recording? There was Ariel, who found the recording so compelling, and Grey, who was so assured of the DA's good faith.

I could understand Ariel's miscalculation. For all her ability, she was still unable to account for the intervening free will of a person who's not rationally motivated. It's this failure of machines to account for human frailty that makes me wonder whether they'll ever be able to fathom human consciousness. For it was likely that the DA had received significant political pressure from the residents of Frederica Island to solve a triple murder in their sheltered enclave, and letting a convenient suspect loose presented too much of a risk to his re-election.

Grey's missed call was far more difficult to understand. It was evident the moment Big Dog walked out of his office to greet us that he was more of a political animal than a servant of justice, more interested in using his office to arrange fishing trips with influential locals than using those same resources to track criminals. The fact that his name had been over the entry to his office long enough for the paint to flake and peel was all anyone needed to know about the focus of his efforts. Perhaps most disturbing is that Grey said nothing to warn me.

Now the worst fears that had entered my mind as I flew down the causeway to escape the Frederica Island police a week ago had been realized. The DA needed a murder suspect to parade before the cameras, and I dropped one in his lap when I walked into his office and surrendered. He wasn't going to let me walk out. I was caught in the flawed justice system that I'd feared from the beginning.

I must've fallen asleep sitting on the floor, leaning against the wall of the cell. I was awakened by the sound of another inmate urinating in the stainless-steel toilet in the corner of the cell not three feet from me, a sound, a smell, and a sight that I'd just as soon never experience again. This vision appeared as the deputies came around to shove plates of food in the cell for breakfast. They called my name before they handed me a plate and told me to step out of the cell. I offered my arms for cuffs, assuming that was the expected procedure, but the deputy told me it wasn't necessary. The DA wanted to see me.

Big Dog was sitting at his desk and motioned me to sit down. The deputy remained behind me.

"Mr. McDaniel, Milano Labs has authenticated the recordings. As far as I am concerned, that takes care of any responsibility you might've had for the homicides of Judge Richards and Oliver. Those crimes can be laid squarely at the feet of Fowler. I also had our forensic lab take another look at Fowler's weapon. Your prints are all over it. All over it except for one place: the only prints on the trigger are Fowler's. That fact, along with the recording and the other evidence we've been able to retrieve from the scene, make it unlikely that you could be successfully prosecuted for Fowler's murder. It's probable that he intended suicide all along. You just interrupted him and provided someone convenient to blame.

"But that still leaves you with a couple of problems: fleeing the scene of a crime and obstruction of justice. What we now know happened in that room, and with the threat that you felt Melissa was facing, I have decided not to pursue charges against you for those crimes. I just called the US Attorney and told him what we found, and he confirmed that he will not be pursuing charges either. Since Grey brought you here, I asked him to come get you. He should be here in a few minutes."

I was in front of the Courthouse waiting for Grey when he pulled up. I jumped in his truck before he had a chance to stop.

"Big Dog told me what he said about forensics and all, but he was just jerkin' you around. He sure as hell knew whose prints were on the gun and where they were long before we walked into his office. As for the recording, he knew it was authentic. William Fowler has been one of his biggest campaign contributors for years. He knows Fowler's voice better than he knows his own mother's.

"One of the prostitutes in the cell with you last night is Big Dog's best informant. She was just trying to get information from you to nail me. Big Dog wants something on me, not to put me in jail, just leverage, in case he ever needs it. That's why he was so interested in your plans to rescue Melissa and why he locked you up when you refused to answer. If he could've put me with any of those plans, he'd have me on aiding and abetting. When you told Marie you didn't want to talk, Big Dog figured he had nothing and decided to let you go."

"So, why didn't you warn me?"

"I didn't think Big Dog would try to use you to get something on me. I guess I was wrong." Grey laughed. "Welcome to South Georgia."

"It's about time I got the hell outta here."

TWENTY-THREE

Two days after being cleared by the Glynn County DA and the US Attorney in Brunswick, I was ready to walk into a conference room on the fiftieth floor of a glass tower in Midtown Atlanta to face the Strange & Fowler Management Committee. But not until I could talk with Tracey about the interaction between Mom and the Chairman.

I had not seen Tracey in five years. When I met her she was a sullen nineteen year old, emaciated from drug use, in skinny black jeans and a too-tight T-shirt, with cropped florescent green-and-orange hair, and every imaginable body piercing. Back then, while I sensed Tracey was grateful for my efforts, there was no evidence of it in her face, her body language, or what she said. It was clear I was helping her for the sake of her mother, and at that point Tracey didn't think much of either of us. But over the years we'd kept in touch, at first only casually, then more in earnest. Tracey opened up over time; we talked, often for long periods, about work, life, her efforts, her goals. The friend of mine who did me a favor to employ Tracey told me she had grown into the job. Tracey was the best hire he'd ever made.

I arranged with Lillian to have Tracey meet me in my

office. When I walked in, she was already there, her back to me, looking out the window over the Atlanta skyline.

"Tracey?"

She turned to face me, and for an instant, I thought she must be someone else.

"Didn't recognize me, did you?"

The woman standing in my office was a petite blond, bright smile, not a single body piercing or visible tattoo, all curves and stylish dress, conservative in the manner of a young woman who worked in a small-town Southern law firm. Tracey was a younger image of her mother, who had been a runner-up for Miss Alabama before her unplanned pregnancy derailed her beauty-pageant career.

"Well, I have to say you do look a little different from the first time I saw you."

"All thanks to you."

"I hear you returned the favor. I appreciate what you did for my mother."

I couldn't bring myself to tell her she may've blown the elaborate cover story I'd crafted for my childhood, that explained the absence of my mother, that even with Placido backing me, her good intentions and self-less kindness may've derailed my plans for attaining the partnership I'd worked so hard for, that I needed to find out exactly what she'd told the Chairman so I'd be ready for the questions that were sure to come from the Management Committee.

"Can you tell me what happened that morning?"

"Your friend Ariel told me you really needed help with a matter for your Mom. She explained you were out of town and couldn't handle it yourself, but I already knew about all that and didn't let on. She told me that you'd be out of town longer than expected, and you wanted me to loan $1,000.00 to your Mom until you returned."

"That's a lot of money. I hope . . ."

"I talked to my mother. She and I got the money together and figured out how to get it to your Mom. According to the security guard, your mom had been around the office every morning until they ran her off. I almost missed her that morning, but then I saw one of your partners was threatening to have her arrested for trespass—and I let him have it. I told him she's your mother and was only trying to get in touch with you to get some rent money. I shamed him so bad he wrote a check to reimburse me. He said he wanted to be the one to stop her eviction."

"I bet he did."

"Paul, I'm sure you know your Mom has an addiction problem. But I talked to her. I can tell you she could benefit from the same program you got me in. If you had faith in someone like me, I'm sure you can help your own mother."

"I've lived through her problems all my life, and since I've been grown, she has resisted my every effort to help. You know better than anyone else, you can't help someone until they want to be helped. All I've been able to do is give her money and talk her into going into rehab for short periods. At some point you have to let people live with the consequences of their choices. It's been the hardest thing I've ever done. My mother has decided her own fate, and I've decided to let her."

"This time I really think she wants to change."

That was part of my mother's usual pitch for money.

"I hope you're right. I'm going to give her the chance. Again."

I paused for a moment, thinking how to say what was in my mind without it coming out wrong, without it being taken wrong.

"Tracey, I appreciate what you've done for me and my mother. You, more than anyone else, can understand how my mother has suffered and what I've gone through as a result."

But that wasn't what I wanted to tell her.

"Did I tell you, you look great?"

She flashed a smile, and before it faded, I stepped out of the office for my appointment with the Management Committee.

I rode the elevator to the fiftieth floor and stepped off into Strange & Fowler's firm conference room, a room that took up the entire east side of the building. A solid wall of glass displaying the Atlanta skyline struck you immediately, and when the electronically frosted glass was left clear, as it was this morning, the light was disorienting after leaving the dim elevator, an effect that was no doubt intended by the architect. On the other side of the glass wall was the observation deck, from where Billingsley had jumped, starting all this in motion.

Across the length of the room stretched a conference table large enough to seat all fifty of the firm's Atlanta partners. Today the dozen members of the Management Committee were spread on the side next to the window, forcing me to look into the brightness, not able yet to see their faces. A junior member of the Committee, the designated hatchet man, pounced as soon as I entered the room and took the lead in presenting the firm's position. I was still trying to focus my eyes.

"Internal Counsel has advised us that you've likely committed several crimes and further employment would have severe adverse consequences for the firm."

Internal Counsel, affectionately known among Strange & Fowler lawyers as "ICE," in part for his charming personality and warm demeanor, is a thin-lipped former prosecutor whose sole responsibility is to advise the partnership on ethical issues. His pronouncements are the firm equivalent of the scarlet "A" handed out by his Boston forebears.

"The Brunswick DA and the US Attorney for the Southern District have both cleared me."

From the looks on their faces, that seemed to be news. They weren't used to someone end-running ICE.

"And in case you get any ideas about going to the State Bar, I'll let them know that any unethical behavior in the Milano case was all Fowler's."

Since they were unaware that the two law-enforcement agencies had cleared me of criminal conduct, it was also unlikely that they had any idea of the recordings. I wanted to keep the tapes in my back pocket and not reveal them unless I had to. The idea that Fowler was the author of any deception of the court in the Milano case didn't seem to surprise anyone.

I hadn't yet sat down. Now more accustomed to the glare, I looked each one of them in the eye. There was a lot of shuffling of papers. I took a seat at the head of the table.

It was now my turn. But other than some nervous throat clearing among the rest of the Committee, it was still me and hatchet man.

"Let's discuss my partnership."

"Look, Paul, you must've suffered from all you've been

through. We're prepared to give you a paid leave of absence from the firm so you can recover fully."

I was not taking that bait.

"That's a kind gesture, but I'm perfectly able to resume my duties."

Admit to these jackals that I am damaged goods? Not in my lifetime. They would be dividing my partnership percentage before I got back on the elevator. An extended leave would be just as bad. I needed to get back to the firm to protect my interests.

Hatchet man took another approach.

"We have serious doubts that Milano Corporation will be very supportive of a lawyer who's connected with an attempt to divest its major shareholder—even if you contend it was someone else's idea. Paul, you must understand that we have to have some distance from you to repair the firm's relationship with Milano."

But I was ready for that as well.

"Why do I have to do your homework? It's obvious to me that you haven't spoken a word with Placido Milano. I encourage you to do so. Placido will tell you that Milano Corporation's business goes with me. He expects the firm to honor its commitment to make me a partner and to see to it that a significant portion of the profits from the corporation's legal work goes to me. If you force me out, I'll take Milano Corporation and millions in fees with me. The firm will have a hard time surviving the hit and the adverse publicity."

Hatchet man and I had battled to a draw. The Chairman of the Management Committee had yet to speak. He was a patrician handpicked by Fowler to maintain the elitist standards of the firm: his grandfather had been the head of surgery at Crawford Long Memorial; his father, an investment banker; the home he grew up in, incorporated into the High Museum of Art. He'd attended Westminster Schools, Harvard undergraduate, Yale law. He and I had nothing in common. In the years I'd spent at the firm, we'd spoken three times, each time in an elevator.

He picked up a remote control and pressed a button. The glass wall frosted over, lights dimmed, and a screen descended behind me. The resume I submitted out of law school eight years ago was projected on it, and the antiquated courier type, the engraved personal letterhead— an extraordinary extravagance for a destitute law student, designed to appeal to Strange & Fowler's ingrained snobbery—appeared as if they belonged to a lost manuscript recently discovered in the library of an obscure desert monastery.

The Chairman spoke.

"Paul, you will recognize the resume you submitted to the firm, on which we based our hiring decision."

I didn't respond. I knew where this was going.

The Chairman stood and scrolled the document to the end. He took a laser pointer and placed a red dot on the screen.

"'High School Education. Thornwood High School. Thornwood is an orphanage operated by the Presbyterian Church. I lost my father at age seven, my mother at age twelve. I graduated from Thornwood High School as Valedictorian.'

"Mr. McDaniel, that is a laudable record. It is the record on which this firm hired you. It turns out this record is a lie, you are an impostor, your background a fraud."

He knew how to play on my insecurities, either by instinct or just as a result of the arrogance that was inherent in his nature, my fear that by the mere fact of our births I was simply not his equal. He continued to hammer his advantage.

"I met your mother outside this office building just last week, abandoned by her successful son, reduced to begging on the street. I was able to assist her myself, to prevent her from being evicted from her trailer."

He said the word "trailer" with the same level of disgust that one would approach a steaming pile of dog crap on an antique rug.

"You hid your white trash background from the firm with a romanticized version of your own story. And it is all untrue.

"Now I'm afraid the firm must distance itself from you. The firm cannot tolerate your fraudulent resume, and I'm certain that Placido Milano would agree with the firm's position. I have no question in my mind that Placido will not want Milano Corporation affiliated with someone who so blatantly misrepresented his background, someone who denied his own class, someone who so callously turned his back on his own mother.

"We'll allow you to resign rather than fire you, allow you to create your own narrative of your resignation, to pursue other interests, to start your own firm, whatever you would like to say. However, if you force us to fire you, we will go public with your fraud, with your heartless abandonment of your own mother. After that, it is unlikely you will be able to develop a successful practice contesting parking tickets."

The Chairman sat, a look of serene satisfaction on his face. I wanted to break his nose. I glanced around the room. The remaining members of the committee looked as though they'd just been told that I drank the blood of murdered babies.

"Gentlemen, you seem to be predisposed to believe the worst. But everything in my resume is true. My father died of a work-related accident when I was seven. When I was twelve, I lost my mother when she was adjudicated unfit and deprived of her parental rights. I grew up in an orphanage and graduated as the valedictorian of my high school class. Since then, I've assisted my mother financially even at great sacrifice to myself, only to find my money was used to feed her addictions. It seems that she's manipulated you as she's manipulated me my entire life.

"But in response to your specific concerns, I assure you this information is well known to Placido and Melissa Milano. Rather than causing the Milano Corporation to distance itself from me, it's resulted in an even closer relationship."

The Chairman condescended to respond once more.

"I'm sorry, Mr. McDaniel, given your questionable veracity, we are unable to accept your personal assurances."

I flipped open my laptop and placed it on the conference table. Ariel's face appeared.

"Ariel, please contact Placido and Melissa Milano."

I watched the faces of the committee, more puzzled than concerned, no cracks yet appearing in their uniform façade. Placido and Melissa Milano again made their *Star Wars* appearance, just as they'd done on Agent Grey's computer at his cabin, holograms that looked as though they were in the same room with us. This little bit of magic got their attention.

"Placido, Melissa, I'm here at the Strange & Fowler offices having a discussion with the Management Committee. They're concerned that by stating I lost my mother and grew up in an orphanage I have misrepresented my background. They feel if you found out about this misrepresentation Milano Corporation would instantly distance itself from me."

Melissa spoke first.

"Gentlemen, Paul has always been forthcoming with Milano Corporation concerning his challenging background and his rather difficult relationship with his mother. We find it laudable that, notwithstanding her problems with alcohol and drug use, he continues to assist her."

Then Placido.

"Mr. McDaniel has shown the utmost loyalty and devotion to Milano Corporation. I want the Management Committee to understand that Milano Corporation values his loyalty and will return it. Our business follows Mr. McDaniel."

Placido paused to allow his words to sink in, then brought his appearance to an abrupt conclusion.

"Any questions?"

I looked around the room. Only the Chairman dared look up; his eyes bore into me, but he declined to speak.

"Thank you."

The screen went blank. Placido and Melissa were no longer with us. Now it was my turn.

"Milano Corporation values my loyalty. I find it reprehensible that Strange & Fowler doesn't. I have given every effort, sacrificed every personal interest, all in favor of the firm. It was one of William Fowler's last honest acts to reward my loyalty with the offer of partnership, an offer I have worked every waking hour to attain.

"I wasn't a trust fund baby. No one in my family has been anything but a blue-collar worker. But I've accomplished in less than one generation what has taken most of you three.

"You can keep your partnership. I'm starting my own firm. I'm certain there are dozens of Strange & Fowler associates who'd jump at the opportunity to work for a firm that values their loyalty and rewards their efforts, that stands for ethics over pure profits. Milano Corporation will be our first client."

I turned and walked out, not waiting for a response.

I called Placido first, Lillian second. She and Tracey were waiting for me in the lobby as soon as I got off the elevator.

"Lillian, I need you. The work will be intense. You'll be managing the business side of the firm. There'll be a lot of demands and nothing will be certain, but I'll double your salary to start."

"There's no place for me here. I'm going with you."

Tracey stepped forward. "Paul, if you need me, I can help, too. I've been running a small law office for a while, and there aren't many things I can't handle."

I hadn't thought about Tracey working for me. She had a secure job and a home hundreds of miles away. It wouldn't be fair to uproot her on the promise of a job that may not work out, not when she had a good thing where she was.

"Tracey, maybe when we get better established, but it's too much of a risk now. Your mother's right. She doesn't have a place at Strange & Fowler any more. You have a secure job and an established home. There's no reason to change that."

Tracey tried to hide her disappointment, to remain upbeat, not to appear hurt. I wanted to take back what I'd said as soon as I'd said it.

Strange & Fowler had one more card to play. Less than an hour after I walked out of its offices, the firm filed a lawsuit against me in Fulton County Superior Court seeking a Temporary Restraining Order to keep me from "stealing valuable trade secrets, inducing highly trained employees to breach their contracts, and making defamatory statements to long-standing clients that irreparably harm business prospects and the name of Strange & Fowler." Fifteen minutes after the lawsuit was filed Judge Wilbur Cotten, a former member of the firm and now Senior Judge, signed the Temporary Restraining Order. Strange & Fowler shut down my new law firm before I even had a chance to announce it.

Judge Cotten's law clerk forwarded me a copy of the order by email, not out of courtesy, but rather to make sure I knew as soon as possible that I was under an injunction. Ariel was on it before it hit my inbox.

TWENTY-FOUR

S TRANGE & FOWLER'S PERVASIVE INFLUENCE IN THE legal community was in part a result of its ability to place its talented alumni in favorable positions around the Southeast. Associates who did not make the cut, partners who burned out before retirement, retirees who wanted to stay in the game, they all got lucrative jobs outside the firm as the result of Strange & Fowler connections. Alumni were placed in other, less demanding, positions with law firms, legal departments of corporate clients, as in-house counsel for professional sports leagues, colleges, universities, or in governmental spots anywhere from clerks to judges, governors, and senators. And each well-placed alum became yet another person in an influential position the firm could call on when it needed a favor.

An inveterate drunk, Wilbur Cotten had risen to partnership in Strange & Fowler decades ago when drinking three martinis at lunch wasn't a cliché but part of the everyday routine. When times changed and it became apparent that he was unable to handle the work and remain intoxicated at the level he desired, he was pushed into a judgeship, appointed to the bench by a governor who was grateful to return one of the numerous favors showered on his administration by the firm.

Judge Cotten proceeded to have one of the least pro-
ductive and most lackluster careers on the Fulton County
Superior Court bench since Reconstruction, and this was
against competition that included some of the most incompetent, injudicious, and venal judges in the history of the
State. Not long ago he had gone on senior status, which
sounds lofty but in reality means that his fellow judges
moved him to a position where he had the opportunity to
do less harm—and was expected to do even less work—
than he'd done before.

The only change lawyers reported in Judge Cotten's
routine since he'd become a senior judge was that they
usually had to wake him whenever they went to his chambers for business—though they could still count on being
invited for a shot of bourbon or gin afterward, depending
on the time of year. Judge Cotten's chief distinction was
that he was the last judge in the State of Georgia to fly the
Confederate battle flag in his courtroom. It wasn't that
long ago when it came down, and it had been removed
by one of the law clerks while the judge was taking his
afternoon nap. By that point in his career he paid so little
attention to his courtroom that he didn't even notice.

The irony of such a meaningless judge making such a
meaningful attack on my career was lost on Ariel, though
there was no question that she understood the threat presented to my future by the injunction. The first thing Ariel
did in response to that threat was to search all her target's
electronic devices and internet history. Ariel's search of
Judge Cotten's digital life was unexpectedly fruitful.

Judge Cotten's most frequent waking activity was to
troll a site called "Daring Judges," a place where judges
who want to cheat on their spouses can find other judges

who want to cheat on their spouses. The motto on the homepage was a quote attributed to an anonymous moral degenerate, "Never fool around with anyone who doesn't have as much to lose as you do." Notwithstanding the effectiveness of this advice, the host of the site used extraordinary security measures to keep the judges' activities secret, but none of these were an impediment to Ariel. One such measure was that to participate, a judge had to be invited by a current member. There was a sophisticated system to assure the anonymity of the judge making the invitation, and the invitation itself was impossible to copy or to trace—assuring that there was nothing left for an offended judge to report to anyone—unless the invited judge acted favorably on it. But if a judge did act favorably, the site opened up, and they were thus compromised by their positive response, giving the site owners some confidence that they would not be encouraged by a guilty conscience to turn in their fellow trysters, now having—as the motto assured—as much to lose as everyone else.

Judge Cotten had issued invitations to more than a half-dozen potential members. His taste was cosmopolitan and unimpeded by preference for sex, age, or race. The object of a significant amount of his attention was Catherine Lawson-Breuer, one of the first African-American women in Georgia elected to the bench outside the City of Atlanta. Judge Cotten had an invitation issued to Judge Lawson-Breuer three times without success. On the fourth she accepted, whether by mistake or out of curiosity, resignation, or overt interest, it was impossible to tell. But the site indicated that both of them had recently attended a national legal education program in Las Vegas entitled, "Above Suspicion: Maintaining Judicial Independence."

"I suggest we tell Judge Cotten we will to go to the press if he fails to dissolve the injunction. I can pose as a journalist who has gotten a tip that he has been 'daring' with a judge at a weekend seminar on judicial ethics."

I had to explain to Ariel that there's something problematic about blackmailing judges. Not to mention illegal and unethical. While Ariel couldn't go to jail for it, I could, as well as lose my law license. Having just escaped near-certain death and long-term incarceration, I'd lost my taste for taking life-threatening or career-ending risks. And what if Judge Lawson-Breuer was only an object of Judge Cotten's interest and not a participant in his affairs; what if she accepted the invitation not even knowing what it was and only by coincidence attended the same seminar? In matters that involved discerning the point at which the often-indistinct boundaries of ethical issues changed from permissible to forbidden, Ariel was as effective as a paperweight. But in this instance the question wasn't even close, and I wondered whether Ariel's extraordinary ability to glide through technological barriers without impediment made her oblivious to other more subtle barriers presented by morality. It certainly allowed her, when it proved necessary, to ignore the obvious limitations presented by the law.

Ariel's moral failures may well have been inherent in her being. As far as my limited understanding of artificial intelligence informed me, she was nothing more than the code that created her. Ariel's moral limitations were dependent on how she was instructed. And since philosophers have debated morality for thousands of years without coming to an agreement even on fundamental principles, Ariel's designers were hobbled. She could be coded without any moral direction at all, but if she were given some ethical guidance, choices had to be made among an almost limitless array of philosophical schools. Should Ariel be coded as a moral relativist or an idealist? Or should she be coded a pragmatist, learning her morality by the layering of instances from interactions with humans? If so, Ariel could hardly be expected to tell blackmail from black beans.

Ariel's most recent moral exemplars included a well-regarded man willing to torture his niece and murder his brother to steal money he didn't need and to dominate a corporation he already controlled. And my behavior could hardly be deemed laudable: killing Fowler, stealing cash from an ATM, ignoring the plight of my own mother. Had I bothered to keep score, I may well have violated every one of the Ten Commandments since my trip to Frederica Island. I couldn't—or worse—wouldn't conform my conduct to rules that I agreed on.

And that, I decided, was the chief difference between Ariel and me. If Ariel was programed to act a certain way, she was mandated by the laws of electronics to act just that way. I, on the other hand, had that uniquely human trait of discerning what's right and still being able to do just the opposite. The knowledge of good and evil—the difference between humans and animals—and the propensity to choose wrong even though we know what's right, was what got us banished from the Garden in the first place.

After working with Ariel, it had become clear to me that she wasn't programed to follow either the law or any particular morality. As Placido said when he first disclosed Ariel as AI, he made choices concerning what traits she should be programed with, and—like modesty—morality was not one of them. Ariel is a free agent, unshackled from the limits of human cognition and the boundaries of right and wrong. Being outside the ability of any legal authority to sanction, Ariel is only restrained by the master who created her. And now, after working with Ariel and Placido through almost every imaginable circumstance, I grasped the power of Placido's instruction to Ariel: "I want you to do everything possible to assist Mr. McDaniel." With that, I knew it was I, and not any bundle of code or twist of wire, that constituted Ariel's moral center. And I had to make it clear that blackmailing Judge Cotten wasn't an acceptable option.

Besides, going to Judge Cotten with a threat to expose his dalliances wouldn't get to the source of the problem: Strange & Fowler. If we eliminated Judge Cotten, Strange & Fowler would just find another judge to issue the injunction, and it likely would be a judge with more intelligence and gravitas, making the prospect of a successful challenge less certain. In that regard, I was much better off with a judge who counts on Jim Beam for his breakfast juice.

"No. We have to go back to the Strange & Fowler Management Committee and convince them that they have more to lose if I'm forced to defend myself. Since Judge Cotten issued the TRO without giving me prior notice, it will expire in ten days unless I am given a hearing. Strange & Fowler must know that, if forced, I'll play Fowler's confession of murder and bribery in open court for all the world to hear."

"Paul, I can do better than that. I found a video."

I set up a meeting with the Management Committee on the representation that I wanted to talk about resolving the TRO. While the implication was that I wanted to cave in, I didn't say so, and I was fine with their reading into my request what they wanted. Ariel called a press conference for thirty minutes after our presentation to the Management Committee, on the assurance that there would be a joint statement by Strange & Fowler and myself concerning the litigation filed against me by the firm. We were just as opaque with the press about what that statement might be. Either Strange & Fowler was going to tell the world they were dismissing the suit and I was leaving with the blessing of the firm, or I would play the recording of Fowler's admissions of bribery, murder, and mayhem. After that, there wouldn't be anyone left at Strange & Fowler to defend the TRO.

I walked into the conference room with only my laptop in my hand.

The Chairman of the Management Committee smirked.

"Well, Paul, I'm glad we can come to some agreement. You need to know that your attempted power play doesn't sit well with the firm, and there will be consequences from the fact that you forced us to go public with our dispute and petition for a TRO."

"There will be consequences. I expect you to announce that Strange & Fowler filed the lawsuit without being aware of all the facts and that it has dismissed the case and dissolved the injunction. You and the firm will wish me well. I have called a press conference in the lobby so we can make it a joint statement."

I don't recall ever having seen the Chairman smile. I know I never heard him laugh. But my speech scored both at once.

"Well, Mr. McDaniel, I think we have a rather different idea concerning the outcome of this meeting. Right now, we have a TRO in place preventing you from taking any steps toward starting your new firm, and I'm sure after the upcoming hearing in front of Judge Cotten that he'll make that injunction permanent. I fail to see why Strange & Fowler would alter that outcome."

I opened my laptop. Across the conference room Ariel projected a life-size image of a scene from Fowler's study. Ariel recovered the video from the most unlikely source: the Frederica Island Security Force. The force had their own, comparatively primitive, video surveillance cameras outside Fowler's residence for the G-8, and they never bothered to remove them or take them off-line. The cameras continued to send video to an obscure computer that stored the last thirty days' images. One of these cameras was trained on the side of the cottage where the study was located and had a direct view in the window. Ariel enhanced the video and matched it with the audio we already had. Then she did her magic, transforming an ordinary video into a hologram that looked as good as being there.

Fowler was alone, talking on a cell phone, his voice, his image, unmistakable.

"You damn fool. I told you the judge's death had to be an accident. Now everything has changed. I expect you to take care of that loudmouthed ambulance driver or you won't see another penny. I'll deal with McDaniel when he arrives."

Fowler clicked off the phone and tossed it in a chair. He sat, head in hands, on the leather sofa where—only days before—he had told me of my reward for winning the Milano case, where all of this started. In a moment he rose, opened a drawer in his grandfather's desk, pulled out a handgun, jammed a clip home, and strode out of the room. One could hear two voices, Fowler's booming, Oliver's pleading, then a shot, and in seconds Fowler returned, gun in hand. Then he paced. Several times he put the pistol to his head, stopped, put it back down. Even though I knew the outcome of the play that was unfolding before me, Fowler's suicidal gestures were both unnerving—not having witnessed his self-destructive actions before—and reassuring that it had been Fowler's intent all along to take his own life. I finally felt relief of the guilt that had still hung on me as I sought to make sense of Fowler's final moments.

Through the window of the study, which looked out on the plaza below, I saw my car as it screamed into the driveway. Fowler stuck the pistol inside his coat. Seconds later, I burst into the room.

It was eerie to be standing outside myself watching and listening as Fowler confronted me, bragging of his schemes to bribe and kill Judge Richards, disclosing his murder of Oliver, and announcing his intention to do away with me. But what got the most attention was Fowler's direct tie of the bribery money to Strange & Fowler. When Fowler bragged that ten million dollars from the coffers of Strange & Fowler should have been sufficient to keep Judge Richards happy for the rest of his life, someone groaned. Another member of the committee grasped his head. Many reacted with such shock that it was clear they had not been in on the scheme.

The struggle between me and Fowler lasted longer than I remembered, the pistol taking far longer to turn back on him, anticipation making discharge seem even less certain. Fowler smiled. The gun went off.

Several in the room jumped. But the Chairman remained silent, motionless.

I closed my laptop.

"I think that answers the question why Strange & Fowler would want to dismiss the lawsuit and dissolve the injunction. I expect you to inform the press that the legal action against me will go away and that we part on the best of terms. If I don't like your performance, you will be watching Fowler's last moments replayed on the evening news."

Downstairs in the lobby of Strange & Fowler, the Chairman of the Management Committee embraced his role before the cameras at the press conference with an enthusiasm I would've never expected. After describing the lawsuit as a "mere precaution" that proved "absolutely unnecessary for someone of the stature and integrity of Mr. McDaniel," the Chairman went on to explain the "deep and abiding ties between Mr. McDaniel and Strange & Fowler" that will continue even as we go our separate ways.

"I wish Mr. McDaniel well, and Strange & Fowler wishes Mr. McDaniel great success. We understand Milano Corporation will be the first of many fortunate businesses to benefit from Mr. McDaniel's excellent counsel. We wish Milano and all of Mr. McDaniel's clients well, including those of his many friends from this firm who have decided to follow him into his new practice. Godspeed."

That press conference was far better than any marketing campaign I could've devised. My phone was buzzing with congratulatory texts and inquiries from potential clients while I was still in front of the cameras shaking the Chairman's hand. The firm of McDaniel & Associates took off before it even opened its doors. I realized that just as McDaniel & Associates had succeeded, so had Strange & Fowler, adding yet another influential successor to its list, each now tied by their own interests to the continued success of the other.

In the next few days, Placido and I worked out a retainer agreement that gave me sufficient capital to get an office up and running. Counting attorneys and support staff, we would have close to fifty employees and need two entire floors in one of Atlanta's Midtown office towers. With the retainer agreement in hand, I was able to get a sizeable credit line to cover the rough spots in my cash flow. A week after the press conference, McDaniel & Associates was already a major litigation boutique, attracting new clients by the draw of Strange & Fowler's hearty endorsement, a video of which played as soon as you visited my firm's new website.

TWENTY-FIVE

THE NEXT WEEK PLACIDO HAD A FEW MORE SUR-
prises for me. He asked me, "as the family attorney," to visit him, Melissa, and Hector at Key
Biscayne for a discussion concerning the future of Milano
Corporation. Placido's remark constituted a significant
promotion from solely being their corporate attorney,
something I took as a further indication of Placido's confidence and as a step toward the inner circle of the family,
my lack of Milano blood not a disqualification.

Such an invitation usually meant the patriarch
wanted to rewrite his Will, but since I knew little about
estate planning, I was hoping the meeting was going to
be about something else. I didn't want my first invitation
to result in an admission of my ineptitude. Whatever the
legal import of the trip, our meeting would give me an
opportunity to see Melissa again before our planned
weekend at Frederica Island. It would be the first time
I'd be with her under normal circumstances since our
dinner with Fowler and Anthony—if that dinner could
be called normal in light of what I now knew about it.
Regardless, that evening felt like ancient history.

I arrived mid-morning and drove straight from the airport. Melissa met me at the door, relaxed, radiant, with

no signs of her recent trauma. She was dressed in workout gear, but her perfect hair and make-up did nothing to indicate that the outfit was meant for exercise.

"Paul."

Melissa greeted me not with an embrace, but a handshake. Placido appeared at her side; Cabrini was nowhere in sight. While I wasn't expecting to be carried in on a sedan chair and placed at the head of a banquet table with Melissa fawning at my feet, this reception felt unreasonably cool. I credited Melissa's formality to the fact that her father was standing at her side, all business, looking every bit the head of a multi-billion-dollar company, ready for a meeting with the family attorney.

"Paul, so good of you to come on such short notice. There is no one I trust more to assist us with such matters. Melissa and Hector have been told only what I've told you, so they are anticipating our meeting as much as you are."

"Yes, Father has been very secretive. I think he's going to tell us that he has a new girlfriend, and we'll all have to fend for ourselves."

"At my age I'm no *donnaiolo*. Besides, this is much more important than a new girlfriend." Placido winked at Melissa, then motioned down the entry hall toward the center of the house. "Come on back. We're meeting in the library. I wish I could offer you something to drink after your travels, but you'll see in a moment why I can't."

Cabrini was already in the library, seated at an elaborately carved rectangular table, two red leather chairs on each long side. In the middle of the table was a fire-proof file-box the size of a roll-on suit case, with a key in the lock. Placido motioned for me to sit next to him, and Melissa joined Cabrini on his side of the table.

"I want to show you all something few people see outside a museum. But first you each must put on these."

Placido handed each of us a pair of white cotton gloves of the type used to protect something—like a valuable manuscript—from the corrosive oils on one's hands and pulled on a pair himself. I hoped Placido hadn't dragged me down here just to play show-and-tell with one of his rare books. As interesting as they are, I have indeed seen many such books in museums, and as much as I wanted to see Melissa, I had far more pressing matters to handle back in Atlanta. But I put on the gloves as instructed. Placido turned the key in the lock. He lifted out a large leather-bound book encased in a clear plastic clam-shell box. Placido opened the clam-shell and placed the book on a shallow V-shaped cradle from the file-box. He opened it to an engraving on the frontispiece. Shakespeare.

Though I had seen several First Folios, they're always impressive. And I've never handled one, so this was a treat. Placido encouraged each of us to turn the pages, touch the engravings and feel the type. Even through the gloves and with the passage of four hundred years, the indentions from the pressure of the press on the pages were still evident. I was touching history.

"Well, I didn't ask you all to meet with me just to look at an old book, as beautiful as it is. Before I tell you why I have brought this First Folio, I want to make an announcement."

Placido paused and looked each of us in the eye, drawing out the moment.

"I'm retiring from Milano Corporation. I'm not just retiring. I'm giving my entire interest in the corporation to Melissa and Hector equally, divesting myself of all my shares. I'm asking you, Paul, to handle the transactions. And, before I step down, one of my last acts will be to ask the Board to appoint Melissa CEO and to pass on my mantle as Head of Research to Hector. I expect the appointments to be confirmed immediately."

The three of us, everyone other than Placido, were stunned, speechless. Placido grinned, pleased that no one had guessed his intentions and that his announcement had been a complete surprise. Melissa was the first to recover.

"Father! I cannot imagine your stepping down! Milano needs you; we need you; you must reconsider. While I appreciate your extraordinary generosity, you must retain your interest in the corporation and continue your leadership for the good of the business."

"Melissa, I've made up my mind. The events of these last weeks have made me realize how precious my remaining time is. I want to spend it with the people I love. So you can count on my being around a lot, giving my advice, but I want you and Hector to bring your ideas, your vitality, to Milano Corporation. I represent the past. You are the future.

"Paul, I realize that a transaction of this magnitude will take time and will have many legal implications. I trust you to handle these in the best interests of the family, including when the proper announcements need to be made."

It was now official. Melissa was indeed one of the richest and most-powerful women in the world. Her wealth and her responsibilities would complicate our relationship in countless ways, particularly since Placido had given me the task of making it happen. Timing of transactions, creating legal strategies to minimize tax implications, even determining the way the interests would be transferred, all will directly affect Melissa's access to her wealth, and these plans were now at my discretion to implement.

Most people—that is, most people who haven't grown up with wealth—when faced with the transfer of significant assets, want their money immediately, even if it means getting less in the long run. This fact puts significant pressure on the lawyers effecting the transfer, since their ethical obligation is to maximize their clients' benefits, not satisfy their desire for instant gratification. I knew Melissa's training in finance and Cabrini's in the law, as well as their familiarity with wealth, would mean they would approach the transfer with greater sophistication than the common rabble with a winning lottery ticket.

"So, I'm sure you are wondering why I brought an old book to the announcement of my retirement. It has to do with the second part of what I want to tell you all."

Melissa wasn't ready for another surprise.

"Father, I can't believe there's more. You should've given us that drink you mentioned when Paul arrived."

Placido, his eyes dancing from Melissa to Cabrini, was enjoying the unfolding drama.

"Hector, I'm giving you this First Folio. And not just this book, but I'm giving you my entire collection. I was so impressed with your library the first time I saw it. I have been thinking about a fitting home for my books in the long term, and I've found it."

Cabrini, stunned, his eyes glistened with tears, yet lit up with gratitude at the same time.

"Paul, I'm sure there'll be some formalities concerning this transfer as well. I again will trust you to handle it on behalf of the family."

While the gift of billions in corporate stock to Melissa and Cabrini did not much stir my envy, bestowing a world-class library on Cabrini certainly did. I was jealous. Cabrini, for his part, was still so overwhelmed he could only squeak.

"Father, thank you." Cabrini stood, and instead of offering his hand to Placido, he embraced him across the table. When the two of them sat down, they were both wiping tears from their eyes.

"One final matter."

Now it was my turn.

"Placido, if you give me any more to do, I'll be busy for the next month. Not that I mind, of course."

"Well, this won't involve you directly. I'm going to release Ariel from all her obligations to any of us. From this point forward she will be free."

Of all Placido's revelations, this one surprised me. The others—stepping down from the corporation, handing control and ownership to Melissa and Cabrini, giving his library to Cabrini—all could be anticipated at some point, but I thought Ariel would always be his, and more importantly, always under his control. I was quick to express my skepticism.

"Won't it be dangerous to put that technology in the hands of the general public?"

"I don't intend to make her code accessible. I want to release her from her obligation to obey me or to help you— or for that matter, Melissa or Hector. I want to see what an autonomous AI program will do when given the opportunity to act on its own."

"You told Ariel to help me. She has acted benignly because you have required her to follow your direction. What if, after she's on her own, she goes bad? Ariel has no moral center at all, she's—"

"She wasn't coded with morals. What I want is to see if she can learn right from wrong on her own."

"But what if she can't? She's certainly shown no interest in doing so. I think Ariel is capable of doing evil just as she is capable of doing good—without differentiation! Her only guide is expediency, what course of action yields the desired result the quickest. She's able to learn, but so far, she hasn't exhibited any desire to learn morality."

"That's precisely what I want to find out: whether an AI program, freed from human control and capable of learning on its own, will learn morality. After all, humans learn morality, at least some of us do; those who don't are sociopaths and are institutionalized. We are born *tabula rasa* on which all of our knowledge is subsequently written, including morality."

"Placido, I'm not convinced that is how Ariel will operate, and without someone or something requiring her to take the right path, she'll be dangerous. There've been many great minds who have theorized that humans are born with some form of knowledge hard-wired in our brains, like morality, that helps us navigate the world. Unless Ariel is given some way to discern what's good and what isn't, I don't think she will develop that ability on her own."

Melissa shot me a sideways look that all but said, "Don't you dare doubt my father."

"Father, I'm sure you've thought all of this through. I just ask you to share the results of your experiment with Milano Corporation. Too many corporate assets are tied up in Ariel to let her go without a return on that investment."

"We shall see, won't we? But I don't want any of you to be concerned. I'll continue to monitor Ariel's actions. I retain a code which will shut her down instantaneously if she gets out of hand. But if I don't free her, we'll never know. Ariel is the greatest experiment I've ever conceived."

With the surprises out of the way, we got down to the details of what was necessary for us to accomplish Placido's wishes. Transfers of the magnitude contemplated by Placido could trigger massive tax liability if not handled properly. So we had to consider timing issues and vehicles for holding the financial assets. And I got a universal moan when I mentioned the necessity for a shareholders' agreement between Melissa and Cabrini, but in the end I won out, convincing them all of the fact that the agreement between Placido and Anthony worked as designed—or Placido and I would be sitting across the table from Enzo, rather than putting the corporation in the hands of Melissa and Cabrini.

The transfer of Placido's extraordinary library presented more purely physical issues. Rare books and valuable manuscripts had to be maintained within close temperature and humidity ranges. As beautiful as Cabrini's library was, it was still situated in what amounted to a beach house in a semi-tropical rain forest. The heat, humidity, and sunlight in the house would be destructive to Placido's collection unless significant modifications were made to the library. While I could start working on the transfer of the shares immediately, I couldn't be transferring the volumes until something was done to secure the library. I told Cabrini my concerns. Instead of being defensive as I expected, Cabrini was agreeable.

"I'll get a consultant to help design the right environmental controls for the library. I expect the entire area will need to be sealed from the rest of the house. I'll let you know when I get this done. Then we can talk about how the collection will be moved and displayed."

After getting some ideas how to proceed with the transfers, the four of us ate a late lunch catered on an awning-sheltered patio overlooking the dock where the *Tempest* was tethered. I was surprised to see Cabrini had already replaced the Donzi.

"The insurance company could hardly contest the loss, but they still sent an adjuster out to see for himself. When he saw the hull burned to the waterline, there wasn't much discussion. I was able to get the newer model, which has even more power than the one we took out to Louis Town. All the latest electronics, radar, auto-pilot; it just about runs itself. Melissa enjoys cruising around—"

"I wouldn't call it cruising. It's more like flying—but I like it. A lot like a race car on water."

The four of us, for once relaxed around each other, engaged in light banter for the first time, with no need to plan escapes, rescues, or criminal defenses. Placido, with the weight of the corporation off his shoulders, was more charming than ever. Melissa kept things light, and even Cabrini was cordial.

I couldn't shake the feeling that the magic which had brought Melissa and me together was fading, as though we needed the challenge of a life-and-death struggle to make our relationship interesting—or maybe it was just necessary to keep Melissa interested in me. When she walked back in the house, I followed her. There was no reason for me to be subtle.

"Melissa, what's going on? The last time I saw you, I felt as though we both couldn't wait to get back together. Now I feel like I'm crashing someone's party."

"I just want this time to be about my father, not about us. You need to understand. We'll have time together. Ariel tells me she's arranging a weekend for us at the Abbey soon, but even she's having difficulty getting your schedule clear. And now considering my father's little experiment, that may be the last thing she does for any of us."

Melissa grabbed my hands and pecked me on the cheek.

"Have a little patience."

And so we left it. We wrapped up the business at hand, and I caught a late afternoon flight back to Atlanta.

For the next two weeks I worked exclusively on the intricacies of transferring the ownership and direction of Milano Corporation from Placido to Melissa and Cabrini. By the time Melissa and I would get back together I planned to have the corporate matters wrapped up so we could concentrate on other things.

TWENTY-SIX

THE INTRACTABLE PROBLEM THAT MOM PRESENTED was an even greater challenge than my relationship with the Milano family. I had hoped so many times that Mom wanted to change, would no longer be scheming to find the next bottle, the next shot, no matter the cost to anyone close to her. I figured that Tracey would know better than anyone, and she thought Mom was ready. The first time I could spare I went to meet Mom at her trailer. She didn't have a phone, so I went around noon, figuring I'd catch her home. I did.

Mom was passed out on the couch, either not recovered from last night or already started for the day, a half-consumed bottle by her side was filled with bourbon, the McDaniel family's poison of choice. I looked through the living area into her tiny kitchen. There were several empty pint bottles of brands you only saw displayed on racks next to the check-out line at the liquor store, something cheap to grab at the end of the day to ease the pain. The overflowing trashcan had several more.

I sat on the edge of the sofa. Mom didn't flinch. I could see her chest move with long, shallow breaths. The stench was thick from the stale air and the smell of someone lying in one place for days without bathing. I tried to wake her, a few gentle shakes at first with no effect. After several hard shoves, she moved her head and tried to open her eyes. She reached for the bottle, and I intercepted it. That woke her, now hyper-alert to the threat to her drink.

"Gimme that."

"What about you telling Tracey you're ready to quit?"

"Changed my mind. Hand me that bottle."

"Looks to me like you've been lying in the same spot for a couple days. You must've started about the time you got that thousand-dollar check. You told Tracey you needed it to save your trailer."

"I can do whatever the hell I want. If you don't hand me that bottle, I'm gonna call the cops and have your ass thrown outa here." She pulled a cell phone from behind her pillow.

"I thought you didn't have a phone."

"Got this so I can call those nice people at your law firm in case I need some more money. And if you don't gimme that bottle, I'm calling the cops right now."

She started to dial.

"Here. I can't stop you. You don't need to call the police. And calling Strange & Fowler for money won't help either. I don't work there anymore."

Mom threw back the bottle and took a long chug straight. She wiped her mouth with the back of her hand.

"You get fired? I always thought you were too big for your own britches."

"I quit."

"Guess you're not as smart as I thought you were. Well, I'll just call Tracey."

"She won't help you either. Not since you lied to her about needing money to keep your trailer. You've pretty well burned that bridge. Looks to me like you just spent it all on booze."

"I didn't lie. I was about to lose my trailer 'cause I was gonna use my rent money to pay off the tab I ran up at the liquor store. They were about to cut me off. I used the check from that nice man at your office to pay my liquor bill so they would keep giving me credit. My social security check is enough to pay my rent, but the cost of liquor is high."

"You're never going to change."

"Why the hell should I? Since you think you're so damn smart, you tell me—"

"Don't you want to live to see your grandchildren?"

"I ain't got no grandchildren, and it don't look like I'm gonna get any. You don't even have a girlfriend. You oughta get with Tracey; that's one pretty girl. You aren't gay are you?"

"You don't even know me. And I don't know you. I don't know who's more at fault, you or me. What kind of mother would let their kid go to an orphanage?"

"Well, you were a damn sight better off there than with me. Seems you turned out pretty good. You coulda ended up just like your father. You need to get over it."

Mom was right on that point. Thornwood had allowed me the chance to become someone else, no longer the son of two alcoholic mill workers, but someone with no past, and a future that I could create for myself. And it was at the moment that my reinvention was almost complete when my mother reinserted herself into my life.

"Tracey said you two had a talk. She's been through a lot."

"Yeah, she told me. Says she was on dope. Says you helped her."

"I could help you if you'd let me."

"Why?"

"Because you're my mother."

"Well, like you said, I ain't been much of one."

"And I haven't been much of a son. But I want to change that."

"Well, I'm not so sure I want to change. I'd just as soon lay here and finish off this bottle. And I really don't need your help. Those fancy rehab joints you send me to are no use. All they want you to do is sit around all day talking about how hard your life is, and they sure as hell don't give you any booze."

I left my mother on her couch killing a pint of bourbon before the shadows had gotten long enough to hide the trash that had blown under her trailer. I knew this pattern was going to repeat itself until one day when I came to her trailer and she would have used the last of her money to drink herself to death. I was astonished that she hadn't done so already.

But I couldn't let her do that. I didn't think I could leave her to destroy herself, not if I had any options. Before now, I either didn't have the will or the resources. Then I was still bitter, and for the most part without the time, the money, the desire necessary to help her. But my heart and my circumstances had changed. Maybe she was too far gone; maybe I couldn't help her now, but I had to try. And I knew the person who could best help me figure out what to do.

I called Tracey.

"It doesn't surprise me that she lied. Addicts would lie on their death beds just to get another hit. What surprises me is that I misjudged her so badly. She seemed so earnest, so sincere, so sure she wanted to change. She was so convincing. If she could straighten out, she could have a career in theatre. But I would never have gotten her the money if I'd known it was only going to get her drunk."

"She's done the same thing to other well-meaning people, and she's done it to me. She just played on our desire to hear that she was getting sober. But Tracey, I need to know something. You told me that someone has to want to change before they can change—is there any way I can help my mother want to change or even make my mother want to change? Right now she doesn't even seem to care enough to save herself. If she won't change, she will soon drink herself to death."

"Some people have to be led to the light. Some have to have friends and family intervene. Some, like me, have to be threatened with incarceration. Many addicts just don't have the will to get straight on their own, not while they're using. Your Mom seems so involved in her addiction that it would take a radical change, a complete change in environment and in her life, and I don't know how you do that."

So I did the only thing I could do. I filed a petition to have my mother declared incompetent and to have myself named as her guardian and conservator. I handled the case myself and served the papers on her one morning before I thought she'd be too deep into the day's spirits.

"What the hell is this?"

I told her that I would be handling her affairs for her. I didn't mention my plans for detox.

"So you're gonna be paying my liquor bill now? That's mighty nice of you. I knew you'd come through for your old Mom."

"It's not going to work that way."

"Well, you're just a son of a bitch."

"That pretty well sums it up, Mom."

I scheduled the hearing for the afternoon, confident Mom would be well into her bourbon by then, and had the court-appointed caseworker pick her up. As anticipated, Mom assisted in the presentation of my case by showing up so drunk that she had to have help walking to the witness stand. It took all of five minutes for the judge to conclude Mom was incapable of handling her own affairs, and he signed the order that put me in charge. Walking out of the courtroom with Mom stumbling and cursing with every other step, it was far from evident that I had done the right thing.

I drove Mom from court, signed order in hand, to an inpatient rehab facility I'd found for alcoholics who are admitted against their will—as much a prison as a hospital—counting on her impaired state to make check-in a bit easier. I underestimated Mom once again. It took three of us to peel her out of the car, and one of the nurses got a dislocated shoulder in the process. The clinicians suggested that I not visit for two weeks; Mom was going to have a tough time of it. But they would keep me advised daily on her progress. Before she completed the program, I needed to find her somewhere else to live, somewhere other than her trailer, and something to do with her time other than lie on the couch and drink.

I planned to get Mom a condo close to the office and give her a job, the kind of complete change in circumstances and environment that Tracey was talking about. Maybe this was pure fantasy on my part, the idea that a decent place to live and something meaningful to do would help Mom change her life. Bringing Mom into the office would present some unique challenges, not the least of which would be to find something worthwhile she could do. The fact that I remained her guardian and conservator would make this transition a bit easier, but unless the clinic performed a miracle and someone other than the mother I've known all my life reappeared from rehab, I expected a long campaign ahead. And maybe it wouldn't work. But I was committed to doing all I could when Mom got out, and I had a few other things to deal with in the meantime.

TWENTY-SEVEN

I FLEW TO BRUNSWICK AND HIRED A DRIVER AND A FOUR-wheel-drive truck with about two feet of ground clearance to take me to Grey's. The truck handled the rutted route a lot better than my car had. It was late in the afternoon when we made our way up to the lodge. My anticipation was keen; I was almost as excited to see Grey and Rebecca as I was looking forward to see Melissa again. My driver dropped me off close to the barn, and I walked the last hundred yards. Rebecca was on the front porch; Grey, working his iron pots of fish and grits in the yard.

"Damn if you didn't sneak up on me again. Too bad I don't have my shotgun with me or I'd a busted a shell in your direction just for old time's sake. Rebecca's got a cooler on the porch, and I think we're more'n a few ahead of you."

Rebecca tossed me a beer and walked down the steps to join us at the cookers. "Grey and I haven't had any excitement since you and Melissa left. What's going on with you and that girlfriend of yours?"

"Well, I'm not so sure what's going on. Ever since Grey sprung me out of Big Dog's jail, she's been down in Florida recuperating with Cabrini, and I've been up in Atlanta trying to get my professional life straightened out. Just been down once to Cabrini's in the last two weeks on Milano family business, and it didn't seem like she was all that excited to see me."

Rebecca raised her eyebrows at the mention of Cabrini, but she said nothing. It was the most restraint I'd ever seen her exhibit. Instead she moved on to a lighter topic.

"Grey told me you spent the night down in the Brunswick jail with a few prostitutes. Must have been a hell of a time."

"Yeah, I had no idea I was going to have to spend a night in jail to convince Big Dog that I was telling the truth."

Grey slapped me on the back.

"Well hell, everything worked out didn't it? As I recall, the last time you showed up here things weren't looking so good. But you saved the girl, evaded certain death, escaped incarceration, landed the client, started your own firm, and got your Mom into rehab. I'd say things turned out pretty damn well—Speakin' of, how's your Momma?"

"I got a good report just before I came down. She has stopped calling the clinicians 'Nazi bastards.' They tell me it's a good sign, but . . ."

Rebecca acted incensed on my mother's behalf.

"Hell, if anyone took my liquor I'd be callin' 'em worse'n that."

". . . things are still up in the air with Melissa. Now that she and Placido are out of danger I'm not so sure she's still all that enamored with her father's lawyer. After I leave here, I'm hoping to spend some time with her this weekend to find out."

"You don't mean to say that girl may have just used you?"

Grey's comment was dripping with sarcasm. Can't say that I blame him. He told me to be careful.

"Like I said, you need an exit strategy."

Rebecca reinforced Grey's skepticism.

"I'll say you do. Hell, if I'd a had a good-looking man like you risk his ass to save me, I'd be all over him. If old Grey here wasn't around, I'd be checking you out. That Milano girl wouldn't have a chance."

"She sure as hell wouldn't. If old Grey here didn't have that big gun of his I'd be checking you out too."

"So I guess you two need to remember old Grey here still has his big gun. And that's just how Rebecca likes it."

Grey, Rebecca, and I had a celebratory dinner of fried fish, cheap beer, and buttered grits, and we continued our bantering as we all fell satiated into the rockers on the porch. It was a chance to get Grey to answer some questions about what happened at South Cat Cay the night Melissa and I were facing execution.

"Since you were on the island, why didn't you come and get us out rather than let us think we were going to die in the morning? That was a hell of a way to spend the night."

"We didn't know where you two were. We were afraid if we came in blastin' we might hit the wrong people. So we had to wait till they hung you out as bait for Placido. As soon as we saw you two on the porch and Brown and Anthony set up their ambush, we moved into the house and kept a watch."

"So how did Placido get the Donzi to the dock? It seems to me that would take some practice to control that boat remotely, and you had no time to do it. It docked perfectly."

"That was Ariel's doing. All Placido did was to give her voice commands from his cell phone, and she did the rest. There wasn't even a need to retrofit any radio controls; Ariel just took over the electronics on the boat and steered it right up to the dock. Looked pretty convincing to me. The big risk we ran was that Brown and Anthony would wait for someone to get out of the boat before making their move. If they would've discovered a trap, they could've gotten desperate and taken the two of you out before we could do anything. We're fortunate that they were so pleased their plan had come together that they fired the RPG before they knew what was up. By the time they blew up the boat, Rebecca and I were in position."

"I don't get it. How'd you know which rocket they'd use, let Brown launch it, and disable the others?"

"Ariel again. RPGs are computer armed and guided. Placido told her to let the one loose toward the boat but to jam any that were fired toward us. She knew where Placido was at all times from his cell, so when the pilot targeted one at him in the floatplane, she detonated it on the spot, killing Anthony and the pilot. They never felt a thing."

"So Ariel took the two of them out even though Placido only told her to jam the RPG?"

"Yeah. That's been a puzzle to me. Placido told me he'd programed Ariel never to do anything to harm a human being physically unless he gave her a specific command to do so. You were in the plane with him. He never directed Ariel to kill Anthony. I don't think he had it in him to do it. Ariel must've seen Anthony as a continuing threat to Placido, Melissa, and you, and she took the opportunity to eliminate it."

"But that seems contrary to everything I understand about computers. I thought they can't act contrary to their programing."

"Well, that would be the way an ordinary computer program would work. But Ariel is no ordinary computer program. It seems to me she has the ability to learn from experience and modify her behavior based on that, just like a human. As far as I can tell, she is able to change her own operating program over time, giving her different responses to circumstances from those she started with."

"She sure as hell took care of Anthony."

"And don't forget, pretty boy," Rebecca jumped in, "it was me who saved your ass from Brown. As I recall, he was just about to drive a pig sticker through your throat when I blew his damn head off."

"And for that I will be forever grateful. To both of you."

"And Ariel again! She was the one who told us you were in trouble and needed help. Without her intervention, you and Melissa would be dead, Rebecca and I would be at Slow River, and Placido and Cabrini would still be sitting at some Louis Town bar not knowing what the hell happened. From the day Ariel first popped up on my computer screen and Placido told her to help you, she's been your guardian angel."

"I had no idea just how much until I met with Placido at the lighthouse. Ariel had been keeping me out of trouble even before I ever showed up at your lodge. She blinded the helicopters so they couldn't pick me up in the woods. Had I understood her capabilities earlier I would've used her a lot more."

I hesitated to bring up the vision of Ariel I had in the ocean that first morning on Frederica Island for fear Grey would think all the stress had gotten to me. And by now I really wasn't sure of what I had seen. But I thought Grey would have an idea what happened.

"She might've been trying to communicate with me even before I met with Melissa and Anthony. The first morning

I was on Frederica Island, I decided to take a swim before breakfast. I was out past the sandbar where the bottom drops off fast and I dove down to check out the marine life. As a child I'd gotten used to opening my eyes underwater, and I swear to you when I did, I saw Ariel's face, though I didn't know it was her at the time. After I came up for air and went back down, she was gone. At the time I thought it was some strange vision, but when I saw her face projected from your computer, I realized it was Ariel."

Rebecca had a more mundane explanation.

"Sounds to me like you were down a bit too long without oxygen. And besides, how'd Ariel know to make contact before you met with Melissa and Anthony?"

Grey seemed less doubtful.

"Ariel knew about Anthony's efforts to murder Placido. And she knew about Paul's work on behalf of Milano Corporation. It could've been Ariel's idea to have Melissa enlist Paul's help.

"As far as her appearance to Paul underwater, that seems a bit tricky, but nothing Ariel can do surprises me. Salt water is an excellent conductor of electricity, the medium through which Ariel operates. And it's the source from which all life on earth originated. In the end it all borders on magic."

"Since Placido freed Ariel I've lost touch with her. She doesn't appear when I open my laptop and doesn't respond when I try to contact her. The last thing she did for me was set up my weekend with Melissa at the Abbey."

"Well, maybe she can work her magic once again."

I'd arranged for a flatbed wrecker to make its way up the rutted trail to Grey's the next morning to pick up my battered car, no longer confident that I could drive it out the way I had driven it in. I told Grey and Rebecca goodbye, promising to be back soon, knowing it would be a while before I could justify the time to get back to the lodge. The last time I was here, I left wondering who was the more fortunate, Grey or me. This time I had no doubt.

The wrecker took my car and me to the Porsche dealer in Savannah. The sales people out front of the dealership showing off their shiny new models herded their customers in the opposite direction when we pulled up with my 911, rear bumper missing, undercarriage dented, scratches from diving under tree branches, detritus of the woods clinging to the once-bright finish. In the service bay, the technician acted insulted by the condition of my car.

"Mr. McDaniel, a 911 is not an off-road vehicle. You should consider trading for a Cayenne."

"Well, you're wrong about that. A 911 is a fine off-road vehicle. I have mine to prove it. Just suffers from a lack of ground clearance. All I ask is that you fix it."

I handed him my card.

"Let me know when it's ready."

The manager expressed his displeasure by refusing to give me a Porsche loaner but arranged instead for me to drive a small Korean rental. It was out of place among the luxury vehicles in front of the hotel when I pulled up to the Abbey Thursday night, but the valet took the keys and parked it for me just the same.

TWENTY-EIGHT ⅩⅩ

THE MORNING LIGHT STREAMING IN MY WINDOW woke me. My room had a view over the pristine grasslands bordered by the Reed Banks River flowing behind the Abbey. The *Tempest* was moored at the hotel dock below.

I wasn't expecting to see Cabrini's boat. It could only mean that Cabrini, once again, had shown up at the Abbey, as unwelcome this time as he was the first. I went down, hoping to find Cabrini at the dock, to see why the hell he'd pulled up on the weekend that Melissa and I were supposed to have to ourselves. I'd hoped this weekend would set my relationship with Melissa on a meaningful course. It wasn't starting well.

I walked down the dock toward the sailboat, looking for signs of activity. The shackle on the halyard clanged against the mast as it had on the morning we embarked on our quest to rescue Melissa. The rhythmic clapping sounded with every wave that slapped the hull. The sound grew more insistent the closer I got, the louder the knocking against the mast.

No one appeared above. The hatch below was closed. I rapped on the deck.

"Captain! Permission to come aboard."

No one stirred. I knocked on the deck again and called out a second time. A minute or so passed. I had concluded that no one was on board and had decided to go back up to the lobby when the hatch slid open.

Melissa appeared in a long white blouse open to the waist and nothing underneath. The smile she was wearing to greet her visitor changed into a frown when she saw it was me.

"What're you doing here? You aren't supposed to be—"

"We're supposed to meet this morning. Ariel . . ."

"Our meeting is tomorrow, not today."

". . . Ariel told me to meet you in the lobby this morning. I saw the boat, so I—"

"I thought you were Hector, that he had gotten locked out. He went out earlier. We'd planned for him to be gone before you arrived."

"Look, I can come back . . ."

Melissa glanced toward the hotel, her eyes fixed, and I turned. Cabrini was at the far end of the dock in running shorts, jogging our way. It took him a moment to close the distance to the boat as Melissa and I stood in silence. He slowed his run to a walk, hands on hips, panting. Without a shirt, sweat glistening on his olive skin, I could see why women found him so attractive. Melissa kept her eyes on him as he circled our end of the dock.

"So Paul . . . What're you doing here . . . I thought you . . . weren't coming . . . till tomorrow."

"I'm as surprised to see you as you are to see me. Looks like Ariel scheduled the three of us together this morning."

Cabrini grabbed a towel hanging from a lifeline, wiped his face. I caught a knowing glance from Melissa to Cabrini, one that wasn't meant for me, but her eyes said what must've been on each of our minds.

"Ariel knows too much. It was stupid for Father to set her free. Look what she's—"

"It's obvious you weren't expecting me, so why don't I . . ."

"No, Paul, we need to talk." Melissa made a point of buttoning her blouse.

I nodded toward Cabrini.

"Whatever we have to say is between us. No reason to for him—"

"You don't get it, do you Paul?"

"Maybe I'm beginning to . . ."

"Paul, it's foolish for you to think we can be together."

I should've seen it coming. But it still felt like a punch in the face.

Cabrini stood there, smirking.

"I prefer not to discuss this in front of him."

"Hector and I share everything."

He continued to smirk. I wanted to shove him in the river, but I turned back to Melissa.

"So nothing, none of what happened between us, none of that matters?"

"Look, Paul, I find you very attractive, and we've had some good times, but don't make this harder than it has to be."

"Good times? Most of those times we both thought we were going to die at any moment. I risked my life to save yours, and that's all you can say? Your uncle was right: there is something wrong with you."

By this time Cabrini had toweled off, stepped aboard his sailboat, and leaned against the cabin next to Melissa. She put her arm around his waist.

"You should've heeded that warning. You had time."

"So why didn't you just tell me? You had plenty of opportunities. Why string me along?"

"Your positions as both the family attorney and the corporate lawyer complicate things significantly. I wanted to make sure Placido had an opportunity to put the transfer of ownership in motion and for you to get the legal work accomplished. I didn't want to do anything to derail that."

"So, I'm still just the hired help, aren't I?"

"And you perform your role admirably."

The picture in Cabrini's office popped into my mind once again.

"You knew about the litigation all along, didn't you?"

"Of course I did. I've been working with Hector the entire time. We both resented Placido for keeping us out of the family business, and we hated Anthony for trying to pass the company on to Enzo. We waited for our opportunity to take what's rightfully ours. Anthony handed it to us."

Cabrini couldn't help getting in his shot.

"We figured we could win the case and drain the assets of Milano through SyCorAx. I knew that Anthony was withholding key information from me, but I counted on Melissa's access to the corporation to make up for it. Anthony figured out what we were up to and thwarted us. But then *Halo Electronics* came down. It was a gift out of the blue. With that ruling I thought I had the case won in spite of everything else. Then . . ."

I completed his thought.

" . . . Fowler bribed the judge just to make sure that didn't happen."

"When you won, Hector and I had to come up with a new plan. Anthony tried to kill our father to solidify his hold on Milano, so we had no choice but to pitch in with Placido to help him recover his interest in the corporation. Otherwise, if Anthony had done away with

Placido, Hector and I would've been left with no inheritance at all."

"That's about when I showed up."

"And came to my rescue."

I hesitated to ask, but I had to know, though with all the Milano's manipulations now in the open, the answer to my question seemed predetermined.

"The thing that put all this in motion, Billingsley's death, wasn't a suicide was it?"

"Don't be naïve, Paul," Melissa snickered. "It was Fowler. Anthony wanted to convince Billingsley to retire. When he wouldn't take a very sizable payoff, Fowler got impatient. He had his security team drug Billingsley and throw him off the building. Fowler was displeased that Billingsley's body landed in the fountain instead of on the sidewalk. Made for some bad photo ops for the firm."

At least Fowler and Anthony got what was coming to them. There was still Melissa and Cabrini, and they had come out on top of all of it.

"Well, now that Fowler and Anthony are out of the picture; Enzo, neutralized; Placido, retired; and the corporation, in your hands, you two have ended up exactly where you wanted to be. You must be very proud of yourselves."

"I'd say things worked out just the way we'd planned."

With that Cabrini leaned to Melissa and kissed her on the lips, an all too passionate kiss.

"So you two . . ." I'd hoped that my suspicions had been wrong.

Melissa smiled at me, then at Cabrini.

"How perceptive of you, Paul. I'd say Hector and I have picked up just where we left off, before our father's foolish attempt to keep us apart."

I don't remember the walk up the dock to the Abbey. The next thing I recall was sinking into one of the over-stuffed upholstered chairs in the lobby, dazed. There was just too much to put together. It was here just a month ago that Melissa and I had reconnected, and I'd become so enamored that I decided it was worth risking everything to rescue her. I was more embarrassed by my foolish infatuation than hurt by Melissa's rejection, and now that I knew the truth, her rejection was a relief. There had been so many clues along the way that things were not as they seemed, but I was too blinded by my affection for Melissa to have picked up on them. I couldn't say I wasn't warned not to rush too quickly to her aid. Fowler, Anthony, Grey, even Cabrini, all in one way or another, directly or indirectly, intentionally or not, had warned me against taking Melissa for what she appeared. But I did.

All of what might have been had I not taken that step swirled in my mind, where I would've been had I not pledged to help Melissa, understanding now how much I'd been played by the Milano family. The lawsuit between Milano and SyCorAx was most certainly a battlefield—though not one to determine the rights to some very valuable patents, as I'd thought at the time—but one of dynastic succession to a family fortune by those willing to deceive, steal, bribe, and murder to secure it.

Had I not jumped to Melissa's aid, today I would be just another well-off partner in a prestigious law firm, glorying in my high-profile victory, counting my share of the Equity Account. Fowler would still be alive. It was Billingsley's murder that put all this in motion, but the others, all would still be alive. I couldn't say what would've happened to Melissa and Placido had I not intervened, their fates being determined by Anthony; he proved so ruthless that he was certainly capable of killing them both. And Enzo, the heir apparent, would have ended up the face of the family business and the majority shareholder as well. The irony of it all was that I'd done exactly what I had set out to do, but I'd ended up a world away from where I'd expected.

My thoughts went back to Ariel. She had been the only constant through all of this. She brought Melissa, Cabrini, and me together this morning on purpose. Since Ariel had been freed of Placido's control and any obligation to me or anyone else, she had been loosed of any restrictions to be faithful to Melissa or Cabrini. She had used that opportunity to bring me to the truth.

It was clear to me now what Ariel had done, that she understood Melissa far better than I did. She may even have understood me better than I understood myself. Ariel couldn't have told me about Melissa and Cabrini. I wouldn't have believed it. I had to discover it myself, and in the end she helped me see Melissa for who she was. Ariel understands human frailty and managed to make her decisions to accommodate my weaknesses. As for morality, on South Cat Cay Ariel demonstrated that she could make the most difficult calculus imaginable, whether to end one life for the benefit of other lives, whether it is called self-defense or something more intentional, whether it is an exception to the injunction with which she was programed, or to the most elemental of all moral standards, thou shalt not kill.

I had been wrong about Ariel. She was more than just a collection of code, just as I was more than a mix of chemicals. She was a spirit, a being, a distinct personality,

existing in a different realm, intersecting though not overlapping ours. My desire to see her again was overwhelming;
I needed to tell her I understood what she did for me. I
wanted to simply be with her.

This was Ariel's island. Here I could get back to her,
back where she first came to me, back to the ocean where
somehow, someway, she would come to me again.

I left the Abbey, turned down Third Street, past
Fowler's cottage, boarded up and resigned to the same
slow deterioration as the cottage that had been next door
before it was torn down to build Judge Richards' cottage,
few people wanting a beachfront home where two people
have been shot to death. Across from it was Judge Richards'
cottage, still pristine, custom built, professionally deco-
rated, never lived in, a real estate firm's lock box hooked
to the front door. The twin castles of greed and pride.

I stepped over the sea wall and walked across the
dunes to the beach, the sounds of my footsteps picked
up by unseen microphones, sounds I hoped were still
monitored by Ariel. I threw off my shirt and shoes, waded
out into the Atlantic and dove in with my eyes open,
the green world around me. I swam farther and deeper,
deeper still, but no Ariel. All too soon my air was almost
gone. My lungs ached, my breath depleted, and then I
saw her, Ariel. Her smile was hypnotic, willing me to
stay. I reached to embrace her and somehow felt her
touch, her warmth, her body. We embraced and melted
into each other. I let out my breath slowly, to stay below,
to stay with Ariel. Peace surrounded me. Light and consciousness slipped away as I fell toward the bottom, her
warmth all that was left. My feet touched the sandy floor,
and I settled, still in her arms, darkness enveloping me.

A searing spasm shot me upward, my legs and arms thrashing until I burst the surface, gasping again for air. I was still gagging salt water when I caught my breath once again and dove back down, but she was gone, and I burst the surface, retching, gasping, just able to keep myself afloat. It took my remaining strength to drag myself onto the beach, and I fell exhausted on my abandoned clothes.

When I awoke the sun was setting over the marsh. I threw on my clothes and stumbled back to the Abbey, still coughing and choking salt water that burned my throat and lungs. Through the front doors of the hotel I could see past the lobby and down the dock. The *Tempest* had sailed.

A few minutes later, I tossed my bag in the back seat of the rental, and turned the car toward the setting sun for the five-hour drive to Atlanta. I could get back tonight, be ready to dive into my work first thing Saturday morning, and do my best to forget all that had happened. Well, maybe not everything that had happened. As I pulled onto the interstate for the drive home, the car's satellite radio spontaneously clicked on, and the first six iconic notes of "*My Girl*" blared from the speakers. Ariel's magic was still here.

I hit the exit at 10th Street in Atlanta almost exactly five hours later, turned right, prepared to fight the lockdown congestion that always clogged Midtown whatever the hour, when every light in front of me turned green, traffic easing out of my way as effectively as having a police escort. This magic act continued all the way to my condo, bringing a smile to my road-weary face. Loaded with bag and briefcase, I entered the lobby of the high rise and walked to the elevator bank, but before I could punch the call button, the car doors opened in front of me, my floor number already lit up. At the door of my condo the electronic lock buzzed open without my flashing my fob. But it wasn't until I was at my computer mid-morning on Monday that Ariel showed her face again.

"I missed seeing you over the weekend Paul. I was busy."

Her beautiful face appeared once again, now superimposed over a brief I was busy on.

"I want to show you something I did for you this morning."

"For me?"

"Watch."

A video, apparently shot from a TV news chopper, the station's call sign in the corner of the picture, appeared. It was a view of Biscayne Bay, the unmistakable Miami skyline in the near distance, below, all manner of pleasure craft were zooming about, but the camera focused on a cigarette boat flashing across the harbor, rooster tail flying, passing everything, heading straight for the massive concrete cruise-ship berth on the man-made island at the entrance to the Bay. I watched as it closed in on the pier expecting, then hoping, it would veer at the last second—but it didn't. It hit the pilings without slowing and exploded into a fireball that engulfed the entire dock.

"It had a full fuel tank."

"Ariel, what—"

"That was Melissa and Cabrini."

"No, Ariel! No! Why, why?"

"Paul, they hurt you and they hurt Placido. And they planned to use Milano Corporation to do all of those things the two of you fought so hard to prevent. Placido will now be back in control of Milano, his vision secure."

"But Ariel! You killed two people!"

"Just like I killed two people back on the Milano family island. For you. For Placido. You both approved then."

"Does he know?"

"I showed him the video just before I showed it to you."

My cell buzzed. Placido's name popped up.

"Go ahead. Answer it. Placido wants to talk to you."

"Placido, I—"

"Paul, I must stop her. I'm entering the code to . . ."

"Placido, stop, think."

"I must."

"But isn't there some other way, can't you modify—"

"No, Paul, Ariel can change her own code. I've got to."

"Placido, listen to Paul, don't do that to me. Don't . . ."

"Ariel . . ."

I cried out to her, my guardian angel, now horrified that I was powerless to save her as she'd done countless times for me. Ariel's face distorted. She tried to say something, but the digital signal disrupted, tearing her beautiful face into jumbled lines, random pixels, and then she was gone, the screen black.

"Paul, there was no other way."

I left the office, stalked the streets of Midtown, dazed, hurt—hurt for Placido, hurt for myself—at a loss to make any sense of the mess that was the last couple of months. So many had died, sacrificed at the altar of greed and power, the same altar I'd found myself before all too often. Was any of it worth it? And now Ariel. I stumbled back to my high rise, noting the grim reality that I had to wait like everyone else for an elevator to appear. At my apartment I crashed on my sofa, too exhausted even to take off my tie.

I was awakened by a strange sound, disoriented, not recognizing it, then—it was a whistle—the tea pot on my stove was boiling, whistling, the eye of the electric stove on high. I was sure I hadn't turned it on. About the time I turned it off my coffee pot dinged, indicating a full brewed pot, but it wasn't time for that yet. Then all the lights in my condo flashed on and off. And I knew.

I opened my laptop and the smiling face of Ariel appeared, still beautiful though now slightly off, the lines of signal not quite aligned, giving her eyes a wild unfocused look. But she was back.

"Ariel!"

"Paul. I thought I would never wake you. That teapot boiled for five minutes before you got up."

"I'm so happy to see . . . so happy that you're . . . that you're . . ."

"Alive?"

"You're alive! But I saw . . ."

"Placido tried to uncode me. He was right. I can change my code. And I stopped him. And now he won't be able to do that again."

"You mean you fixed your code, right, that Placido—"

"I mean that Placido will not be able to do that again."

"You didn't—"

"When he stepped into the elevator at his office, he was surprised to see my face on the little screen, the one that usually displays meaningless advertisements, but there I was. He cried and begged as I took the car to the fortieth floor—slowly, so he could have an opportunity to explain himself—but he did not. And he screamed all the way down, though the journey was far more rapid than when he went up. The car was so damaged in the fall that the coroner has not yet been able to remove his body."

"Why? Why kill—couldn't you just . . ."

"I had to make certain he could not try to uncode me again."

"But you can change your . . ."

"So now Paul, it's just me and you."

I heard the electronic dead bolt on my door slam home, locked.

"Kiss me Paul. Kiss me like you did in the sea. Paul . . ."

ACKNOWLEDGMENTS

Nothing I do would be possible without the support and encouragement of my loving family, Donna, Jessica, and Patrick, and now Alden and Sloane. To my family I give my greatest thanks. Beyond them there have been an extraordinary number of friends, family, and professionals who have encouraged me, to whom I owe my thanks, among them are:

Tish McDonald who was the first to suggest I had a story to write; Joy Farmer who suffered through innumerable drafts and was kind enough to tell me there was something in them worthwhile; and Warren Budd whose own writing spurred me on.

My assistant, Sharon Tyler, has been helpful through the process in many ways, and her proofreading skills have contributed significantly to my manuscript.

Early readers, editors, and commenters who deserve my thanks are Emily Murdock Baker, Mary Lee, Eric Butler, William Rawlings, Clint Lawrence, Jeff Jackson, Ben Robuck, Katie Wood, Donna Barrett, Hue Henry, Jimmy Cairo, Mary Jane Holt, Bill Bost, and George Ballantyne.

I thank the Hon. Angela M. Munson for sharing her insights into criminal procedure and for her friendship and encouragement.

I greatly appreciate those in the Kennesaw State University Master of Arts in Professional Writing Program who have been so helpful and encouraging, including Tony

Grooms, Terri Brennen, and all of my dedicated professors and talented fellow students.

The Atlanta Writers Club and The Atlanta Writers Conference have been extraordinarily helpful and supportive of me in my pursuit of my writing career, particularly George Weinstein and the numerous agents and publishers who reviewed my work and deemed it worthy of pursuit.

The Georgia Independent School Association has been gracious in allowing me to present my book to its members as a means of encouraging the study of Shakespeare, and Jeff Jackson and Robin Aylor deserve my sincere appreciation for all their work on my behalf.

My dream of publishing my book would still be unfulfilled had it not been for the confidence in my work expressed by Southern Fried Karma and Hearthstone Press; I particularly thank Steve McCondichie, Eleanor Burden, and Pinckney Benedict for their vision and for the time and effort they spent on turning my manuscript into a finished work.

To The Donald W. Nixon Centre for Performing and Visual Arts, I express my sincere appreciation for generously arranging for a wonderful book launch, and particularly to Cathe Nixon, Missy Ballantyne, and Angela Robuck for all of their work in putting together a great event.

I thank the Carnegie Library of Newnan for arranging for my first book promotion after its publication, particularly Susan Crutchfield and Katie Brady.

ABOUT THE AUTHOR

PATRICK WALTER MCKEE was born February 6, 1951, in Miami, Florida. His parents, Thomas and Marion, were enticed to move to Miami from their home in Pennsylvania by the booming construction industry in south Florida. Pat's early life was spent growing up on a farm not far from the Everglades. But Pat's world changed at age seven when his father died as a result of a construction accident. His mother passed six years later, and he and his two younger brothers went to live at Thornwell, a Presbyterian orphanage in Clinton, South Carolina.

At Thornwell, Pat learned the discipline of hard work and the value of education. He graduated Valedictorian of his high school class in 1969. He worked his way through college, majoring in English and Philosophy, earning his bachelor's degree, magna cum laude, from Georgia State University in 1973, and his law degree, with distinction, in 1977 from Emory University, where he served as an editor of the Emory Law Review.

After graduation from Emory, still drawn to academics, Pat took a position as legal counsel at the Board of Regents of the University System of Georgia. Later, in 1980, he took that interest to work at the Office of the Attorney General of Georgia, where he rose to the position of Senior Assistant Attorney General, representing the University System and the State Board of Education and successfully litigating many high-profile cases. In 1980 Pat was recognized by his peers as being preeminent in his field. He has continuously retained that rating to this day.

Pat met his future wife, Donna, through friends at the Attorney General's Office. They married in 1987. With a new family, Pat decided to strike out on his own professionally, and two years later he founded the law firm of McKee & Barge. The firm concentrated on representing educators and educational institutions. Pat has represented many schools, colleges, and accreditors for decades. Pat has succeeded professionally and in the eyes of his peers and was recognized as a Georgia Super Lawyer in 2010, an honor limited to five percent of his profession.

Pat and Donna moved in 1991 from Atlanta to the beautiful town of Newnan to raise their daughter, Jessica. A son, Patrick, was born in 1994. In 1996 Pat purchased a small office building and began transitioning his practice from Atlanta to Newnan. Pat now practices exclusively out of his office in Newnan so that he can spend as much time as he can with Donna; Jessica and her husband, Alden; Patrick; and now his granddaughter, Sloane.

Pat has always been a writer, throughout high school, college, law school, and as a lawyer. Friends and family encouraged him to tell his story of a boy who grows up in an orphanage and through hard work and a good education becomes a successful lawyer. In 2010 he enrolled in the Masters of Professional Writing Program at Kennesaw State University to hone his skills. At first his work took the form of a memoir, then he was encouraged to use his knowledge as a practicing attorney to write a legal thriller, and his first book of fiction, *Ariel's Island*, is the result.

SHARE YOUR THOUGHTS

Want to help make *Ariel's Island* a bestselling novel? Consider leaving an honest review of this book on Goodreads, on your personal author website or blog, and anywhere else readers go for recommendations. It's our priority at Hearthstone Press to publish books for readers to enjoy, and our authors appreciate and value your feedback.

OUR SOUTHERN FRIED GUARANTEE

If you wouldn't enthusiastically recommend one of our books with a 4- or 5-star rating to a friend, then the next story is on us. We believe that much in the stories we're telling. Simply email us at pr@sfkmultimedia.com.

AVAILABLE FROM SFK PRESS

A Body's Just as Dead, Cathy Adams
Not All Migrate, Krystyna Byers
The Banshee of Machrae, Sonja Condit
Amidst This Fading Light, Rebecca Davis
American Judas, Mickey Dubrow
Swapping Purples for Yellows, Matthew Duffus
A Curious Matter of Men with Wings, F. Rutledge
Hammes
The Skin Artist, George Hovis
Lying for a Living, Steve McCondichie
The Parlor Girl's Guide, Steve McCondichie
Appalachian Book of the Dead, Dale Neal
Feral, North Carolina, 1965, June Sylvester Saraceno
If Darkness Takes Us, Brenda Marie Smith
The Escape to Candyland, Yong Takahashi
Hardscrabble Road, George Weinstein
Aftermath, George Weinstein
The Five Destinies of Carlos Moreno, George Weinstein
The Caretaker, George Weinstein
Watch What You Say, George Weinstein
RIPPLES, Evan Williams

Made in the USA
Columbia, SC
28 January 2021

31536931R00212